NO GRIT

By

Elaine Calloway

Copyright & License Notes

Connect with Elaine Calloway at http://www.elainecalloway.com

Acknowledgements

To my family, friends, and fans for the support. Y'all keep me going!

To Carol Foster and Terry Poca who provided feedback and always cheered on this story, even when it was in its rough stages.

To my editor Dori Harrell, Breakout Editing, for taking my story and making it shine.

To my cover designer Taryn Knight, Leafbreeze Creations, for yet another fantastic cover. You are talented, artistic, and patient! I am lucky to have found you.

To Cathy and Jerry King, for the fun evening of weapons research & setting me straight on guns/bullets.

To one of my favorite cities in the world, Savannah, for being such an ideal backdrop to this ghost story. Locals will notice that several locales are fictional. However, beautiful landmarks like the Savannah River, the Squares, and Bonaventure Cemetery are included in the backdrop too.

Thanks to the artists who generously allowed me to use their quotes in this book: Bruce Lee, Roger Drawdy, Dodinsky, Ashleigh Brilliant, Dick Gregory.

An additional thanks to Roger Drawdy, whose incredible Irish music and passionate onstage performances inspired the character of Riordan O'Shea.

CHAPTER ONE

The bitterest tears shed over graves are
for words left unsaid and deeds left undone.
~ Harriet Beecher Stowe

Boston 1997

Brianna McNeil spent years talking to the dead, sharing secrets with those who passed through her family's mortuary. But the day one talked back, everything changed.

It had happened on her fifteenth birthday, at Declan's burial. If only her big brother had been the first to whisper from the grave, she might have handled things better. But no, the first voice was creepier—threatening, even—and without a body attached.

Her Irish clan stood around the grave, huddled together under umbrellas. Uncles sipped Jameson and spoke of Declan's bravery. Aunts sobbed and held each other. Across the lush cemetery, Celtic crosses and winged cherubs loomed over gravestones, protecting the dead with their vigilant watch. Now they would protect Declan, her confidante and idol.

In the chilling drizzle, Brianna approached the coffin. An American flag cloaked the long box like gift wrap. Maybe the stars and stripes were supposed to be comforting. They weren't. She didn't need a hero. Just her big brother back.

Leaning over so no one could hear, she whispered, "Your life was cut short, but I'll make a difference with the time I have left. I promise."

Lightning crackled across the sky, followed by an ominous voice. "Be careful, Brianna. No one breaks a promise to the dead without retribution."

If only she'd listened.

###

Savannah, Georgia—Present Day

Lights flickered and cast sinister shadows across the vaulted ceiling in the den. Brianna swallowed hard. *Don't panic.* Faulty wiring could cause such things. She *had* chosen to rent an older Victorian in Savannah's historic district. Old houses had their quirks.

Of course, the dead had their quirks too—flickering lights being one of them. No. No need for paranoia. There must be a logical explanation. That's what her many psychiatrists would say. Back in Boston, shrinks outnumbered friends five to one.

Cool air breezed across her neck, sending a shiver down her spine. Coincidence. It had to be. She took a deep breath. Moving down South had been the right decision. The right time to embrace the living, start anew. Keep her promise to make a difference.

The only dead person's voice she wanted to hear was Declan's.

Declan had loved Savannah, calling it a jewel on the South's necklace. Here Brianna could have a new life, a new beginning, in the city closest to her brother's heart.

It wasn't too much to ask. Was it?

Plato dropped his dog toy, sending it to the floor with a loud squeak. His short legs raced past her, every tendril on his sable-and-white coat flying in the wind created by his boundless energy. When he reached the recliner, he stopped short.

"What's up, boy?"

He plunked his hindquarters onto the floor and gazed at the empty chair like it was the world's largest bone. She watched his hind legs wiggle, no doubt struggling to remain seated. He never obeyed the "sit" command for long. If she didn't know better, she'd think someone was teasing him with a treat.

Yet the chair was empty.

Goose bumps shot down her arms. Relax. Everything's fine. She had a new home, new job, and a new start. Most of all, there were no voices ringing in her ears twenty-four seven.

Plato broke the sitting position and proceeded to do what shelties were known for: barking incessantly.

"Hush, boy. Nothing's there." Maybe she said the words to convince herself, too.

He ignored her. She turned toward the kitchen, ready to dismiss the strange occurrence as another one of his moods. Old homes tended to creak, settle, and make odd noises from time to time. There was a logical explanation. There had to be. The alternative was too frightening to consider.

Plato's bark shifted, became a higher octave.

Her stomach cramped. This wasn't his "I see a leaf on the ground" bark. It wasn't even the "call 9-1-1" bark.

This bark was new—shrill, loud, and unending. To say it expressed panic was an understatement.

She grabbed the butcher knife and wrapped her pale fingers around the handle. Thank heavens she'd unpacked the knife set. So many boxes still needed sorting.

"C'mon, Plato, we're doing a thorough search. I'm calling the landlord. Begley has some explaining to do."

She tiptoed through the house. Plato followed at her heels, offering choppy barks as his toenails clacked against the hardwood floors.

With each step down the long hallway, she braced for long-buried monsters to emerge from a side bedroom. Ridiculous, yes, but she couldn't help it. At least the bathrooms were an easy check. All the homes in Savannah's historic district came with miniscule bathrooms, their size only matched by those in Manhattan.

The next two rooms on the right, the office and guest room, weren't going to be so easy. They had large windows and tucked-in closets, nooks and crannies where a burglar (or something worse) could hide. Why had she picked this house, again? The short walk to work didn't seem so important now.

She approached the guest room. "Plato, forward." She stepped aside for him to enter. He only looked up at her with a "Who, me?" glance.

"Forward. You're the dog. You can sense things humans can't."

With a resigned snuffle, he trod into the room and sniffed the baseboards. After he returned without any barking or weird behavior, she entered the room.

Nothing was amiss. The bed, dresser, and closet remained as neat and tidy as when she'd set them up two weeks ago. The tingling at the nape of her neck subsided. "Two more bedrooms to go, Plato."

She stopped at the master bedroom doorway and took her first relaxed breath in ten minutes. Sunbeams slanted through the bay window behind the headboard and bathed the wood-accented room in a golden light. *This* was why she fell in love with the place, why she'd agreed to pay Begley extra money each month to eventually make the house her own.

Plato scurried inside and began to bark. Brianna's chest tightened. Could something—or someone—be in her bedroom? She gripped the knife tighter, ready to strike. Not that she had any kind of knife training. What was she thinking? She didn't believe in guns, so a knife and a swift kick to the groin would be her self-defense strategy.

She checked under the bed, behind the curtains, around the master bath. Nothing. Plato stepped toward the closet and barked at the closed, slatted doors. "The closet?" she whispered.

Plato stuck his long, narrow nose up to the door slats. Okay. She could do this. She thrust the closet doors open, revealing a thick, black smattering of ash on the floor. What the hell?

Ash belonged in a fireplace, not a closet. While her bedroom did have a wood-burning fireplace, it was at least twenty feet away. How did cinders get into the closet?

Plato refused to sniff the closet floor. Instead, he sat and let out a piercing howl. A howl? Since when had he turned into a wolf?

"C'mon, Plato." He looked up with big almond eyes and lay down to rest his head between his paws. He seemed to be—no, he couldn't be—praying? With flattened ears and drooping brows, he continued to stare at the ash pile.

Brianna knelt and checked the fireplace interior but found nothing. "I'm going to call Begley," she said, standing tall and stretching her back. "It's time for some answers."

###

Two hours later, Brianna put Plato in his dog crate and opened her front door.

“Hello there,” Sam Begley said, his voice slow and smooth Georgian. The South specialized in drawl and leisure, a way of talking in addition to a way of life.

“Thanks for coming.”

Begley wiped his feet on the welcome mat. “No trouble at all.” He stepped inside and winced.

“Are you okay?” For a man in his fifties, he seemed healthy enough.

He bent to rub his left knee. “Too much football at University of Georgia, I’m afraid. No worries.” He stood to full form, about six foot two and a bit intimidating. “What can I help you with?”

Plato spotted him and barked. “Hush,” Brianna said.

When Plato obeyed, Begley arched a blond brow. “That’s a new one. I usually don’t allow my tenants to have pets, but yours is well-behaved.”

“Thanks,” she said, grateful Plato listened to her when it mattered. “Regarding why I called you today—”

“Yes. Is there a problem with the house?”

Depends on how you define problem.

“Please don’t think me crazy, but does anyone else have a key to the property? Perhaps the last tenant?”

Begley narrowed his eyes, their bright-blue tint turning gray. "We change locks with each lease. Why do you ask?"

She'd be honest, even if she sounded absurd. "I've noticed some…strange occurrences. Lights flickering on and off, peculiar smells fill the air on occasion, usually cinnamon and rose hips. It reminds me of my uncle's pipe tobacco."

Begley blinked once. To his credit, he didn't laugh. "These old windows sometimes let drafts in, I'm afraid. Plus, the historic district is a tight fit for all the houses. Maybe your neighbor was smoking at the time?"

"I considered that," she said. "But sometimes, even from the back room without any windows, I smell charred cheese."

"Charred cheese?" This time he didn't bother to hide a sarcastic smile, the kind men in white coats give mental patients. She should know. She'd seen that expression enough. An ache throbbed in her chest at the memory.

"There's also the black ash covering the master bedroom closet."

"What did you say?" The vein in his neck bulged and pulsed with a conga beat.

"The large stain in the master closet. I noticed it this morning."

His ears glowered red. "Show me."

She took her time walking down the hall, with him practically bumping into her. The ash was obviously significant—but why?

She opened the closet door and stepped out of his way. "There."

"I thought you said there was a stain," Begley said, not bothering to hide his accusatory tone.

She glanced into the closet. Only a hardwood floor. No ash. No nothing. She knelt to avoid passing out. "I don't understand. This morning, all the area was black. Honest."

Have I gone crazy? Is it happening again?

Begley scanned the room, eyeing every corner and joint. "Did your dog accidentally play in the fireplace?"

"No. Plato wouldn't even put his nose close to the floor, and I checked the chimney already."

After a long moment, Begley slicked back his perfectly gelled hair with his hands. "Perhaps there are some remaining pest-control issues. I will, of course, take care of this promptly. Will you be home tomorrow for my exterminator to come out?"

"I work until three, but I'm home after."

"Good, I'll set it up." He smiled again, the happiness of a man who had solved a problem—even if he hadn't.

"Can I do anything else for you while I'm here?" He stepped into the hallway and examined the moldings and baseboards. No sense hurrying anymore. He moseyed to the kitchen. Until that moment, she didn't even know what moseying looked like, but he perfected the practice.

Guess she'd have to figure out things on her own. Was this a Yankee's purgatory?

"I'm fine, thanks. As long as you are quite certain no one else could possibly have access to the house."

He plastered a smile across his face. "Don't you go worrying about your security. Why, in Savannah, especially in my properties, you're safe as a baby in its mother's arms."

"Hogwash," a male voice said, its deep tones bouncing off each wall before echoing in her ears.

Holy hell! She spun around, her heart beating ten times faster than usual. No one appeared.

"Shh...did you hear that?" she asked. Breathe. Just breathe and calm down.

"Hear what?"

Begley's brows narrowed at the interruption. He'd been in the middle of an arrogant litany of his business goals, how he'd be the one to put Savannah on the big map, how he'd become the pillar of the community. Obviously, he hadn't heard anything.

She dug her nails into her palms to keep a decent poker face. "It must be my imagination."

Don't let on. *Never* let on about the words without faces. Voices equaled Thorazine and a bed in psychiatric. She wouldn't go back there—ever.

"Carpetbagger!" another voice said, this one female.

No no no! This couldn't be happening. Two voices with no source. Shit. Brianna's knees gave way and she stumbled backward into a chair.

Begley reached out and helped her stand. "You sure are a light-headed little thing, aren't you?"

"I guess I didn't sleep well last night." A lame excuse, but Begley didn't seem to care.

"You just wait," Begley continued. "I'm going to improve this town, and everyone will know my name."

She nodded politely but ignored the rest of his speech. Utter hopelessness ripped through every vein in her body. When it reached her heart, her chest ached.

This move down South had gone terribly wrong. How could she have been such an idiot, thinking she could escape? The voices were back. All hopes of a normal life—gone. What other calamities awaited her in this Southern city?

CHAPTER TWO

I want peace and quiet.
I want it so much I'd die for it.
~ Michael Collins

Morning came like a slap in the face. Brianna had tossed and turned all night, an attempt to ignore the sudden onslaught of whispering voices. Deceased Southerners outdid their Yankee counterparts in the chattiness arena by a factor of ten.

Fumbling out of bed, she slipped into a navy blouse, tan pants, and stud earrings. Standard work attire while maintaining comfort. But when she reached for her white sandals, they were nowhere to be found.

She checked under her bed, in the previously ash-stained closet, and around the house. No luck. Her sandals had gone AWOL, adding fuel to the week from hell.

Plato's jingling collar announced his entrance into the living room. "Did you take my shoes, boy?"

His triangular ears stood erect, and he licked his lips. No, he couldn't have eaten them. Don't be ridiculous. Besides, he'd never been the kind of dog to swipe her things. Like his Shetland Island ancestors, he preferred herding to stealing. But in a residential house without rolling, emerald hills peppered with stubborn sheep, Plato improvised and herded the furniture.

So far, the furniture had behaved.

Plato barked at the clock as it chimed nine times.

"Great, I'm late for work. Edwin won't accept lost shoes as an excuse." With resignation, she picked up her tennis shoes. They'd do for now. She reached for her keys as Plato sauntered to his foam bed, spun around three times, and flopped.

She set up the baby gate to keep him enclosed in the back half of the living room. "Too bad you're not a retriever. You could help me find my shoes."

Plato let out a deep snuffle, apparently not amused by her humor.

She grabbed her purse and swung open the door. A man—no, make that the most gorgeous man she'd ever seen—waited there, ready to knock. He stood tall at over six feet and had a guitar slung across his back. A musician? Her body tingled in places she'd ignored for too long.

He had angular cheekbones framed with black layers of hair that extended past his collar. Long enough to give the impression of a rebel but short enough to blend in when needed. Something inside her yearned to know his story, for she'd spent a lifetime blending in—but at what cost?

His jade eyes—intense, filled with a past—met her own. Maybe Savannah *did* have something to offer.

He had to be lost. Surely, he wouldn't be looking for her, though she wished that was the case. Men tended to dismiss her as odd, a Wednesday Addams type, before running after lankier women. She'd hoped this move to Savannah would be a way to interact with more humans, embrace the living instead of the dead.

She certainly wouldn't object to embracing *him.*

"Can I help you?" she asked.

He rechecked the address. "Am I at the right house? Two twenty-five Oxley Way?"

"Um…" Her purse fell off her arm, and Plato began to bark. Could this mysterious man be looking for her?

"You have a dog? In my house?"

Your house?

She tried to keep her tone nonaccusatory. "You mean, my house. I moved here last week. Sam Begley is the landlord."

He held out a rusted key as if it offered undisputed proof. "Since when? Where are my parents? My sister?"

"Steven?" The voice was tiny, meek, and female. Brianna's head began to ache.

She spun around, eyeing the living room for any sign of a human. None. Why had she expected anything different? That made voice number three in her home.

"Ma'am?" the man on her stoop asked. Such formality coming out of his luscious mouth seemed odd.

"The name's Brianna, not ma'am." *Besides, I'm thirty, not eighty.* "And you are?"

His muscles flexed as he pulled the guitar off his back and set it down. "Steven."

Clammy air slithered down her spine. *Of course you are. Just like the voice said.*

She leaned against the doorframe to steady herself. Voices in her home, followed by this lost musician claiming the house is his? What next?

"What did you mean, this is your house? I'm renting to own it from Begley."

The gleam vanished from Steven's eyes, leaving confusion. For a split second, his rebel-without-a-cause persona was replaced by a confused young boy. A pang shot through her heart. Maybe there was a way to help him?

He reexamined the black iron address numbers on the house. "How can you own my family's home? We've lived here for three generations."

She peered around him to check for cameras. Could this be some kind of twisted joke?

"I don't know, Steven." The hair on his muscled arms looked soft and appealing. And his shiny watch—crap, his watch. Nine fifteen. She was even later for work.

"I need to go," she said, shutting and locking the door behind her. *As much as I'd like to keep you here.* "Why don't you contact Begley about the details? His office is on Johnson Square. He'd know more than me."

Steven's shoulders slumped and a sense of despair washed over his toned body. "Of all the damn luck. Where could they have gone?"

She was tempted to ask why he didn't know his own family's whereabouts but decided to not go there. No sense volunteering to deliver bad news. If the voices she'd heard were his family, one thing was abundantly clear: they were dead.

The stress lines on his face caved crevices of pain and worry. Think, Brianna, think. Figure out a way to help. At least figure out a way to see him again.

"I'm late for work, but the director's wife is a history buff. She knows the ins and outs of all the historic homes. I could see if she knows anything about your family."

"Thanks." He tilted his head, his inquisitive face studying hers. "The director? You work on a film set or something?"

Brianna bit her lip. Whenever she told men her occupation—cosmetologist at a funeral home—they ran and never looked back. She'd hoped the move to Savannah would change that pattern.

"Director, boss, whatever," she said. Maybe he would shrug off her answer as one of those cultural differences between north and south. *Don't dismiss me just yet.*

"Talk to Begley. I'll be home around four, so why don't you come by then and I'll let you know if Margie knows anything about the house."

A flicker of hope crossed his face, and he tilted up one side of his mouth in a smile. "I appreciate it, ma-am, um, Brianna."

She chuckled softly. "You Southerners can't help it with the ma'am thing, can you?"

His large eyes clouded with fear, the black pupils blocking out the green hue. "I'm not sure I deserve to call myself a Southerner, not anymore."

Hmm…why?

Before she could ask, he offered a polite smile and left. She jingled her keys and stared after him for a long second. If his family had lived here and were now ghosts, why didn't he know they'd died? Why hadn't anyone contacted him about the estate?

She wanted to help him in more ways than one. But haunted house or not, she had no plans to abandon her new home.

###

One great thing about her house—even if it was haunted—she had a short walk to work. No more bumper-to-bumper traffic jams on Boston's expressways. With Savannah laid out in a grid, walking was great exercise and an ideal means to get to work. Main thoroughfares provided easy access from the bars on River Street to the serene Forsyth Park, bookends of the historic district.

She sprinted past sage and violet homes, through the city's plush squares adorned with live oaks covered in Spanish moss, and continued up Habersham Street. Restful Oaks Funeral Home sat on East Bryan Street, one block off Warren Square. Once a Victorian plantation, Restful Oaks had a wraparound front porch reminiscent of the Old South. The narrow front walkway was flanked by marigold blossoms and fresh mint sprigs, welcoming visitors and employees alike.

She gingerly opened the front door and tiptoed inside.

"You're late, Brianna."

Damn. Most days, Edwin stayed in the back office and only Margie, his wife and admin assistant, sat in the main lobby area.

"I'm sorry. There was a problem with my house."

Edwin glared at her over gold-rimmed spectacles. His slender frame, dark suit, and deep voice reminded her of a macabre Kermit the Frog. "What kind of problem? We're slammed and the phone keeps ringing. I almost had to outsource work to another place."

"It won't happen again. I promise." *Please don't fire me. I need this job.*

Edwin rubbed his narrow chin with a bony finger. "Go to the preparation room. Start on Mrs. Jenson. Then plan to stay late to make up the time."

Stay late—except she wanted to be home by four to meet Steven. She sighed under her breath. Yet another chance to get to know someone—someone alive—ruined. She couldn't risk losing her career, even for Steven's tempting physique.

"Brianna?" Edwin prompted, irritation lines forming between his brows.

"Mrs. Jenson, absolutely. You can count on me." Brianna hurried to the preparation room. Her questions for Margie would have to wait.

Sandra Jenson, ninety-one, had died two days prior. Her coarse, white hair had frequented too many beauty parlors, making the ropelike strands harder to style. After several attempts, Brianna finally managed a French twist.

"Let's hope your family likes the hairdo, but we all go into the afterlife with bed head, I'm afraid." She smiled. Working in a funeral home suited her, even though it gave most people the creeps. She liked the solitude. The dead never complained, never expected too much. And the ones at work never talked back.

She cleansed Sandra's face, guessing they would've shared a laugh if Sandra were still alive. Dead women came in three categories: the happy, the bitter, and the Botox. Wrinkles never lied, and Sandra's age lines were etched in a smile, evidence of how she lived.

"You spent your days entertaining the grandkids on the front porch, didn't you?"

Brianna glanced through the file, proud of her accuracy. "Four children and eight grandchildren. Let's get you prettied up for those precious grandbabies."

She applied the facial foundation with precision and ease, making sure to blend the colors and avoid a splotchy appearance. Restful Oaks used a mixture of oil-based makeup as well as store-bought brands, just like her family's funeral home in Boston where she'd learned the business.

The eye shadow choice proved tricky but she decided on matte gray. Once Sandra was placed in the visitation room, the canned lights with red bulbs would make her appear more flesh toned. One of the many tricks of the trade, so bodies looked more human.

"Is the body ready?" Edwin asked.

Holy crap! He seemed to appear out of nowhere. She coughed and caught her breath.

"I'm about to apply the lipstick."

He nodded in approval. "I'll greet the family. Be sure to page Margie when the body's ready."

"Will do," she said. *The body.* Why did people in life have names but in death became a generic noun? Shouldn't individuals have a name, a voice, after their death? *Heaven knows they have voices. I hear them all the time.*

She applied the lipstick, avoiding any smudges to the facial makeup. There, Mrs. Jenson was ready. Brianna stole a moment of silence. "I wish you the best, wherever you may be. If you see my brother Declan, tell him I miss him. Tell him I'm doing just fine."

Her stomach clenched, twenty years of pain churning into a vortex. What had she done? She'd asked a dead person to lie for her, lie to the brother she loved and missed.

"I'm sorry," she whispered. "My life isn't just fine. I spend more time with the dead than the living. Voices reverberate in my ears. I want to connect to someone, but I'm petrified. People dismiss me as strange. I've never fit in."

A terse male voice sliced through the air, his words carrying the precision of a salute. "You made a promise, Brianna."

She stumbled backward and crashed into the instruments' table. Ouch. She rubbed her hip to alleviate the pain. "Hello?"

No one was in the room except her and Mrs. Jenson. The voice had been male. What's worse, she'd heard it before—at Declan's funeral.

She grabbed her wrist to check her pulse. Yep, racing like a thoroughbred in the Derby. Breathe. Just breathe. The dead hadn't talked to her at work. Until now. Odd, considering funeral homes would be the ideal place for conversation.

She choked out what words she could. "I haven't forgotten my promise."

"What have you done to keep it?"

She didn't know what to say. *Life had been busy* sounded as lame as the excuse it was.

"Speak the promise, Brianna."

A lump formed in the back of her throat. "Why?"

"Because the spoken word has more strength than the silent one."

Was this the spirit of someone who wrote fortune cookies? She didn't want to repeat her promise—she had failed miserably at keeping it—but ignoring the dead's command would be worse.

She wrung her hands together and inhaled deep. "I promised to make a difference."

The room fell silent for a long minute, the only sound being the secondhand of an old clock. Tick, tick, tick—a haunting rhythm of broken promises and failed dreams.

"Please ask Declan to forgive me."

"Not my area," the curt voice said.

Not his area? This was not her favorite dead guy.

“What do you want?” she asked.

“Keep your promise. Make a difference.”

“I have the soup kitchen phone numbers at home, and I planned to volunteer at the animal shelter—”

“Make a difference with your gift.”

Gift? What gift? He couldn’t possibly mean hearing voices. Since when had never getting a moment’s peace been considered a gift? If anything, it was a curse.

“What if I can’t?”

“Are you done with the body yet, sugar?” Margie’s thick accent came over the intercom. “Edwin’s having a fit, and you have three more bodies to finish up.”

Brianna paused, longing for an answer to her question. “Hello?” she whispered.

“Hello?” Margie replied.

Brianna waited a long moment. Only silence. How was she supposed to use this *gift* to make a difference? She sent the dead into the next realm with careful skin care. It’s not like live folks were lining up on her doorstep for help.

Wait. Steven had, in a way. Maybe she could help him? Help him find out what happened to his family?

Brianna pressed the intercom. “Yes, Mrs. Jenson is ready.”

Now to find out if I am.

###

The clock showed 6:30 p.m. What a day. One stunning musician, four dead bodies prepped, one prickly male ghost, one broken promise she’d better make good on. This was a day to end with beer.

On her way out, Brianna stopped by reception. “Margie, you know a lot about old houses in the historic district, right?”

Margie looked up from her computer. “Sure do. Why?”

“The house I’m renting, two twenty-five Oxley? Do you know who lived there before Begley bought it?”

Margie took a sip of her coffee and left a ruby lipstick smudge on the cup. Then she leaned forward to beckon Brianna closer. “James and Virginia Grayson, both upstanding members of the community. He was an engineer. She was the busybody type. Very Old South.”

Margie’s gossip didn’t warrant the secretive air she’d given to the conversation. Maybe there was more to learn?

“Did they have kids?”

Margie brushed a rebellious strand of coiffed hair behind her ear. “Two kids, Steven and Amy. Folks claim Steven moved off to California and became a prostitute.”

Brianna suppressed a laugh. Steven, the guy with the guitar who'd been so concerned about his family—a male hooker?

"What else?"

Margie grinned. "He didn't even say good-bye, much to the dismay of James and Virginia, believe you me. There was a big ole hubbub when he left town."

Brianna began to understand how this gossip thing worked. Apparently people had to work for it. No one just offered information. One had to pry.

"What about Amy?"

Margie used her manicured hands to fluff up the back of her hair. "Such a beauty. The whole thing was a real shame."

"What whole thing?" Brianna asked, surprised at herself for whispering. Apparently it was contagious.

"Rumor was, James and Steven had a huge blowout, something about the family business. Steven skedaddled and James went mad. Killed his family. Burned them all in a house fire."

House fire? Alarm bells clanged in her mind as she remembered the black ash.

"What do you think happened?" Brianna said. She knew Margie kept a pulse on the beauty parlor gossip chain.

Margie leaned back in her chair and shrugged. "The fire made the newspapers, but the rest is speculation. Some folks even say Steven had come home to visit, that he died in the fire too. The police never found his remains, but that doesn't mean he wasn't there."

Yes it does. Steven hadn't died in the fire, if her morning visitor had told the truth. Brianna didn't volunteer this tidbit though.

"Can you tell me more about him?"

Margie pondered a moment. "Steven always was one of those types that heard a different beat than everyone else. Difficult position to be in, here in proper Savannah. That boy got into some wicked fights with James, always about how he should run his life."

Familiar story, Brianna thought. Her father did the same with Declan, only Declan gave in to parental pressure. He died trying to get their dad's approval.

Margie continued talking. "No one's been able to find that boy in years, and the house fell to probate without a will. I reckon Begley bought it at auction."

Yet Steven was alive—and in town. When he learned about his family, he'd claim the house was his, no doubt.

Before she could pry further, Margie peered over the desk and glared at Brianna's tennis shoes with disdain. "What are those?"

"Sorry about the casual shoes. My white sandals went missing, and I was already late for work."

Margie raised an eyebrow. "Labor Day's long gone, sugar."

"So?"

"Sweetie, you can't wear white after Labor Day."

Brianna smiled, feigning professional courtesy. She liked Margie, but Southerners could be really strange about some things. The dead were so much easier to talk to—provided they didn't talk back.

"I'll wear professional shoes tomorrow, I promise." She clutched her purse and headed for the front door.

"You do that, dear. People round here are required to keep their promises," Margie called after her. "It's a Southern bylaw, you know."

Brianna pretended not to hear. She had more important promises to focus on, and she sure as hell didn't need any further retribution.

CHAPTER THREE

There are three classes of people: those who see,
those who see when they are shown, those who do not see.
~ Leonardo da Vinci

The full moon had risen in the autumn sky before Brianna got home. No sign of Steven—figures. Maybe he'd stopped by earlier and would try again. She liked to think so, but who knew?

You idiot. You should've asked for his cell number. Her chance to connect with a living man—such an attractive one too—had slipped through her fingers like old dust.

She went inside, tossed her purse on the couch, and unhitched Plato's baby gate. He hopped off his bed and sprinted toward her, his front paws knocking her knees with enthusiasm. "Yes, I missed you too, boy."

After she walked him in the backyard and returned inside, he rolled onto his back and rubbed himself against the carpet, grinning and making happy barks when she rubbed his white belly. If only reality was that simple.

"Okay, Plato. Mama needs a beer." She walked to the fridge and he followed at her heels. After uncapping an icy-cold Smithwick's, she collapsed on the couch. Long day. Maybe something decent was on TV.

Before she could reach for the remote, Plato snatched a rolled-up newspaper she'd left on the coffee table. The issue contained interesting

Savannah history she wanted to peruse when she had the time. He carried it in his mouth and dropped it at her feet. Hmm. He'd never been one to fetch the paper. She'd never even trained him how.

"Thanks, boy." She flipped on the TV and let the *Jeopardy* questions wash over her tired mind.

Plato pawed at her foot.

"Stop, Mama's tired."

He pawed again, whining.

"Is there something you want me to see?" It was a ludicrous question. Why would her dog care about the newspaper? But he barked twice and stuck out his tongue in what could only be construed as a dog smile.

Why not? Things couldn't get any weirder. She leaned down and picked up the newspaper to read the headlines: "Real Estate Deals Skyrocketing in Savannah," "Hit-and-Run Accident Shuts Down Bull Street." Buried on another page was an ad—Take Charge of Your Future: Psychic Readings by Clara.

Plato barked twice when she read the advertisement out loud.

"A psychic? C'mon, Plato. The palm-reading tarot crowd isn't my style."

He lifted his head and howled three long notes—chilling, haunting cries—that sent shivers through her. *Was* he trying to tell her something?

"Plato?"

He whimpered and locked his almond gaze on her, reflecting back her own curiosity.

She double-checked the psychic's address and considered the option. Not one she would've thought of on her own, but what did she have to lose? Maybe this so-called psychic could eliminate the voices, or at least tell her a way to block them out. Not to mention, psychics were also misunderstood by society. No fortune-teller would call the men in white coats without risking committal herself.

The place was on River Street, a short walk from home and work. She could stop by tomorrow after dinner. Maybe Plato *did* know something she didn't. Anything was worth a try at this point, wasn't it?

###

After a long Friday spent beautifying the dead, Brianna meandered past praline shops and Irish pubs to the quieter, eastern end of River Street. A psychic's sign dangled from a red brick building, an ominous welcome into the unknown—or perhaps the fraudulent. But she had to do something, take some action. Even the questionable held a powerful credibility tonight. The full moon's beams glinted across the cobblestone walkways, adding to the evening's surreal mood.

She approached the river's edge, stalling for a few minutes. Neon lights from River Street bars cast reflections onto the Savannah River, making colorful ripples of green, purple, and gold. The river seemed as wandering and mysterious as the city itself. A gentle breeze lifted off the water and blew across her face.

As the wind rustled through the oaks, she heard the faint notes of a violin.

"Violins again?" *I thought only the voices had returned.* She sighed, her breath blending with the cool night air.

"You're hearing violins, dear?" a hoarse voice said.

Brianna turned, unnerved. She hadn't heard footsteps. No one had approached in the last few minutes. Yet, as if out of thin air, a crotchety-looking woman stood not two feet away. Tan age spots and blisters covered her face, and her matted hair was doused with baby powder or theatrical makeup, resembling a helmet more than a hairdo.

"Pardon me?" Brianna asked, stepping back a few feet. Best not stand too close.

The woman prodded forward, invading the personal space Brianna had tried to protect. "I asked if you were hearing violins, dear."

"Yes." Not to mention other things.

"I see. And you're planning to see Clara?" she asked, pointing to the psychic's doorway.

"Yes." Brianna shifted her weight from foot to foot, feeling awkward for admitting such a thing. While many Irish clans embraced the paranormal to a degree, her own parents did not, which was why they'd admitted her to a mental hospital at sixteen.

The old woman's intense stare pierced into Brianna's soul. "Clara caters to the tourists. You're local, aren't you?"

How did she know? "I need to find out what's going on with my house." *I'm here because my dog suggested it. Go ahead. Call me crazy.*

The woman smiled, revealing decrepit teeth. "You're not crazy, Mo Éireannack Cailín."

"What did you just call me?" Brianna asked. The words sounded familiar and dangled on the fringes of her imagination. Had she actually heard them before?

"Clara won't be able to help you," she said, ignoring Brianna's question. "Only one person can." She offered a piece of old, buff-colored paper in her wrinkled hand.

Brianna opened the note and read it aloud. "Five five five Julian Street, in one hour. Get the answers you seek." She stared at the calligraphy letters on the parchment. "I don't understand—"

But the woman disappeared, leaving only the lapping sound of the river behind.

###

The crusty old woman had been unnerving. Brianna paced along the river's edge for fifteen minutes, debating whether to drive to the mysterious address. She had no desire to walk there, not in the dark. River Street was different, being the central hub of activity, tourists, and bars. But show up at some random place based on what an old hag had suggested? No, her metallic-blue Volkswagen Jetta would be better—not only to get there, but to provide an easy exit.

Besides, the old woman knew about the violins—something Brianna had never told anyone. Not even in the psych ward.

Five five five Julian Street turned out to be a dilapidated house set off the main road. Several boards of the gray siding had provided regular entrees for termites. Some boards had separated from the house, barely dangling from rusted nails. The front door had a mesh screen with a giant spider-shaped tear in the center.

This didn't look good. Brianna turned around, ready to leave.

A woman called from inside. "Are you the one who hears violins and voices?"

Brianna stopped midstep. She hadn't said anything about hearing voices. Before she could stop herself, she replied, "Yes. My name is—"

"Brianna," the woman replied. "And my name is Anzhela."

Brianna's heart skipped a beat as she peered into the dark doorway. She swallowed hard. "How did you—?"

"I know your name, Mo Éireannack Cailín." A young, gypsy-looking woman appeared in the doorway. She wore a teal camisole, flowing eyelet skirt, and long dangly earrings—perfect outfit for autumn in Savannah.

"The old woman by the river called me that. What does it mean?"

"My Irish girl," the gypsy said. "Didn't your parents ever speak Gaelic?"

Gaelic? Her parents had cut themselves off from so many of the old ways. Declan occasionally had spoken in Gaelic to her, but only in limited phrases. "Maybe. I honestly don't remember."

"A pity. Such a beautiful language." Anzhela tilted her head and studied Brianna's face. "Come in."

Brianna crossed her arms and took a deep breath. Enter a stranger's house? *Keep it together. This might be your chance to get answers.* She followed Anzhela inside and stopped short, surprised to find an exquisite interior. From the outside, she never would've guessed.

In the living room, antique mahogany tables were tucked in corners, ornate perfume bottles and azure-blue pottery covered every surface, and the air smelled sweet like freshly cut grass in summertime. Shelves lined the walls, all filled with books on the arcane sciences.

Anzhela smiled and picked up a rose-colored teapot from the kitchen counter. She poured a dark-pink tea into delicate china cups. Its aroma instantly permeated the room with rose hips, coriander, and strawberries.

"What do you think is happening to you?" Anzhela asked as she sat down across from Brianna. A small, antique table stood between them.

Brianna leaned back in the mahogany rocking chair and pretended to sip the tea, which smelled like strawberry-flavored honey. Tempting, but she wasn't about to drink anything that could be laced with a hallucinogen. Or worse, poison.

"The voices followed me down South. Something, or someone, is now living in my house."

"Your house?" Anzhela repeated with a raised eyebrow.

"It is mine." Did she sound as defensive as she felt?

"Never mind. Tell me why you think someone is living in your home."

Did she want a whole list, or just the top ten?

"Things fall on the floor without reason. Strange smells fill the air. Lights switch on and off. My dog sits next to the chair and barks at nothing for thirty minutes."

Anzhela's silver bracelets clanked as she set down her cup. "Perhaps he can detect things you're not ready to see."

Brianna's face heated. "What should I be seeing? I've heard voices and violins since I was fifteen. Men find me strange. People avoid me. Most of my energy is spent convincing myself that I'm not certifiably insane."

A large Persian cat strolled in, curling its tail around Anzhela's ankles for attention. She petted its arching back and said, "Do you know we humans are the only species to question their instincts? Think about it. Cats know when to approach, when to flee. Birds don't argue with themselves whether to fly south for the winter. Their instinct tells them to do it, and they listen. Dogs listen, like yours. People are the only creatures who second-guess their way out of following their instincts."

"I hadn't thought about that before."

"And perhaps your instincts will lead you to the people you're destined to meet," Anzhela said. "A love interest, perhaps."

Brianna's mind wandered to Steven. The point of moving to Savannah was to keep her promise to Declan, to make a difference. Perhaps she could figure out a way to help Steven—if she ever saw him again.

"We aren't alone on this Earth," Anzhela said. "Spirits from other worlds and realms surround us, watch out for us. Most humans are blind to their forces, but a few people have the ability to notice."

Anzhela had a point, but she didn't see the bigger picture.

"But I want to get rid of the voices," Brianna said. "I want a normal life.

Anzhela's eyes radiated patience. "Normalcy is overrated."

"Please, I need to figure this out, make it stop."

"When you're ready, things will be revealed. If you can hear the violins, you're on your way."

And this helps me how? Brianna sighed, wishing she'd never made the promise to Declan. She didn't want such a strange gift. She wanted silence.

"Why do you claim it's your house?" Anzhela asked. She leaned back in her chair, seeming at ease not only in this eclectic home but with who she was. What Brianna wouldn't give for such inner peace.

"Because I'm the one paying rent?" Such a practical answer seemed out of place amid the mystical atmosphere.

Anzhela thought for a moment. "If these spirits think the house is theirs, your monetary exchange means nothing."

"How do I get rid of them?"

Anzhela's eyes widened in surprise, as if she thought eliminating any kind of spirit was crazy. She stood. "Wait here a moment." She walked out of the room and returned seconds later with a pink, marble-looking gem on a chain.

"What is it?"

The gypsy woman handed Brianna the necklace. "This pendant is made from powerful crystals—azurite, fluorite, and aventurine. Protective crystals."

Brianna ran her fingers across the smooth surface. "Will this help me get rid of the voices?"

She didn't comment but said, "I notice you're wearing a Saint Christopher medal."

Brianna stiffened. "I won't take it off. My older brother gave it to me."

Anzhela smiled, serenity beaming from her gaze. "I'm not about to break a bond between siblings. When you wear this pendant with yours, you'll achieve the inner peace you seek."

Yes! Inner peace. Finally, a cure for this supposed "gift." She would never take it off.

"Be careful to never lose it." Anzhela turned and gazed out the small window, watching leaves blow to the ground. "Autumn always brings about change. Scarlet reds, warm golds, and ash browns paint the Earth, telling us things are changing. You should go now, and be careful."

Brianna fingered her new necklace. "Why do I hear violins? I don't understand."

"You will in time. Be open to music and its influence." Anzhela gave a knowing smile.

Be open to music? As in, Steven would become part of her life? She would welcome the opportunity.

"Thanks for your help," Brianna said. Coming here was the right decision. The pendant would silence the voices, and she might have a chance to get to know Steven. Tonight, she would get a good night's sleep, something she hadn't had in a week.

They walked to the doorway. With a parting smile, Anzhela said, "Remember to trust your own voice. Animals don't question their instincts, and neither should you."

Brianna treaded down the creaky steps to the sidewalk. Wait a minute. What if she needed to speak to Anzhela again? Brianna bounded up the steps and knocked on the door.

An unfamiliar gentleman answered. "Yes? May I help you?"

Brianna rechecked the address, which now said 553 instead of 555. "Excuse me, but I was just speaking to Anzhela? Is she inside?"

His eyes narrowed. "There hasn't been a woman living here since my wife died ten years ago."

What the hell? Color faded from her hands until they were ghostly white, and her pulse thumped in her ears. Impossible. She hadn't dreamt this encounter. There had to be a logical explanation. "Her address was five five five Julian Street—"

"Lady, you've got the wrong house. The city redid all the addresses years ago. They skipped five five five on purpose."

"Why?"

He shut the door a few inches. “Legend says a woman at that address went insane over three hundred years ago. The developer didn’t want the headache of selling a doomed property, so they skipped the number.”

Brianna hugged the porch post to maintain her balance. Maybe the doctors in the psych ward were right about her—schizophrenia accompanied by hallucinations.

“Lady, are you okay? Should I call someone?”

“No, thank you. I’ll be fine.” She stumbled to her Jetta with Anzhela’s words circling around her like a haunted Ferris wheel.

This wasn’t my imagination. She grasped at her neck. The pendant was real. Fingers trembling, she pushed the key into the ignition. *I’m not hallucinating. I just had tea with someone in a house that doesn’t exist.*

She sped past gigantic live oaks lining every street. In the moonlight, their scraggly branches intersected like an old woman’s hands. Given the eerie events of late, maybe the branches *were* a woman’s hands—Anzhela’s, or some other dead spirit?

Streets blurred as she drove down Bay and turned on Habersham. *Focus. Keep my promise to Declan. Get out more. Enjoy life in Savannah.*

She pulled into her driveway, relieved to see her own house hadn’t moved. With steady fingers, she held the pendant and closed her eyes. *This will bring inner peace, Anzhela said. Meaning all voices and violins are now silenced.*

Goose bumps multiplied across Brianna's arms. *At least, I hope that's what she meant…*

CHAPTER FOUR

If God sends you down a stony path,
may he give you strong shoes.
~ Irish Saying

"I'm sorry, Steven," Begley said. He leaned back into his leather office chair. "Your family is dead."

Steven couldn't speak. Couldn't think. He'd been trying to meet with Begley for days, only to learn his family was…dead?

Steven clutched a hand to his tightened chest, hoping to alleviate the stabbing pain. He was too late. Amy had died. His little sister. A warm numbness spread through him.

"Wait…what happened? How did they die?"

"House fires are claiming many of these old Victorians, I'm afraid." Begley used a casual tone, as if discussing the weather or which tie to wear. He didn't even rise from his chair or offer a handshake as a show of respect. There was no sense of sympathy, no reverence. Just a cool and collected bastard sitting behind an ornate desk.

"When did it happen? And why wasn't I contacted? I'm next of kin."

He had to be dreaming. All these years he'd been gone. Running away, as he'd done far too often. Now he'd returned—intending to make amends and see Amy—and they'd all burned to death?

Begley continued filing papers and receipts. "Been several years now. I ran ads in the Savannah paper and the *Los Angeles Times*, trying to find you."

"I lived all up and down the coast. Never in L.A."

For the first time, Begley looked him in the eye. Well, not looked. More like glared.

"Lived, as in past tense?" Begley's pupils grew bigger. "I hope you don't intend to relocate back to Savannah. Try to claim your family's home. It's my property now, and I have a tenant."

"What do you care where I live?" Steven said. He had no intention of returning, but why volunteer the information? Let Begley sweat a little. "Besides, I called Amy every holiday and on her birthday. Couldn't you have looked up the phone records?"

Begley's mouth tightened and the little vein in his neck bulged. "What was I supposed to do, Mr. California? You left this town. James and Virginia couldn't find you for years. They died in the fire, with no will recorded. I checked every law office in Savannah."

Steven bit the inside of his lip. Feeling guilty over leaving would do him no good now. He'd had a reason—a damn good one—for leaving the South. He had good reason to return. Begley didn't deserve to know either one.

"Tell me how the fire started."

Begley shrugged. "You can obtain a police report. It claimed faulty wiring."

Bullshit. His dad was the epitome of an electrical engineer, complete with all the nerdy traits. Dad designed the wiring for the house to prevent fires, not ignite them. The rewiring had been the last project they'd worked on together, before things grew irreparable between them.

Steven kept his suspicions to himself. There was something quirky about Begley and his manner of handling legalities. No way could the house have burned due to faulty wiring. Meaning something else contributed to their deaths.

Begley furrowed his brow and grabbed some folders. "I apologize, but I do need to get to work. Would you like me to set up a memorial service with Edwin, the town funeral director?"

Too little, too late.

"I want my family's house. The young woman is only renting it, right?"

Begley smiled wide, revealing the bleached teeth of a man fond of appearances. "I see you met Brianna. Quite an interesting gal, don't you think?"

Now it was Steven's turn to shrug. "She's all right. Now about the house—"

"Son, if I was younger, I'd be chasing that skirt. Unless you're blind."

"I'm not blind," Steven said.

Begley obviously wanted to avoid discussing the house, and mentioning Brianna's beauty was a stalling tactic. Not that Begley was wrong on this point. Brianna did have stunning features: black hair, ivory skin, blue eyes. Definitely a change of pace from the blonde clones he'd grown accustomed to dating.

But she lived in the house he wanted and that didn't exactly put him in the mood to snuggle up to her.

Begley continued to stack papers and buzzed his secretary for coffee to go. "I really do need to return to work, and I'm afraid I need you to leave. Should I set up the memorial for your family?"

You're a dirty bastard. I just can't prove it yet. "Let me get back to you. How long have you rented the house for?"

Begley pursed his lips. "Six months, but she's renting to own. Paying me a hefty penny above and beyond the home's value for the privilege."

Aha! So money is what will make the difference. "How about I pay you more?"

"Can't. I'm partnered with several Realtors and we're transforming the whole city block. I like keeping it rented for now, but we'll eventually be restoring those homes."

"You mean changing them." Steven's mother would roll over in her grave. In fact, he was sure she was doing precisely that right now.

"Change is what Savannah needs," Begley said with a hyper enthusiasm reserved for televangelists and Amway salesmen.

"Not always." Steven balled his hands into fists and stormed out.

###

Like a stray dog without a home, Steven roamed across the Savannah squares to pass the time. He'd waited for Brianna at the house, like she'd suggested, but she never showed up.

The meeting with Begley had been a bust, and the cops had given him the runaround on attaining a police report. He'd filled out a request, but their computer system was on the blink. The bouffant-haired woman at the desk said it could take weeks to obtain the report.

Did everything move slower down South? He'd forgotten that part. Not that San Francisco was the epitome of fast-paced, but it was more progressive than Savannah.

Hell, every place was.

Each square-shaped intersection contained its own little bit of history, all draped under live oaks covered in Spanish moss. The South did have a few redeemable qualities.

Just not enough.

He ambled toward a stone bench in Troup Square, one of his favorites. Under the large tree limbs, people brought their dogs to drink from the doggy water fountain, an ornate structure created just for them. Damn,

Brianna owned a dog, in his house. He'd heard the pooch barking while Brianna stood in the doorway. He hoped it wasn't a destructive breed or a chewing machine.

Brianna didn't have a Southern accent, and he thought he'd detected a bit of Northeast clipped speech. He chuckled, knowing his mother would have a cow with a Yankee in the house. Why had Brianna moved here? Maybe she was one of those snowbirds, people who longed for warmer weather.

The South was a double-edged sword though. If she hadn't figured it out yet, she would soon. People weren't always what they seemed—Begley, in particular.

A blue dragonfly with delicate wings flitted nearby before landing on the adjacent bench. As he watched it resting in the afternoon sun, an animal at peace with its surroundings, he made a promise. He would learn what happened to his family—what really happened. He would make amends, somehow, for not protecting Amy like he should have.

And if Begley was hiding something, Steven would learn the truth—no matter what.

###

On Saturday morning, Brianna slept in until nine. Plato wouldn't let her rest any longer, with his pacing and muffled snorts.

She rubbed her eyes, grabbed her slippers, and snapped on his leash. The backyard wasn't entirely fenced in—she planned to finish it once the house was hers—and she didn't want to start the morning by sprinting across Savannah to chase him if he eyed a rabbit or squirrel.

They hurried into the chilly morning air. "C'mon boy, do this quick today, and I'll make us both breakfast."

He searched the grass, every movement fastidious. If he were human, he'd be quite the anal-retentive male.

After a few lingering seconds, she ushered Plato inside and unhooked his leash. "Now for some coffee."

As she wandered into the kitchen, he barked and raced around the den furniture three times at top speed. She cracked a smile. Her little sheep herder hard at work.

Coffeepot in hand, she turned on the faucet—and froze. Two large pots, both caked with enough grits and butter to feed an army, soaked in sudsy water. Pots she hadn't used. Pots she'd never seen before.

Where did they come from? Adrenaline ripped through her chest and tasted metallic in her mouth. Breathe. Be logical. Find an explanation.

An intruder? Not likely without Plato noticing. Maybe when she'd taken him outside? No. The back wall of the house had two double-hung windows overlooking the backyard. She would've noticed. Besides, they'd only been outside for five minutes. Not enough time to make mounds of grits.

Damn, what did she know about grits? She didn't even know what a stupid grit was. What kind of intruder breaks in only to cook a Southern dish?

Plato continued to herd the furniture, oblivious to her panic.

"Some guard dog you are."

He stopped midrun, intelligence beaming from his eyes as if he understood her. He cocked his head to one side and barked twice, seeming to say, "What are you so worried about?"

If Plato wasn't bothered, did she need to panic? He'd always kept her on high alert for any danger. While he'd be more prone to herd a burglar than attack one, his bark never gave away such truths.

Begley had the only other house key. Wait, not true. Steven had an old rusty key. But Begley had changed all the locks. No way would Steven's key still work. And even in the best fantasy where Steven would show up and take her in his arms to kiss her, grits weren't part of the equation.

"What the hell is happening?" she said, her high-pitched tone ringing in her ears.

Plato sauntered over and pawed at her foot. He barked three times.

"What?" she asked. He was becoming quite the mysterious dog. "What are you trying to tell me?"

His eyes sparkled like they held a secret. She thought she saw his mouth curl into a smile, the same kind as when he'd fetched the newspaper.

Was he saying the grit-caked pots were left behind by paranormal forces? No. Not possible. The dead don't cook grits.

He howled once, his narrow nose aiming to the ceiling before returning to focus his gaze on her.

"Are you telling me what I think you're telling me?"

Am I honestly asking my dog to confirm my hallucinations?

He barked twice and spun around, mischief radiating from his wiggling body.

A throbbing pain started behind her eyes and spread down to her stomach. It felt like a gut punch, and she gripped the hunter-green countertop edge.

Dead spirits in Boston had been different. They hadn't been able to touch things in the physical world, and they definitely couldn't use cookware. The Southern dead were a new breed. A new breed indeed.

Coffee. The morning chaos had happened precoffee. Maybe she was sleepwalking? Oh, to have such a simple explanation. Not with her luck.

One thing was for certain: Caffeine would make everything better. She prepared a potful, adding extra grounds. Strong coffee to cure a strange morning. Hell, a strange week.

She glared at the two pots coated in white clumps. "No. Not just no, but hell, no!"

Not on her turf. The living have a right to fight for what's theirs.

She grabbed both pots, carried them outside using two fingers—like she was transporting a dead rodent—and tossed them into the garbage bin.

Out of sight, out of mind.

Yeah, right.

Anzhela had lied to her. This was not achieving inner peace! This was schizophrenia on steroids!

Damn. How could she have believed the voices would go away? Some hippie-looking woman gives her a necklace and suddenly there was hope? Preposterous. She'd been so desperate to believe things would get better.

They'd gotten worse.

The coffeemaker gurgled. She poured the aromatic liquid into a large mug, knowing all the caffeine in the world wouldn't be enough to prepare her for things ahead.

CHAPTER FIVE

Valor grows by daring, fear by holding back.
~ Publilius Syrus

Brianna tossed a Lean Cuisine into the microwave. On autopilot, her fingers hit four minutes and start. As the chicken piccata cooked and spread the smell across the kitchen, she poured a large glass of ice water and brought it out to the coffee table in the den. Plato lay at her feet, unusually quiet.

Another Saturday night, complete with a frozen dinner and a DVD. Her usual routine. Saturday night meant dates for others, but she'd do what she'd always done—relax. Alone. Over the years, Saturday evenings had been her escape, time to recharge her batteries for the week ahead.

So why was there a tugging in her chest?

Steven's sudden appearance into her world made her wish for something different, something she'd craved since Declan died—a connection to another human being. When she saw Steven on her front porch with his guitar slung across his shoulder, her stomach had fluttered—actually fluttered—like butterflies coming to life for the first time.

Why hadn't he returned? Had he tried to stop by when she worked late? She racked her brain to think of ways to contact him. Maybe she could reach him through Begley's office? If Steven talked to Begley about his family, he might have mentioned where he was staying. Perhaps Begley had jotted down a cell number to follow up on any legality?

It was worth a shot. She'd call Begley's office on Monday. Meanwhile, she needed to start going out more. Savannah offered so much to experience. She wanted to meet the jewel city Declan had written about in his letters home. Connect with his favorite places, walk in his footsteps to see the mysteries and beauty.

Plato yawned and rose from his bed. "Time for a chick flick," she said. One plus of having a dog—especially a male—he didn't roll his eyes at the mention of movies that dripped with estrogen.

She scanned the DVD tower, searching for an old favorite, *Chocolat.* The survival story of a woman who enters a small town and influences the way people view the world. Brianna looked in every DVD slot.

No use. Only an empty slot where the DVD should be, meaning she wouldn't have any peace tonight. Great, now her movies had gone missing? Who steals white sandals and DVDs?

The microwave beeped, and she raised an eyebrow at Plato. "Did you move my DVD the other night when I saw Anzhela?"

He wagged his tail and circled the furniture. Brianna sighed. "Guess not."

She walked to the kitchen with Plato nipping at her heels. "Stop it, boy. I'm tired." She tossed a toy down the hall, hoping he'd chase it and leave her alone.

He didn't.

When she opened the microwave door, the steaming chicken smell permeated the kitchen, reminding her of chicken soup her mother made when she was sick. But it was the sudden tingling along her right forearm and icy gust shooting down her back that caught her undivided attention.

"Brianna?"

She turned to Plato, suddenly wondering if he could talk. With the strange events lately, who knew? But Plato only spun around, performing dog tricks for no one in particular.

There had to be a logical explanation. She pushed away the psychiatrist's mantra. To hell with logic. She'd been trying to use logic her entire life. Bottom line: she heard voices. She heard violins when it was windy. There were grits in her sink. This was her pathetic life, and it was high time she took control of it.

With smooth strokes, she rubbed the pendant Anzhela had given her and shut her eyes, squinting hard to concentrate. *Trust my instincts. Find out what the dead want and maybe they will leave me alone.*

Seconds later, she opened her eyes. And gasped.

"Hello." A semitransparent older man with white hair and a well-trimmed mustache stood in front of her, smiling with yellow-tinted teeth. He wore a faded gray suit and a plaid vest and smoked a cranberry-colored pipe. *It's official. Sherlock Holmes lives in my house.*

The voice was the same as the one she'd heard when Begley had been there, but now the apparition sounded pleasant. She stumbled back a few feet. "Who—who are you?"

Stay calm. Embrace my gift. Then get these ghosts the hell out of my house.

"James Grayson, ma'am. I'm pleased to meet you."

The man who supposedly burned the house down? She swallowed hard and rubbed the pendant again. *I've spent years talking to the dead. They talked back. Now I can see them?*

Despite his see-through state, she could easily decipher his expression. His eyes twinkled, as if he could read her innermost thoughts. "I didn't kill my family. Despite all evidence to the contrary, you're not crazy."

Somehow, a dead spirit telling her she had all her mental faculties seemed comforting. Oh, the irony.

"I don't know why you can see and hear us," James said. "But you're the first tenant who can."

Not surprising. "So Anzhela was right? You've lived here all along."

He nodded. "Some ghosts can touch things in the human world, not sure why. I left the newspaper out for Plato to find. My wife, Virginia, left the pans in your sink. I do apologize for the mess."

Brianna backed up, clutching the oak kitchen table to sturdy herself. This was too surreal. But at least she wasn't crazy. Slowly, she let her muscles unclench.

"I knew something was up. Plato knew before I did though."

She walked into the den with James floating behind her. "So who took my DVD?"

"I did." The voice was female, young, and lyrical sounding.

Brianna spun around. A teenage girl, also semitransparent, sat on the bay windowsill, twisting her long auburn curls around her fingers. She looked like a porcelain cat grooming herself. "I hid your things so you'd listen to us."

I've been listening to your kind for far too long. It's what earned me a bed in psychiatric.

Yet the desperation in the young girl's stare fired straight to Brianna's heart. The girl's life had been cut short, just like Declan's. Was this why Steven seemed so confused, wondering where his sister had gone?

"What's your name?" Brianna asked.

"I'm Amy. Sorry if we scared you, but we need your help."

The pendant round Brianna's neck grew heavy, almost like it was trying to get her attention. Anzhela mentioned the importance of remaining open to new spirits. Was this what the gypsy had meant? Brianna stumbled to the couch and sat down.

"Help with what?"

"We're trapped here," Amy said. "We can't leave the house until things are set right. Believe me, we would if we could." When she spoke, a wisp of fog lingered in the air. Ghost breath?

There had to be more to this situation than missing shoes and DVDs. "What are you not telling me? How can I help? I'm just a cosmetologist for the local funeral home—"

"Restful Oaks. Yes, we know," James said and glided to the recliner.

Strange how the dead enjoyed similar comforts to the living. She remembered Plato growling at the empty recliner in recent weeks. Damn, dogs did know more than humans.

"How do you know where I work?" she asked.

"We know many things. More importantly, we know your landlord is Sam Begley, one of the most corrupt men in Savannah. He started the rumor about me killing my own family. I would never do such a thing."

James's breath smelled like peppermint and pipe tobacco, the same scents she'd noticed in recent weeks. The evidence had been there all along. She just hadn't seen it.

Now, with Anzhela's pendant, her senses had kicked into overdrive.

"Nice to meet you," she stammered. *I'm seeing ghosts in my den. There's a yacht in my therapist's future.*

"Thank you," James replied, a courteous Southern tone encasing his words. One of sincerity. When Begley talked, his accent sounded put-on, a means of keeping up appearances.

"So, where is Mrs. Grayson? Virginia, is it?" May as well meet the whole family, right? The woman's voice she'd heard the other night must have been Virginia's.

James took a puff from his pipe and cast a nervous glance toward Amy. "Well, she's—"

"Indisposed," Amy said. "Now, about how you can help us…"

Brianna stared at the TV. She'd never get *Chocolat* back until she listened, and she longed for a movie to wash away her worries. "Fine, but no promises. Tell me about Begley. You say he's corrupt?" She sat on the arm of the couch.

James moved smoothly from the recliner to the couch. When he reached toward Brianna's arm, the air turned cold.

"Begley killed us, Brianna."

"*What?*"

She rubbed the back of her neck to get rid of the goose bumps. Her landlord was a murderer?

“Begley wanted our house,” James said. “One day we’re minding our own business, and he shows up and demands we sell. I told him no repeatedly. Virginia is proud of her family homestead. She wouldn’t move five feet outside Savannah.”

Steven had mentioned the house had been in their family for three generations.

“What happened? How did Begley kill you?” Brianna asked.

Amy glided effortlessly and sat next to James. “He cornered us in the back of the house. He maimed Daddy first and then killed Mama. He started to go for me—”

“When I hit him in the knee with the fireplace poker.” James’s eyes glared with rage.

Brianna shivered, remembering how Begley winced when he stepped into her house. “He told me the bad knee was from playing college football.”

James laughed. “The closest that wuss ever got to college ball was being the towel boy. He’s lying.”

Brianna’s head throbbed. Too much input. She grabbed the glass of water and took several swallows.

“Why not take revenge yourselves? Why do you even need me?”

With a weary gaze, James said, “We tried to leave, but some kind of force always pulls us back. We’re literally tied to this house, at least for now.”

Three permanent houseguests? Brianna shoved away the thought. Anzhela had been right—the pendant worked. Though certainly not how Brianna had expected or Anzhela led her to believe.

What had Declan always said? *Be careful what you wish for.* Why had she not listened to the things he’d taught her so long ago? She’d always resisted, and she’d always wound up having to learn the hard way.

“If Begley killed you,” she said, “then how is he not in jail? Why is he renting houses to unsuspecting people like me?”

James puffed on his pipe, filling the room with sweet clover. “Once Begley had us trapped in the back of the house, he set the fire. The master and back rooms burned, and the front had some damage. Since we’d burned to death, there weren’t any autopsies. The man is dangerous. Be careful.”

She had to admit, James had an old-school wisdom she admired. But the thought of Begley wandering around Savannah killing people? Illogical.

“I’ll be fine.” She took a sip of water. “Not to pry, but what about Steven? He came by the other day, but I haven’t seen him since. Where was he when you all died? Why didn't he know anything about the house?"

Amy muffled a sob and James stared at the floor. Obviously, Steven was a sore subject.

"My son made his bed and has to live in it." A rotund woman with facial wrinkles like a shar-pei appeared from the kitchen. "And that's enough of your questions, Yankee woman."

Yankee woman?

James blushed, likely embarrassed by his wife's crass behavior. "Brianna, this is my wife, Virginia."

"Nice to meet you," Brianna said, her tongue almost halting on the lie. What *had* happened to Steven? Why didn't his family want to discuss the matter? How did he not know his family had died?

Virginia gave her the once-over glance and frowned. Even semitransparent, Virginia's prudish eyes held judgment that wouldn't go away anytime soon.

"I'm Virginia Grayson," she said with the smooth authority one used to address ladies' league meetings. She'd probably given many speeches in her day. "Welcome to my home."

Your home? Brianna's neck stiffened.

"I need to know what you want, how I can help," Brianna said. *So I can get my house back, thank you very much.*

Virginia's heavy sigh fogged up the mirror hanging on the wall. "Must we solicit the Yankee's help?"

Amy shot her a dirty look. "Mama, you promised to behave."

Great, not just ghosts, but dysfunctional ones. *This just keeps getting better and better.*

James sat forward and cleared his throat. "We think Begley continues to commit crimes. Our house wasn't the only one he wanted."

"He did say he wanted to put Savannah on the economic map," Brianna said.

"Yes, but at what cost to human lives?"

Brianna looked down at her hands stained by eye shadows and other creams she'd used for work. "I put makeup on the dead. What could I possibly do to help the three of you?"

"Sneak into Begley's office, review his estate contracts, gather evidence against him, and anything else you can," James said.

No, Your Honor, the devil didn't make me do it. The ghosts did. Somehow, she didn't see any judge buying such a lame excuse. And since when was this her responsibility? She'd moved to Savannah to get away from strange events, not walk right into them.

"I have a six-month lease. Begley's offered me a rent-to-own option. Why would he do that if he wanted the property for himself?"

James paused for a long moment. “You may want to reread your house agreement. Chances are, Begley’s just collecting extra money and never intended to let you own this place.”

Brianna choked on her drink.

James sat up straighter. “We never had the chance to see Begley brought to justice. You can make that happen. Maybe, once justice is served, we’ll be free to leave.”

Brianna reached down to pet a docile Plato. Was she seriously considering their proposal? The only reason to do such a crazy thing would be to get them out of her house once and for all.

“Our family loved Savannah,” James continued. “We were happy once. And then that bastard—”

“Language, Daddy,” Amy said.

James offered an apologetic smile to his daughter before turning back to Brianna. “He stole our lives, our home. Now he’s stolen our peace. I want him exposed.”

The pride in those wise eyes flickered into sorrow. “You can say no. I realize we’re putting you in an awkward position, but we’d be forever in your debt.”

She glanced at the kitchen cabinets, the wallpaper border, the home that, until recently, she presumed would be hers. What would happen if she said no? She’d likely be stuck with these ghosts for the rest of her days.

Not a good option. But spying on Begley, trying to take someone as powerful as him down, accuse him of murder? Not ideal either.

"I don't know," Brianna said. "This is all so bizarre."

James nodded, took out a handkerchief, and dabbed his eyes. Did ghosts tear up? What else could they do?

After he put the white linen in his pocket, he gazed at her with pained eyes. Eyes of an old soul. "I understand, but you could make a difference, Brianna."

Make a difference. Her promise to Declan chimed in her ears. Maybe this is what Anzhela meant when she said to listen to her instincts. Would doing so bring inner peace? But was Brianna supposed to keep her promise by spying on her landlord, possibly losing her house in the process? Couldn't she just give money to charity?

"I need time to think about it," Brianna said. She hoped she sounded more put together than she felt.

Amy nodded, her auburn curls bouncing off her shoulders. "We understand. We'll leave you alone so you can mull it over."

If anyone could convince her to help, Amy had the best chance. A life cut short was a tragedy, especially with someone so young. As Declan had been.

"I'm not saying I will help," Brianna began. "But if I do, I have one condition."

James's eyes twinkled. For a split second he resembled a shopping-mall Santa Claus, a jolly old gentleman who could grant anyone's wishes. "Anything."

CHAPTER SIX

In Ireland, the inevitable never happens
and the unexpected constantly occurs.
~ Sir John Pentland Mahaffy

On Saturday, the early morning sun ruptured through a slit in the hotel curtain and positioned itself on Steven's face. He shifted and rolled over, but the light followed, sending a warmth across his eyelids even though he'd shut them tight.

Time to wake up. Get things done. He didn't want to hang out in Savannah any longer than necessary. Learning the truth about his family's death would take time. The cash reserves from the band's breakup wouldn't last forever.

The breakup. It was like losing an arm or leg. The rest of his body tried to function, but some integral part was missing. His jaw clenched at the memory. Electric guitars in an array of colors, amps blaring through massive speakers, and the thundering applause of the crowd going wild. So many thrills, from hearing his songs on the radio to the first time the band squeezed into the top-ten hits.

Without those essentials, without his routine of practices and gigs, the days faded from one to the next. Returning to Savannah skewed his timeline even more. Home always had.

He stumbled out of bed and yanked the curtains open. Damn, what a view. The Hyatt had upgraded him to a river-view room based on the many points he'd earned playing gigs up the California coast over the years. The landscape in Savannah took his breath away.

The serpentine Savannah River glimmered with sunlight as the port city came to life. A rusty behemoth of a ship carrying multicolored containers crept toward the docks where yellow cranes were already in place to lift them onto land one at a time, like Tetris pieces.

Home wasn't *all* bad. To the left, the Talmadge Bridge—resembling a string guitar, with bridge cables fanning out from the tall arches to the base—carried the weight of cars on their way to South Carolina.

Damn, he needed to get back to his music. His mind was on full tilt. Even seeing musical instruments when he looked at a bridge? If he didn't return to his passion soon, he'd be one of those guys who only saw guitars when staring at inkblots.

He dressed in jeans and a white T-shirt in a matter of seconds. Computer in hand, he took the elevator out to the private River Street exit and zigzagged the two blocks to the Artisan Café. At least a few of his favorite places remained. They'd added free Wi-Fi, making the spot ideal for morning research.

First, he'd gather what info he could on the house fire. Second, check out Begley's business doings. The bastard was dirty. Third, stop by his old house. Or rather, Brianna's place.

A bell chimed when he entered the café, and an ache rolled in his gut. Brianna's place. The words just didn't sound right. The house was meant to pass down through generations, not rent to a stranger. Not that he'd ever planned to raise a family down South. He always assumed Amy would, but was that fair to her?

She'd only been sixteen when she died. He had his chance to leave home, spread his wings, and see other parts of the world. She never had the opportunity. Aside from the guilt nagging at him for not protecting her, of not following up with her when she didn't return his calls, the thought of her unlived life haunted him the most.

He waited in line behind a young couple, their hands intertwined with leftover passion from a night spent together, he guessed. Watching their intimacy, his thoughts turned to Brianna.

Begley had been right about one thing. She had a rare beauty. He couldn't let her looks distract him, however. Would she be open to moving? He'd have to get past the legal Begley crap, but if he got that far—would Brianna be willing to let him have his home back? Not that he planned to sell it right away since he didn't want to make Savannah his home base. But the home had belonged in his family. He had to figure out something.

Stop. Thoughts running amok wouldn't solve anything. Especially before coffee.

He ordered dark roast, thanked the barista, and settled into the back corner. The café was quaint, tucked away past the bars and gift shops, with assorted colorful art on the walls. Flavorful aromas tickled his nostrils as he glanced around. An empty, old stage sat off to the left, cluttered with stacks of spare chairs.

A long-buried wish stepped out of the shadows. With the band in California, he'd lived the rock-star routine: loud music, large crowds, fame and fortune around every corner. But amid the earsplitting noise, he'd longed to try an acoustic, coffeehouse approach to music. Hell, he'd written several ballads over the years. The band hadn't been interested; they'd wanted to keep the rock-and-roll branding.

Maybe Savannah could offer him the chance to do something different. He could try and convince the café owners to let him play a few nights a week. If he had to be back home again, why not incorporate music? Nothing fancy or overdone, just a small connection to what he loved while he figured out what happened to his family.

Coffeehouse gigs had more ways to connect with the audience than the neon nightclubs anyway. The Artisan Café seemed more…what was the word? Alive? Eclectic groups of people from all walks of life traipsing through, creative energy in the espresso-scented air, and quirky chalkboards with questions of the day written in hot pink: *If your life were a rollercoaster, what would its name be?*

Train wreck.

Shake it off, man. Don't think that way. There's still time to change, make amends. Even if Dad wasn't alive to see the effort, Steven had finally returned home.

He took a big swig of coffee, hoping to calm his thoughts.

From his position, he could keep an eye on anyone entering or leaving the establishment. Paranoid? Not exactly. But something wasn't right. Best to be on guard until he learned what the hell had happened in Savannah since he left.

He flipped open his laptop and Googled Savannah house fires. Seven links appeared, most from the local paper. He read each article and typed a few notes in an open document. All the houses were older Victorians, homes whose families had owned the properties for generations. Just like his. Hmm, interesting. All fires were within a three-block radius. Some homes were completely destroyed. Others, like his parents', only had partial damage but had required extensive remodeling.

Begley mentioned wanting to redo parts of the city. Could his redevelopment plans be motive for arson? Quite a stretch, especially when the historic district was close-knit anyway. But when it came to Begley, anything was possible.

The moron hadn't even searched phone records. If he had, he'd have seen how Steven called Amy on her birthday and holidays. Wouldn't the average Joe put two and two together? Granted, Steven lost touch and had left messages on voicemail the last few times he'd called, and too much time had passed since he'd reached his little sister. But calls from California would still appear on the phone bill. Who else from California would have called Amy?

Steven took another swallow of coffee. Without proof of wrongdoing, he couldn't do anything about Begley—yet. He scanned a few more story links, diving deeper into the incidents. A name jumped out at him. Dennis Stuart? Every journalistic piece had been covered by a Dennis Stuart. Could it be the same guy? Drummer Dennis, the guy he used to jam with in high school? Steven had assumed his old buddies had split the South just like him. Could Dennis have stayed? More importantly, could he become a resource to learn what really caused the fire?

###

An hour later, Steven knocked on the lime-green door. A clean-cut guy answered, with a slicked-back receding hairline. Steven waited a long moment. Had he approached the wrong house again? The Dennis he knew wore kinked hair down his back and played drums until all hours of the night. This corporate-banker-looking guy didn't resemble his old friend.

Not at first.

A flicker of recognition crossed Dennis's brown eyes. His mouth dropped open. "Steven? Holy shit, man! What the hell are you doing here?"

Steven gripped his buddy's hand. "Long story."

"C'mon, come in." Dennis opened the door wider.

"Thanks." Steven followed him to a fairly neat kitchen. White cabinets, indigo countertops covered with every kind of electronic gadget on the market—iPad, cell phone with zoom screen, coffeepot with cappuccino maker.

Dennis grabbed two bottled waters from the fridge and offered one. "What's up? I didn't know you were in town."

Where to begin? They hadn't talked in so long. With his own band's recent breakup, Steven wasn't feeling super confident.

"I didn't know you still lived here," Steven began. He pulled out a black bistro-style chair and sat by the tall table. "Thought the whole gang split the South just like me. Then I saw your name in the paper. You're a journalist now?"

Dennis sat and pointed to stacks of papers and files lined against the wall. "Yep. The paper trail never goes away, even if the world is digital."

Steven took a sip of water, contemplating how to approach the real reason he'd come. "I hear that. Listen, I want to catch up—how you've been, what's been happening—but I did come here with a specific question."

"Ask away." Dennis's expression held no trace of animosity or confusion about the past. Good. Made the question easier.

"I noticed you covered the story of my family's death—"

"Aw, man. I was so sorry when that happened."

"Thanks." Steven bit his lip. No reason to divulge too much too soon. "I know I've been away a long time. I didn't even know they'd died until I returned to town last week. Can you give me any details, anything suspicious you noticed? Help me piece together the puzzle, so to speak."

Dennis didn't say anything for a long moment. When he spoke, there was an unmistakable earnestness in his voice. "I wish I'd have known more back then. I might've been able to stop that corrupt asshole Begley from buying the house."

Steven swallowed hard. "Tell me more about Begley."

"What's to tell? He's unbelievably corrupt. Hell, he's evil incarnate. The historic society is pissed off because he purchases so many homes. Always gets around the preservation laws, and he has corruption in his genes. All those fires so close together—"

"Do you think it was arson?" Steven asked. A leap in motive, yes, but perhaps Dennis could provide the missing pieces.

"Brother, I'm sure it was. But good luck proving it."

Steven clasped his hands around the cold water bottle. The coolness seeped into his fists, fists that yearned to pound Begley into a wall.

"I went to see the bastard, figuring I could learn what happened. He blew me off, told me he tried to locate me in a few cities. Jackass didn't try very hard."

Frown lines crossed Dennis's face. Something was wrong.

"What?" Steven said.

"I tried to find you for months, man. Even had a few leads tying Begley to corruption and fraud. When my editor got wind of it, she ordered me to bury the story."

"What? And you did? Didn't you even try to follow up?" Damn it, did everyone know more than him?

Dennis leaned forward. "Look, I was a rookie then. Didn't even know what I had in my hands. I've been trying to build a case against Begley since, but proof is hard to come by. The man may be an asshole, but he covers his tracks with precision."

Steven clenched and unclenched his fists. Let go of the anger. He needed friends right now. Dennis shouldn't have buried the story, but

Steven had made enough mistakes over the years. Who was he to judge anyone else's?

"Want some help with nailing Begley?" Steven asked.

"Are you serious?"

"I'm not leaving town until I get the truth." Steven felt his body stiffen. *Besides, it's not like I have a band to return to in California.*

"Then you'd better plan on retiring in Savannah." Dennis shook his head. "I cover the main stories to pay the bills. All those files"—he pointed to the paperwork lining the wall—"are done on my own time to bring that sack of shit to justice."

Steven's gaze wandered across the wall. Stacks of papers, ledgers, boxes. The paperwork nightmare from hell. But if it would get Begley behind bars, so much the better.

"I'm in," Steven said.

"Sounds good, man. Where are you staying?"

"The Hyatt on River Street."

Dennis pointed down the hallway. "If we're going to take Begley down, you'll go bankrupt at a hotel. Want to crash in the spare room? It ain't much, but it's yours if you want it."

"I don't want to impose—"

"Nonsense, brother. Truth is, I've missed hanging out with you. Remember all those band jam sessions in high school?"

“You still have your drum kit?” Steven asked, a wave of nostalgia sweeping over him.

“In the garage.”

“Ever do gigs anymore?”

Dennis shrugged. “Since the gang left town, I haven’t found anyone I wanted to pursue gigs with. Nothing matches our old group.”

“Hard to believe. We were just kids.”

“Maybe we can jam some now that you’re back.”

Steven smiled. Being home was starting to look up. “Count me in.”

###

They spent the afternoon hours reviewing all the history on Begley. How did someone get so much power? A better question: How were they supposed to take someone down who had such influence?

Dennis’s research proved Begley had corrupt cops, city officials, everyone in his pocket. Dennis was right. This would take time. Good thing for the free place to stay. The spare room was decent, a basic bed and set of shelves. Great for now.

Dennis went to the fridge and brought back two Cokes. “So tell me something. Why come back now, after all this time? I didn’t think you’d ever return.”

Steven set down the file he’d been holding. All letters, documents, and legalities had begun to swirl together. He needed a break.

"Amy." Steven rubbed his eyes and brushed his fingers through his hair, hoping to keep himself awake. "I was in a band, a great one, out in San Fran. Gigs four nights a week, top pay, great apartment overlooking the ocean, you name it."

"Sounds terrible," Dennis said, smirking.

"I was on top of the world." Steven drank some Coke, letting the bubbles tickle his throat on the way down. "Then I, um…"

"Then came a woman," Dennis said.

Steven chuckled. His buddy always did know how to fill in the blanks. "Yes, only she was the lead singer's younger sister. Kate."

"Ouch, brother. You got a death wish?"

"Maybe. I didn't intend to fall for her. It just happened. We were on one of those long bus rides, the kind where you spend hours talking to someone? She was amazing. Beautiful, bright, and longing for life on the road."

Dennis nodded, clearly knowing where this was headed. "But lead singer didn't want his little sister being a tagalong in the rock 'n' roll way of life."

"Exactly." Steven suppressed a smile. He'd been right in looking up Dennis, who wasn't only an old buddy but someone who could fill in the missing gaps without Steven having to go through the agony of saying it. Theirs had been the perfect friendship once. Maybe it could be again.

"Let me see if I have this right," Dennis said. "You tell top guy you're going to keep dating his little sister. He freaks out. Insert lots of arguments in a slew of cities, ending with your band splitting up."

"Yes."

Damn, Dennis *was* a journalist. He didn't know the full story, but the basic explanation was enough.

Dennis scratched his chin. "So you decided to return home to visit, just like that? Nah, man. I don't buy it. Why'd you really come back?"

Should Steven tell him? Dennis was trustworthy. They'd known each other all their lives. And anyone who was Begley's enemy was Steven's best friend.

"I returned for Amy, mainly."

"Your little sister," Dennis said.

"Yes. Granted, I suppose part of me wanted to make amends with Dad, but I didn't have my hopes up. I wanted to see Amy. Make sure she was okay."

Dennis tilted his head, confusion and curiosity etched on his face. The look of someone who knew there was more to the story.

Damn, Steven had missed his old friend who didn't let him get away with anything.

"The girl," Steven began. "Kate, the younger sister of the lead singer—"

"What about her?"

Steven blinked back tears. *Just say it.* "Kate was killed by a drunk driver two months ago."

"Aw, man. Sorry."

"Thanks." Steven took a swig of Coke. "I was so stunned after it happened. Then Tyler showed up and gave me right hook to the jaw." Steven rubbed it, remembering the pain from Tyler's hurtling fist. "It got me to thinking. I adored Kate, but she was someone's younger sister. How would I have reacted if he'd wanted to date Amy? I began to see his side of things."

Dennis nodded. "So you came back to check on her."

"Yes. I called her on a regular basis from California. Things became busy and I missed reaching her for quite some time. When I tried again, the phone had been disconnected. I figured something had happened and I'd better get back to Savannah. Making amends with my father would be a bonus, but Amy is why I came home."

"Can I help in any way?"

Steven stared at the floor, trying to focus. "Just help me figure out what happened to my family."

"You got it."

Dennis hadn't hesitated one second. Steven realized right then, he was one of the lucky ones.

"Thanks."

Dennis stood up. "You want another soda?"

"Nah. Let's finish going through these files today. Tomorrow, I need to go by my family's house."

"Did Begley find a tenant?"

"A woman named Brianna."

"You met her?" Dennis asked.

Steven nodded. "I showed up at the family homestead to learn Begley owns the property and rented it out. But she was nice. She said she'd try to get me some additional information."

Dennis arched an eyebrow. "Do you think she could be on our side? No person is going to go against their landlord. Not in Savannah, where historic district property is prime real estate."

"Brianna might."

"What makes you so sure?"

Because I saw the look of loneliness in her eyes.

"I have a feeling," Steven said. "Besides, it's worth a shot."

Dennis shook his head. "You always did have a way with women. Let's hope it can help our cause."

"Damn straight." Steven raised his soda in a toast gesture, keeping a casual air about things. He stopped short of saying the words burning on the tip of his tongue. *Because all the women I've cared about have wound up dead. And I can't afford to mess this up.*

CHAPTER SEVEN

Anyone who has never made a mistake
has never tried anything new.
~ Albert Einstein

Any hope Brianna had for sleeping late on Sunday was cut short by the shrill ringtone on her smart phone. Caller ID said Restful Oaks. Edwin? Why was he calling her at this hour on her day off?

"Hello?"

"Good morning," Edwin said in his usual mortician yet Southern drawl. The man would make an incredible narrator for a haunted house.

"Morning," she mumbled. "Is something wrong?"

"I hate to ask this—"

"You need me to come into work, don't you?"

Crap. Her hopes of roaming Savannah and beginning to enjoy the city went right out the window. Why was her life two steps forward, one step back?

"Yes," Edwin said.

He sighed so loud, she had to pull her ear away from the phone. "We have a body which requires some…discretion…and the family wants this matter done and settled."

"And this can't be done tomorrow?" she asked. As soon as she said the words, she wanted to take them back. Normally, she'd have bitten her tongue, but he'd woke her up, for Pete's sake.

"No. The family didn't get along, there are matters which need to be cleared up, and we need to accommodate their wishes."

"You're right." She felt a pang of guilt. This was part of the mortuary business. While there would always be job security, people didn't die between nine and five. "I'll be there in thirty minutes."

"Great. Thanks."

She hung up and looked at a wide-eyed Plato. "Sorry boy, I can't take you to the park today."

He whimpered.

No sign of the Graysons. No whispers after she'd gone to bed last night either. Maybe they were in hiding, giving her some time to decide if she would help them. She didn't object, nor was she about to look a gift horse in the mouth. Freedom from voices and spirits was a welcome thing. No sense questioning it.

Forty-five minutes later, she stood in the preparation room next to Edwin, staring at the body on the table. Ian Kendall was only sixteen. The file said he'd run away from home four years ago.

His weatherworn skin resembled an old fisherman's, someone who'd endured Mother Nature's bitter moods. Living on the streets, away from friends and family, tended to age people faster than a presidential term.

"What happened, Edwin? He's only a kid."

Edwin clasped his hands together, an enclosed knot at the end of noodle-like arms. *Ladies and gentlemen, meet the human Muppet.*

"All signs point to pneumonia. He didn't appear to be seeking medical care," Edwin whispered. In the confines of Restful Oaks, Edwin always spoke in hushed tones.

Brianna stared at the boy's Goth appearance. He had ivory skin and thick, black eyelashes. Smudged eyeliner caked his lower eyelids and a plum-colored lipstick had begun to fade from his lips. But it was the multicolored Mohawk that captured her attention.

"I'll need some extra time to work with his hair."

Edwin stepped closer to the body. "I wanted to speak with you about that. Ladies?"

Two frumpy old women entered the room. They held each other arm in arm as if holding on for dear life, like one would slip away into death by walking into a funeral home.

"Brianna, this is Myrtle and Evelyn Kendall. Ladies, this is our cosmetologist, Brianna McNeil. She'll be handling Ian's makeup and hair."

What was Edwin thinking? Standard practice didn't allow relatives into the preparation room. People who saw their loved ones before they were prepped tended to get upset. The flesh color in the bodies hadn't been contoured, and sometimes there was bloating. It was never a pretty sight, so why had Edwin brought these women into the room? Why the urgency in calling her in on a weekend?

The old ladies waddled to the kid's body and began to comment.

"Such a sad thing."

"Yes, indeedy."

"He never listened, always ignored folks. I told him time and time again to cut his hair."

"He caused quite a ruckus."

"Now look at him. With that awful Mohawk."

"He never listened to anyone, not even his own mama. What kind of kid doesn't obey his mama?"

"She was always too permissive, you know."

"That she was. Thank heavens his daddy knew better."

"Sad."

"Tragic."

"I just can't get past that awful hair."

Brianna shifted her gaze between the two frumps like watching a tennis match. The women looked like Tweedle Dum and Tweedle Dee, but without the propeller hats.

"Edwin?" she prompted. *Please take them to your office and let me work.*

He didn't seem to get the hint. Instead, he offered a comforting pat on both women's shoulders. "We will see to it that your nephew is buried with a respectful appearance." He flashed Brianna a stern glare.

The two women gave Brianna the once-over, as if evaluating whether she would obey.

"Please don't cover up my hair," a hoarse voice said.

Brianna jumped and metallic adrenaline surged into her mouth. Yuck.

"Are you okay?" Edwin asked with sincere concern on his face.

"Yes." She dug her nails into her palms. She really didn't need her boss knowing about her gift. When her hands lifted to rub the pendant, movement flittered across the room. When she looked, the young kid's nearly transparent form sat on the edge of the preparation table, his dark eyes shining with hope.

"Can you see me? Hear me?" the ghost asked.

She bit her lip but nodded in what she hoped was a nonchalant way. If Edwin or the clients suspected she was talking to ghosts, she'd be out of a job quicker than she could say *grits*.

The boy's ghost form smiled. "Fantastic, thanks. Please don't let my aunts take charge. Please. They never understood me. My hair was the first thing I had that was mine, something I could control. They never let me have a say in anything. Don't let them have a say in my death."

Brianna leaned toward Edwin. "May I have a word with you in private?"

One of the women marched up to her, leaving no personal space. "You are going to follow our instructions, aren't you? I do not want to see that horrible Mohawk on my nephew. He needs to look respectful for the service, and every single member of our family hates that sinful hairstyle he has."

"Meet my Aunt Myrtle," the kid said. "Such a tolerant woman."

Brianna couldn't help herself. She smiled, even though it wasn't appropriate.

Myrtle frowned, and the lines on her face made her cheeks sag a bit. "I don't think this is funny in the least." She turned to Edwin. "Are you going to make this woman do her job or not?"

Edwin gripped her arm. "Brianna—"

"Of course I'll do my job, ma'am," Brianna said. "Edwin, please give me a moment in private?" *And get your hand off of me!*

He ushered her toward the doorway, leaving the women to their commentary.

“The family,” Edwin said, “wants the Mohawk gone. Use a toupee piece, something that will be a better appearance.”

She took a deep breath. There was a tactful way to make her point without disrespecting her boss. “I understand the family’s concern, but Ian Kendall was an individual. To cover up his hair now means covering up his identity.”

Edwin’s thin lips turned downward. “Yes, but we need to do right by the relatives.”

Why did the living insist on managing everything, including the dead? What about the voices of the deceased?

“I thought our job was to respect the dead,” Brianna said. Working in the funeral business meant compromise, a balance between making the family happy and abiding by the deceased’s wishes. At least, that’s what Edwin had taught her in training. It’s how her own family ran their funeral home in Boston.

“Just do as I tell you on this one, Brianna. Apparently, one of Ian’s relatives is running for office and the family doesn’t need any kind of scandal.”

Politics or not, why was Edwin changing his rule for these horrible old women? They clearly had no understanding of who Ian Kendall ever was.

She looked at Ian's spirit once more. The tension creases between his brows spoke volumes. The kid would never have wanted to be buried this way. Ian Kendall was an individual, not a conformist. She had to try to make Edwin see reason, even if he barked at her.

"This kid left home at age twelve," she said. "He lived and died on the street to get away from his relatives. I'm not saying the hair won't be a problem, but shouldn't we try to compromise?"

Edwin wrung his bony hands together. "This is how we do things. Appearances are important, but I appreciate your dedication to your work. Leave your personal feelings aside and do what's right for the family."

Was there no changing his mind in this? "But—"

"Enough." Edwin's eyes flashed with anger and impatience. In a split second, he changed from serene funeral director to something—else. Something eerie. Mean.

"Restful Oaks is my life," he said. "I've struggled to build my career, and I'm not going to ruin my reputation because you feel empathy for some runaway kid."

Wasn't he being a bit dramatic? She wanted to do her job and respect the dead Restful Oaks sent onward. Always make the bodies look their best—it was the code she lived by. But respecting the individual was paramount.

She lowered her voice, wanting to appear respectful. "I didn't say anything about ruining your reputation—"

"I don't even own the funeral home. Begley does."

She coughed and struggled for breath. "Begley owns Restful Oaks?" Meaning Begley controlled her home and her job? Helping the Graysons could cause her some serious trouble.

Edwin nodded. "He's kept me on as funeral director and manager. We've established a low-rent rate for life, thanks to his granddaddy and mine being fishing buddies. I can't jeopardize my business. Fix up Ian's body and call Margie when it's done."

With that, Edwin's slender hand grabbed her wrist. Ouch—that would leave a bruise. He led her back to the preparation room and escorted the two women out, but not before looking back to give one long, last glare with a clear message: She'd better do as he'd requested.

Damn. Left alone, Brianna traced each colorful spike of Ian's Mohawk with her fingers. His ghost crouched in a back corner.

"I'm sorry, Ian. Nobody seems to understand what you were about."

"Can't you do something?" he asked. The room turned cold when he spoke.

"I can't leave your Goth appearance as is or I'll lose my job."

Ian approached his empty shell of a body. "I don't want to get you fired."

Brianna couldn't stand to look into those dark, individualistic eyes any longer. She had to find a way. "I'll see what I can do."

"Really? Thanks."

She combed the two front spikes down, cut and layered them, and brushed the hair around his face. Leaving the other spikes intact, she moussed them behind his head, adding an extra pillow to hide the orange and green hues. She dyed the front two spikes brown and draped the acceptably colored hair around his face. Instant conformity with a twist. His aunts would be pleased to see the Mohawk was gone, yet Ian's spirit could move onward with individuality undamaged.

Brianna glanced to where Ian's ghost sat. He was smiling. "You do good work."

"Thanks," she said. The dead had never commented on her cosmetology skills before. If they could talk all the time, how easy it would be to ensure she presented the appearance they wanted.

Wait. Why was she wishing for more voices? No. Not good. No more voices, thank you.

She stared at Ian's body on the table. "May you be more understood in your new realm than you were in this life."

Warmth spread across her shoulders, relaxing the muscles. She glanced up. Ian's ghost had disappeared and taken the cold air with him.

She took one final look at her handiwork and smiled. She'd done the right thing. Edwin would never know.

CHAPTER EIGHT

May the road rise to meet you, May the wind be always at your back. May the sun shine warm upon your face, the rain fall soft upon your fields. And until we meet again, may God hold you in the palm of his hand.

~ Irish Blessing

Declan leaned against a massive cypress tree on the front lawn of Restful Oaks Funeral Home. The next soul should arrive soon. After fifteen years of helping the recently dead transition to their new existence, he'd become an expert at timing. He'd also grown accustomed to what the newbies needed. Comfort, first. Answers, second. Honestly, he'd been the same way.

At least he'd made his way back to Savannah. Being dead in Idaho was worse than hell. But here, in this port city with more ghosts than people? Work remained busy and the afterlife was never boring. There were also pirate legends, shanghai tales, and historic buildings—all under a canopy of Spanish moss and massive live oaks. Savannah was…alive…in a way no other place could match. And it took way too many years of overtime to get stationed here.

When the kid's spirit drifted through the funeral home walls, Declan squinted. Were his eyes failing him after all these years of escorting the dead to their next place? Who'd botched the kid's hair? The front appeared average, standard brown hair draped around the face. But the back? Green and orange points spiked upward like a fan. The kid looked like a lost peacock.

Not that Declan was surprised. Young souls came in all shapes and sizes, complete with tattoos and piercings. He'd wanted a tattoo but hadn't dared cross his father's wishes. Kids nowadays were braver, willing to become independent despite the consequences.

"Are you Ian Kendall?" Declan asked.

"Yep. Who are you?"

"I'm Declan McNeil, your very own mentor."

He gave Ian the once-over glance, stopping again at his hair. Strange, but it wouldn't cause complications. Other things would though. "You have any piercings?"

The kid opened his mouth and stuck out his tongue to reveal a silver stud. Declan flinched. This journey was going to be difficult.

"That's gonna hurt when we cross over."

The kid blinked. "Cross over?"

"Into your next realm. Afterlife. Purgatory. Heaven. Whatever you want to call it. Metal gets tangled in the portals."

Ian didn't have much color—he was dead—but what little color remained seeped from his face. "How does metal get tangled?"

Declan smiled. So many things the living didn't know about the next life. Hell, he hadn't either. Those souls who died without any unresolved business were the easiest. Greet them, check for piercings, escort them to their orientation, case closed.

The others, those who'd died without resolution in some form, required more effort. That's why the mentor system existed. Groups of souls, all within a chain of command, working all corners of the Earth to ensure the newly dead could resolve their issues and eventually cross over. Otherwise, overpopulation became a problem.

Declan patted the kid on the shoulder. "Afterlife portals are like an MRI machine. Anything metal or foreign in the body gets sucked out. Last week, I escorted a nineteen-year-old girl across who had five hundred piercings. She almost didn't make it to the end."

Ian stood motionless, seeming to contemplate his upcoming fate. "What, exactly, happens now?"

Declan patted Ian on the shoulder. "Don't worry. You'll learn everything at orientation. Then I'll take you through the portal to your new home."

"Would that be Heaven or Hell?"

Declan chuckled. "Call it what you want. Try to imagine the afterlife as a giant house. I'm the one greeting you in the foyer, and I'll take you to the living room to get your orientation. They'll go over all the rules—"

"The afterlife has rules?" Ian frowned.

Declan shrugged. “Yeah, who knew, right? Same as in life, there are penalties for those who don’t obey the primary laws.”

“Like what?”

“It’s complicated. They’ll teach you everything at orientation.” No sense going into a bunch of surreal laws that wouldn’t make sense at this early stage.

Ian’s eyes widened with curiosity. “Can’t you give me a general guideline? I don’t want to piss anyone off. And hell would be returning to my aunts’ house. My family didn’t understand me in life. I don’t want to be around them now that I’m dead.”

Declan thought for a moment. He didn’t want to overwhelm the kid. “Fine. There are two types of afterlife spirits—indoors and outdoors—and where you died determines where you will spend your time. Since you died on the street, outside, you’ll be confined to outdoor places. You can’t enter people’s homes, but the outdoors is your territory.”

“So no haunting my favorite tattoo parlor?” Ian grinned.

“Not until you earn enough points to exist in both indoor and outdoor places. It takes a lot of time, trust me.”

“What about you?”

“Me?” Declan asked. He wasn’t accustomed to newbie souls asking him about himself. Most were so freaked out by their own death experience, they rarely talked. But Ian was different. He almost seemed at ease, happy.

"I'm an outdoor ghost, like you will be. I died in a plane crash and never had the chance to say good-bye to my sister. I volunteered to work in the mentor program so I'd store up enough privileges to transfer between indoors and outdoors. I plan to find her. That day can't come soon enough."

Ian nodded, seeming satisfied with the response.

Time to move and get the kid to orientation on time. "I do have to ask, before we go—"

"Yeah?" Ian asked.

"What's with the hair? Most souls appear impeccable, but it seems Restful Oaks did a botch job on you."

Ian's purple lips turned into a huge smile. "You don't understand. They did an amazing job."

Really? Had the kid looked in a mirror?

"Then why do you have two hairstyles? Was the cosmetologist a split personality?" Declan laughed at his own joke.

"Nah, man. You don't get it. My overbearing family wanted to make me up like a Bible salesman. Not my style. Never was. But this woman, Brianna, took great care of me—"

"*What?*"

Coincidence. It had to be. No way could his little sister be in Savannah. Could she?

"Brianna, man. She refused to give in. She tucked in my spikes behind pillows so my aunts wouldn't notice. I got to keep my unique look. This gal was fantastic. She really respects the dead."

Holy hell. "Tell me what she looks like."

"Probably in her thirties, shoulder length black hair, blue eyes. She could use a suntan. I don't know. She was great though."

Declan slid down the knobby tree and pressed his back up to it. "I don't believe this."

"What?"

"Brianna's my kid sister. I've been dead for fifteen years. Been searching for her for that long too, but it's not like I get much say where I work. Besides, families are strictly off-limits. Especially to the newbies."

Ian cocked an eyebrow. "So what happens now?"

Declan admired the brazen quality in Ian's appearance. The kid could be quite helpful.

"Now we get to break a few of those rules I told you about."

CHAPTER NINE

Your feet will bring you to where your heart is.
~ Irish Proverb

Brianna heard Plato barking long before she reached the front door. With arms full of groceries, she fumbled with the keys and finally swung open the door. Plato bolted toward her, knocking his paws into her knees.

"Why are you out of your crate, boy?"

He circled and barked.

She looked around but saw no sign of James, Virginia, or Amy. Surely, they'd been the ones to let Plato loose. He didn't know how to jump baby gates.

Maybe the Graysons were still giving her some space. Good thing. Solitude was what she needed, especially if they wanted her help. But she'd insist Plato remain in his gated area when she wasn't home.

She leaned to pet him, when he slipped between her legs and out the door. Oh shit. He wasn't the running-away type. He was the herding type. So why was he sprinting down her driveway?

"Plato, come!"

He stared back at her but didn't obey. Damn it. He'd never run off before. She tossed the bag of groceries and her purse onto the entry table, grabbed the leash, and ran after him.

What if he got hit by a car? She shoved the thought away. No, he was an obedient dog. Most of the time.

"Plato!"

He spun around and barked twice. She slowed as she approached him. If she kept running, he would think she was playing chase. Not good. He could dart into the street and get hit by a car.

"Plato, come here. Now."

This time, he sat down, his ears erect.

She took another few steps. "Let's go home, boy. Doggy treats at home, right?"

When she was only steps away, he rose and hightailed it toward the nearest square. What the hell? She raced after him. Most vehicles didn't speed in the historic district, but there was a first time for everything. *Don't get hit by a car. Please don't get hit by a car.*

She chased him through four Savannah squares. When she arrived in Whitefield Square, she leaned over to catch her breath. There sat Plato, panting and happy, next to Steven. Like nothing was wrong.

Seriously? Had Plato escaped just to play matchmaker? Aching muscles throbbed inside her rib cage and competed with the butterflies in her stomach. Seeing Steven again sent the butterflies aflutter.

"Lose someone?" he asked, winking at her.

Relief washed through her. Plato was safe. She would have to keep an eye on him in the future, ensure she never left the door open for even a second. But her dog was safe.

When she thought she'd caught her breath, Steven's flirty wink made her insides flip-flop. Why did a stranger affect her so much? Or was it the combo of having also raced after Plato for six blocks?

"Plato normally herds people. He's never run off before." She brushed her hair back with her hands to get it out of the way. Breathe. Just breathe.

Steven had Plato by the collar, so she reached out and clipped on the leash.

"I'd planned to come see you today. Guess your dog found me first," Steven said.

She glared at Plato. "Yeah, sometimes he knows more than I do." She didn't know whether to yell at Plato for running off or be glad he brought her to this spot.

"Have a seat," Steven said, gesturing to the bench.

Her breath sped up once again. "Sure."

Plato lay sweet and innocent between their feet, his gaze flitting from one squirrel to another. Overhead, the thick branches from the old oak trees provided shade.

"Did you find out anything about the house?" Steven asked.

"Yes." Had he learned his family had died? Better play dumb and presume he hadn't. "Steven, I'm afraid I have bad news—"

"Begley told me about the house fire." Steven's eyes, a shimmering green like the Caribbean Sea, turned dark. "That my family died."

"I'm sorry."

"Thanks. I don't trust Begley's explanation though."

Neither does your family.

"I asked Margie what she knew," Brianna said. "She claimed your father killed your family after a bad argument with you. The gossip chain didn't know if you were killed too."

"Are you serious?" Steven threw up his hands in resignation. "No wonder Begley didn't try to find me."

She wanted to ask why he'd cut himself off, why he hadn't known his own family had died. Why had he wanted to put so much distance between home and a new life? She'd done the same when she left Boston, but she still kept in touch with her family. Somewhat. Okay, not as often as she should. She made a mental note to call her parents soon.

"Begley hasn't impressed me, either," she said, hoping her nonchalance would encourage Steven to keep talking. The last thing she wanted was to push him away.

Plato dug his nose into a batch of clover and whimpered. Steven reached down, plucked a four-leaf clover out of the group, and stared into it. "My father might have been a control freak, but he'd never harm anyone." Steven rubbed the four green leaves between his fingers. "Not physically, anyway."

Meaning what? Had Steven and James suffered the same antagonistic relationship as her dad and Declan? Had they been part of the ongoing tug-of-war between old and young men, each needing acceptance yet craving independence?

"I take it you and James didn't get along?" she asked.

Steven narrowed his eyes. "How did you know my father's name?"

Oh shit. Think of something. Something besides the truth, that she could see and talk to James just like any living person—even though he was dead.

"Margie mentioned it when I asked about the house." Perfect. Reasonable, logical. She didn't want to lie, but she didn't trust him yet. He might be gorgeous, but she'd proceed with caution.

Steven shrugged and said, "Dad wasn't the best at supporting people's dreams. At least, not mine."

Brianna nodded. "My dad and my brother, Declan, argued all the time. In the end, Declan did what Dad wanted."

She blinked back a tear. Why was she becoming so emotional now, next to this almost stranger? Hadn't she just told herself to be careful?

Bewilderment radiated from Steven's eyes. "You okay?"

She rubbed Plato behind his ears, needing to occupy her hands. "I'm fine. Just a painful memory."

They sat in peace for a moment, taking in the sunlight streaming through webs of Spanish moss. Why couldn't she just say it? A dead sibling was something they had in common. Maybe if she told Steven about Declan, he would feel better about Amy.

"My brother joined the air force to win Dad's approval. He died in a plane crash, a rescue mission gone wrong." She paused. "I know how it feels to lose family."

"I'm sorry," Steven said. The empathy in his warm gaze melted her heart.

"Guess we have that in common," she said. "I'm sorry for your family too."

"Thanks."

Awkward silence fell between them, as if they'd both stripped their souls to the core and now didn't know what to talk about, as they were…practically strangers.

Steven finally broke the silence. "So why'd you move to Savannah?"

Ah, the casual chitchat. She'd do her best to keep topics on a surface level. "Declan worked here for a summer in college. He loved it, wouldn't stop talking about it in his letters. When he died, I tried to make a life of my own in Boston, but nothing ever changed. Same big Irish clan, same old stories, same opportunities, or lack thereof." She watched a squirrel climb a tree and jump to another one. "I guess I wanted something—"

"Something more." His eyes glimmered in the afternoon sun. Damn, he was handsome.

"Exactly. I didn't want to wait any longer. What about you? What brings you back?"

He fidgeted for a moment, shifting his position and leaning to pet Plato. "Family business brought me back. Finding out what really happened is what's keeping me here."

"Really happened?"

Steven nodded. "Police report and Begley say the fire started due to faulty wiring. I know for a fact that's bullshit."

"How?"

More importantly, why hadn't Begley mentioned anything about possible faulty wiring when she signed the lease? Had the Graysons been right? Was Begley a murderer?

"My father designed the wiring," Steven said. "He was an electrical engineer. Trust me, he didn't make mistakes where work was concerned."

"So you're thinking arson?" She hated to admit it, but the possibility seemed more of a probability. What had she gotten herself into?

"Yes, I'm just not sure I can prove it."

Was Steven planning to finish what the Graysons wanted her to do? Prove how they died and bring the culprit to justice? If so, she'd hit the jackpot. She wanted to help the Graysons to get them out of her house. But working alongside Steven? That would be a bonus. A bonus indeed.

CHAPTER TEN

Our deeds still travel with us from afar,
and what we have been makes us what we are.
~ George Eliot

Plato tugged on his leash with brutal force. As determined as he'd been to bolt away, he seemed all the more ready to return. Brianna grabbed her keys from the pocket of her slacks while trying to restrain him.

"Let me take Plato," Steven said. He reached for the leash.

"Thanks."

As she found the right key and inserted it into the lock, she smiled. The South had the rest of the world beat on gentlemanly behavior. Not that those Boston boys weren't decent. Many were. Yet somehow, in this southern pocket of humidity, men went out of their way to make women feel special. She could get used to this. Provided she didn't blow it.

Plato circled Steven's feet, containing them with his leash. *Good boy. Fetch me a gorgeous man.*

"Be careful when you step," she said, and they went inside.

Steven walked slowly, seeming to take in every angle, every nook of the house he once called his own.

"Shell shock?" she asked.

He nodded. "I like the back wall being one large window. When I lived here, it was closed up."

She looked out into the backyard where the hydrangea and azaleas had grown so large, they provided their own privacy barrier between her and the neighbors.

"I want to fence in the backyard eventually," she said. "Make it easier to let Plato in and out."

Steven didn't respond, just kept looking around like someone had dropped him on another planet. She tried to imagine how she would feel if their situations were reversed. How strange it would be to walk through her family's home and see another person living there. An ache rolled in her stomach. The poor guy must be going through hell.

"You want to see the rest of the house?" she asked. Men liked task-oriented ideas. Maybe walking through the house would alleviate some of his shell shock.

"Sure."

She led him through the kitchen. His fingers traced the corners of the walls, as if he was trying to reconnect with his past. What had his years in Savannah been like? What made him leave? She didn't want to seem nosy, but the questions pushed at her.

"If you don't mind me asking, what made you leave Savannah for California?" She led him down the hallway, wanting to keep them both moving, their bodies occupied.

Without responding, Steven meandered through doors and cased-in openings, taking in all the new sights of the home that was once his. They wandered into the den.

James's see-through form crept close to Steven. "He left because of me."

Brianna pressed her lips together. Oh lord. The ghosts were back. And while she wanted to get their point of view for what had happened with Steven, she doubted she could handle several conversations at once. And she definitely didn't need Steven thinking she was crazy for talking to ghosts. Hearing them. Seeing them.

"I wanted to be a musician since I was a little kid," Steven said. He sat in the recliner James favored and leaned forward with his elbows on his knees.

"You wanted to be a rock star with all the filthy lifestyle that goes with it," Virginia said, disdain lacing her tone. She kept her distance from her son.

Brianna turned to them and made the signal to shoo.

"What are you waving at?" Steven asked.

Crap. This whole talking to ghosts and living a normal life had officially become complicated.

"I guess your family didn't support your decision?" She plopped onto the couch and ignored anyone not named Steven. Brianna looked directly at him in hopes of keeping the conversation between them only. No others.

Fat chance.

"Yep," Steven said. "My father insisted I go to business school. He wanted me to join the engineering firm where he worked. Can you imagine? Corporate America? Not for me."

"I never was the cubicle type either."

Steven hunched his shoulders. "But James Grayson, pillar of Savannah, never understood that fact. Heaven forbid anyone chase their own dream instead of living someone else's."

Out of the corner of her eye, she noticed James leaning on the back of the recliner. His shoulders sagged as he watched his son.

"I only wanted the best for him," James said. "What kind of life could he have on the road, trying to make ends meet?"

Brianna pulled Steven up so he could see the rest of the house. Did she really hope to outrun ghosts? Leaving Boston hadn't accomplished that goal. Why did she think walking from the kitchen to the back rooms would allow such a thing?

She stopped short at the master bedroom. What if the ash had returned to the master closet? Anything was possible. What other voices would get added to the mix if she opened that possibility? No. She couldn't go in. No sense tempting fate by opening Pandora's Box.

"Forgive me," she said, blocking his view of the master bedroom. "The master is messy, so why don't we return to the living room? Would you like something to drink?"

"Coke, please. Thanks."

They returned to the front of the house. No Graysons—they had faded out again. Damn, why couldn't she get them to do that on command? Such abilities would make her life so much simpler.

She brought the drinks and they sat in the living room. On the love seat.

"How'd you find this house in particular?" Steven asked. "Did you do a real estate search? Did you use a broker?"

Damn, her window of learning more about him and his family had slipped past. He had returned to casual conversation.

"I searched online," she said. "Because of work, I wanted a place in the historic district."

"What do you do for work, again?"

Crap. Truth time. She couldn't hide what she did forever. "Um, I work at Restful Oaks."

Steven arched his eyebrows. "The funeral home?"

Here it comes. Have the decency to be original with whatever excuse you use to leave.

"I'm a cosmetologist," she said. "I love working with makeup and skin tones."

"Oh." His face was void of emotion. He'd be a great poker player.

"Go ahead and ask. Everyone else does."

Steven smiled wide. "Isn't working with dead bodies kind of…creepy?"

Not as creepy as being roommates with them.

"Be honest with my son, Brianna. Talk of your passion," James said. He'd appeared again, this time from across the room. She couldn't keep track of where they'd show up. She'd rather hoped they would confine themselves to the den. And why would some engineer type care about passion? That's the kind of thing artists speak of.

Steven seemed curious about her career choice though. As much as her past relationships had bombed, she refused to lie about her work. She may as well tell him and gauge his reaction.

"My parents run a funeral home in Boston, so I grew up surrounded by embalming rooms, lamps to bring out the best flesh tones on dead bodies, and everything in between. When Declan died, the cosmetologist we hired did such an amazing job. She made him seem alive—if only for the viewing. It comforted my parents, comforted me."

She took a breath. “I wanted to contribute something important to others like she did.”

“Good job,” James whispered before fading out.

“I like that,” Steven said. He took a swallow of Coke. “One good thing about coming back home is returning to Coca-Cola products. Too much Pepsi in California.”

She blinked. He wasn’t bolting to the door. No excuses? No suddenly remembering his commitment to join the circus? Boyfriend number two had used that whopper.

She studied his angular features, his soulful eyes, and waited for any signal he planned to leave. But he didn’t give any. Wow. She’d waited far too long to start spending time with the living. She should’ve moved to Savannah years ago. Fear had kept her in Boston, fear and inertia.

Out of habit, she felt the need to explain. “I admit I chose a strange career—”

“Who am I to judge what someone wants to do with their life? I chose music, against my father’s wishes. I wouldn’t dare assume to tell others what career to choose.”

The dormant butterflies in her stomach twirled into a happy dance. Maybe a relationship was finally possible. Silence lingered between them for a few awkward seconds. Think of something to say. Stop acting like a schoolgirl. He spoke of career. Since she wanted to learn more about him, she could steer the conversation back.

"When your dad didn't approve of your musical aspirations," she said, "you decided to move to California?"

Steven leaned forward, rested his elbows on his knees, and clasped his hands. "Add in some wicked fights and arguments, but yes. That's basically the reason."

Brianna darted her gaze toward the kitchen. She didn't see James, but she sensed he remained close by.

"You know, if I could see Declan one more time, I would tell him I loved him. I never had the chance to say good-bye." She sipped her Coke and hoped she wasn't being too intrusive. "What would you tell your dad?"

Steven's eyes changed from seafoam to dark green. She loved how the color shifted when his emotions changed. Most men were so out of touch with their feelings.

"Originally, I planned this trip home to see Amy."

Wait a minute. Where was Amy? James and Virginia had appeared and vanished. Why hadn't Amy? If Brianna were a ghost, she would definitely appear to see Declan.

"You travelled across the country because you missed your little sister," Brianna said. *Buddy, your stock just went up about ten thousand points*. In that instant, she knew Declan would have liked Steven if they'd ever had the chance to meet. She was sure of it.

"Yes, we were close." Steven looked out toward the backyard. "I suppose I wanted to make amends with my father too. At least talk to him."

Choked tears erupted from the kitchen. Sounds only Brianna could hear.

"I'm sure he misses you," she said. *More than you know*.

Steven shrugged. "By the time I left, we barely spoke. I don't know if he'd want me to return, honestly."

"I would've said I'm sorry," James whispered. "Sorry for not believing in you."

She leaned down to pet Plato's flanks. Plato arched his body like a cat, aiming his itchy place right at her hand.

"Tell Steven I'm sorry," James said. "Please."

She had to blink back the tears. While she admittedly didn't want to play the role of family therapist, she had the chance to bring peace between a father and son.

"I'm sure your father is sorry, realizes he should've had more faith in you," she said.

Steven arched an eyebrow. "Not so sure of that, but I'd like to believe it."

"Brianna," James urged. "You have to tell Steven about us. I need to make matters right with my son."

No. *Not going to risk losing the most handsome and understanding man I've ever met.* She'd already told the truth about her occupation. That was risk enough for one day.

"Tell him," James repeated.

Since when was she the elected liaison for dead father and live son relationships gone wrong? She'd offered her sincere observation that James cared about Steven. Did she really need to dive deeper?

"I'm sure your dad is proud of you," Brianna said. To her left, James and Virginia were waving their hands wildly to get her attention. No. Not going to go there. She didn't want to scare Steven away.

"Let's hope he is," Steven said. "I figure if I can prove the house-fire theory was a hoax, then maybe, somewhere, my father will smile."

"I already am," James said. "Tell him. Tell him you can see and hear us."

She kept her mouth shut. Did James not understand what was at risk for her? If she wanted any kind of normal relationship, she couldn't tell Steven about her gift. The minute Declan died, she'd given up a normal childhood. Every ounce of energy went into being the surviving child for her parents, who wound up putting her in an institution. Yet she'd still followed in their footsteps and pursued the mortuary arts for a career.

Now the dead were trying to convince her to serve as their liaison to the living? No way.

Couldn't she just have a normal dating relationship without any interference?

"Make yourself useful and tell him about us, Yankee woman," Virginia said.

A normal dating relationship was out of the question.

Yearning to switch topics, Brianna asked, "So how do you plan to prove your theory on faulty wiring?"

"I located an old bandmate who's a journalist. He said he'll help me get some answers."

"I hope you learn the truth," she said.

"The truth is, I'm sorry," James said. "Tell him."

She turned to glare at James before returning her attention to Steven. "I'm sure, if your dad was still alive, he'd be proud of your efforts to make things right."

There. That didn't sound too suspicious. Any empathetic person would say the same. It didn't make her crazy.

"You're not telling him the key factor," James said. He puffed up his shoulders to seem more overbearing. She liked him better when he'd faded out. Or even when he'd stayed in the kitchen.

"Shh," she said.

Steven's eyes narrowed. "Excuse me?"

Crap! Having two conversations at once had put her in serious trouble.

"I'm sorry. I thought I heard Plato whining and I couldn't hear you."

Steven glanced down to a docile and quiet Plato at their feet. "Your dog is right there."

Damn, damn, damn. "Yes, he is. Sorry. Continue, please. I wasn't shushing you. I just…couldn't concentrate. Go ahead. I'm listening. Honest."

He paused, a dubious look on his face. Even if he hadn't bolted away earlier, now he was thinking it. She braced herself for his impending exit.

"Some other time. I need to get back to Dennis's place," he said.

There it was. She would never see him again. He'd dismiss her as a weirdo, like everyone else. Damn it.

Instead, Steven stared at her for a long moment—she could see her reflection in those emerald pools—and he offered a warm smile. "I'm going to Kevin Barry's later to hear an Irish band. Do you want to join me? They have a dining room and a bar, too, if we wanted to grab something to eat first."

The pounding pulse in between her ears stopped short. What? She'd acted crazy and he was asking her out on a date?

"How about it?" Steven asked.

She forced her lips to move. "Sure, I'd love to."

Plato stood, sauntered to Steven, and pawed his foot.

"Apparently, Plato wants to come along too," Steven said, flashing his charming smile.

"Kevin Barry's is the Irish pub on River Street, right?" she asked.

Steven petted Plato behind the ears, eliciting content snuffling noises. Hmm. Wonder what sorts of noises Steven could elicit from *her*. Heat flushed across her cheeks as she considered the possibilities.

"Yep. How about I stop by to get you around six? The pub has an upstairs dining room overlooking the river."

"Sounds great," she said. Stay calm. Don't leap for joy. Not until he's out of sight.

He petted Plato good-bye. "See you tonight."

She waved and shut the door slowly, wanting to watch his muscular frame as long as possible.

When she returned to the living room, Virginia's double chins were quivering. "What is wrong with you? You're supposed to be helping us, not chasing after my son."

"Virginia—"

"My southern-born son, dating a Yankee. Kill me again, why don't you?"

"Aren't you being a bit overdramatic?" Brianna positioned herself on the love seat right where Steven had sat, enjoying his lingering warmth.

"She isn't," James said, once again appearing out of nowhere.

"Will you please stop just showing up out of the blue?" Brianna said. "It's unnerving."

"Humph," Virginia said. "You haven't begun to see unnerving, you damn Yankee." She folded her arms across her ample chest.

"C'mon. I'm going to hear music with him. It's no big deal." Brianna rolled her eyes at Virginia's absurd attitude.

"No big deal? Was the burning of Atlanta no big deal?" Virginia said.

Brianna's mouth fell open. How was she supposed to respond to such a ludicrous question?

"Listen," James said, his voice calm and logical. "We need you to keep your focus. No romantic entanglements. Your job is bringing Begley to justice."

Excuse me?

"James, we talked about this before," she said, righteous indignation lacing her tone. "My only job is to put makeup on the dead."

She paused. Stay calm. Who knew what kind of mess could happen if she lost her temper with a ghost?

"You want me to help your family. I get it. But I never agreed to play secret agent and risk losing my house. In fact, I said I'd be more inclined to help you if you could figure out a way for me to talk to Declan. What progress have you made on my request?"

James sighed, and the air turned cold. Ghosts could replace air-conditioning units across the South. If she were more of an opportunist, she'd harness such knowledge. But she wasn't. She just wanted a little normalcy.

"I'm seeing what I can do on your request," James said. "Don't give up yet."

She studied his face, the wrinkles, the way his eyes turned watery blue when he spoke with emotion. "I'll never give up on wanting to talk to my brother."

"We just want you to keep your focus," James said. "See what you can find out about Begley. That's all."

"Romance puts one's mind in the gutter," Virginia quipped with an accusing pointed finger.

Brianna ignored Virginia's outrage. So did James.

"Brianna, listen to me," James said. "I lost my son once. Begley is cold and dangerous. He killed my family and set us on fire. I can't lose Steven twice. You need to help him. If Begley kills Steven, then I have truly lost everything."

His heartfelt feelings cut her to the core. Damn it, why was she in this position?

"What do you want me to do? I can't tell Steven that I see ghosts. I can't. No. No way."

"Okay," James said.

He was conceding the point? Good news.

"But keep an eye on him," James said. "Get Steven whatever info you can find on Begley. Steven has a journalist friend he mentioned. Why don't the three of you work together?"

Ghosts must have a short attention span. Maybe something happened after death to cause it?

"Remember, going against my landlord will risk me losing my home."

James took a moment and lit up his pipe. "Yes, it will."

"If I lose this place, the next tenant might not be able to see and hear ghosts."

He cocked his head sideways as if the thought hadn't occurred to him. With a steady voice, he said, "I believe in you, Brianna. Despite the risks."

Tears welled again. She blinked quickly. No one had professed such confidence in her since Declan was alive. Now James was saying he believed in her. She wasn't a superhero; she never even played one as a child. Yet James believed she could do it.

"I'll think about it," she said. "I'm not sure how much help I can be, since I don't want to do anything illegal."

"Any insight you can get is a big step forward," James said.

"Okay. In the meantime, I'm meeting Steven for drinks and music tonight."

Virginia cleared her throat. James shot her a dirty look to silence her.

"Please do," James said. "Make a difference, like you said you wanted."

And there was the clincher. The words rose up to haunt her more than the ghosts. Why had she made that damn promise to begin with? She missed Declan with all of her heart, but sometimes, she wished she could take back the original promise that started all this trouble.

CHAPTER ELEVEN

Music expresses that which cannot be said
and on which it is impossible to be silent.
~ Victor Hugo

Steven left his family's house humming a tune. Why did being near Brianna make him miss music so much? Kate had been the same way. Tunes and lyrics seeped into his consciousness when he least expected it. Spending time talking to Brianna, he felt close to himself again—his old self. One he admittedly missed.

The shushing incident had been weird, true. But after the slew of materialistic and psychotic beach blondes, Steven didn't find Brianna's weirdness alarming. She didn't even begin to reach the psycho level of strange. A random shushing was better than a mental breakdown over how many calories were in a meal. And hell, she'd even apologized. The beach babes never did that. Besides, she might be willing to help him. Maybe join him and Dennis to determine what Begley was conspiring.

Steven spent the Sunday reviewing the files Dennis collected, only to stumble upon a few glaring patterns. Ten house fires, all within the historic district, all claiming faulty wiring. Just like the news articles had said.

The properties were far enough apart in time and place that he couldn't prove arson. But where Begley was concerned, any corruption could exist.

The files said a collection of electric companies denied negligence, but Begley's advertising campaign to restore what was broken in Savannah had thrust public opinion into outrage. The cases had heated up the courts, and in the end, faulty wiring had been named the cause.

Not possible. Begley must have the arson inspector in his pocket. Especially since after each case ruling, Begley had purchased the property with the guise of restoring it for the community. Such philanthropy from a sleazy asshole? Doubtful. Steven just had to prove the truth.

At precisely six, Steven knocked on Brianna's door. When it opened, he almost choked. Wow, she dressed up nice. Her hair was down, with long black curls on her shoulders, and she wore a pastel pink top, which accentuated her blue eyes.

"Hi," was all he could say. How lame. He wrote lyrics for a living and all he could mutter was "hi"? He was losing his touch. Yet another reason to return to his music.

"Hi back." She smiled at him and her eyes crinkled with laugh lines. Was she making fun of him? Stop. Don't get defensive. He was back in the South. Things were different. Brianna seemed genuine and down to Earth. This could work out—if he didn't blow it.

Plato barked from the background but didn't appear. "Not taking a chance on him running off again?"

Brianna nodded. “He’s in an area blocked by a baby gate.” She leaned forward and whispered, “Don’t tell him that he can jump over it.”

“I promise,” Steven said, winking at her.

Most women blushed and grinned when he winked at them. But Brianna’s pupils grew bigger, the blackness pushing the blue hues away. Whoa, hold on. Was “promise” a bad word in her mind? Time to change the subject, move things along, and get to the pub.

Besides, all conversations were easier with great scenery and a drink in hand. River Street bars had that appeal—helping men talk to women for hundreds of years.

After a ten-minute stroll and superficial chitchat, they approached Kevin Barry’s. The place was hard to miss with the giant Irish flag of orange, white, and green dangling from the awning.

Brianna stepped up to the first door.

“Not that one,” Steven said.

She shot him a quizzical look. “But it’s the door.”

Memories of his youth came flooding back. “That’s the performance entrance. The next door lets us in the bar.”

He opened the door and waited for her to enter. Two separate entrances to the pub confused tourists. It was one of those things distinguishing the tourists from the locals. Surprisingly, the memory didn’t make him cringe. Was the South changing him?

"Want to go upstairs for a great view of the river?" he asked. He hoped she'd agree. The view was spectacular, plus he wanted the privacy.

"Sure."

He motioned for her to go first up the stairway, and she smiled back at him. Was she not accustomed to the Southern gentleman's ways? This could work in his favor. Impress her with what came naturally to him. Rather, what his mother drilled into his head since he turned three.

Why were the childhood memories flooding back? And family moments? He was in the presence of a genuine Yankee from Boston, and yet the past tapped on his shoulder like a long-lost lover. Savannah had that effect on people. No one could escape the past or the present—the city dripped with history and emotion. Why had he thought he could run from it?

He put his hand on the small of her back, not wanting to startle her but to ease her up the winding staircase to the top level. Her neck smelled like jasmine. He tried to inhale without being too obvious.

Once upstairs, they sat on the porch overlooking the river. She ordered a Black and Tan—classic Irish beer cocktail, she definitely looked the part—and he asked for a Guinness. Together, they watched ships crawl along the water.

The waitress walked upstairs carrying a tray of drinks.

Brianna glanced to the bar area on the second level. "They have to go up and down stairs to serve?"

"The Guinness has a special tap," the waitress said. "Only works downstairs."

"Thanks," Steven said, taking his dark beer with its foamy head.

Brianna frowned. "I didn't mean for us to cause her to go up and down the stairs. We could've sat on the lower level."

Steven tried to look into her face, tried to read her. She seemed so cautious about upsetting anyone. Or rather, inconveniencing anyone.

"They do it all the time," Steven said.

The waitress nodded. "No problem at all. We know the locals love the view up here."

Brianna tried to smile, but her face looked embarrassed. What was her story? Had her family put too much pressure on her after her older brother died? Had she been burdened with their happiness?

"What do you think of the South so far?" he asked.

Maybe if he could get her to open up, he could help her. Because he definitely needed her help, and he didn't believe in being in someone's debt.

She sipped her drink, her pensive face watching the sunset. "I haven't seen as much of Savannah as I'd planned, but Declan loved it here."

Her eyes sparkled when she mentioned her brother. Steven felt a sharp pang in the center of his chest. He missed Amy. If only he'd come home sooner. Maybe he could've saved his little sister. Kate, on the other hand…there was no going back.

"Sounds like you two were really close."

"We were." She pushed back a long black curl behind her ear and grinned. "You should've seen how petrified I was of going to school for the first time. All the neighborhood girls came home crying, saying they'd been teased on the playground. Kids stole their crayons and pulled their hair. That decided it. School was not the place for me."

Steven felt a surge of warmth pass through him. He'd heard a version of this story, but from a different point of view.

"A terrible place, eh?" he said.

Brianna nodded. "Those girls came home with rumpled braids and scuffed knees. I vowed to never go to school, and I locked myself in my room."

He grinned at the image. She definitely had a stubborn streak. This could come in handy. "So what happened?"

"Declan was the only one who I'd talk to. He sat down next to me, against this huge stuffed bear I had. Mr. Wimbles was his name, I think. Declan told me school wasn't as bad as I imagined."

"Sounds like a great older brother to have," Steven said.

The kind he wished he'd been. Why did he always have to run away when things turned complicated? That's the one thing he would've told his father if he were still alive. That he was sorry for running away when he did. He hoped Amy had forgiven him.

"Declan was an old soul, even at fifteen," Brianna said. "He said if anyone hurt me, he'd take care of it. He always wanted me to have more faith in people, and when he said it, I did. I believed everything Declan said."

Steven couldn't help but smile. He remembered the days when Amy felt the same way. Then he'd been an idiot and left town.

"So no one tugged on your hair or hurt you in kindergarten?"

She smiled. "Of course they did, but I managed." She pulled out a pendant around her neck and showed him. "That same day, he gave me this Saint Christopher necklace, said it would protect me. Years later, he gave me this Celtic cross."

Steven admired the necklaces while getting another brief whiff of her jasmine perfume. Or perhaps it was soap? Either way, she smelled nice.

"And has it worked? Has the pendant protected you?"

Her smile faded. "Until Declan died, yes."

"I'm sorry." Steven reached out for her hand and squeezed her fingers.

She met his gaze. "It's okay. Cynic that I was, I asked him what to do if the pendant didn't work."

"What'd he say?"

Brianna smiled, and her eyes glistened with the beginnings of tears. "He told me I didn't get it. Said he would always protect me, no matter what happened." She paused and took a swig of beer. "The strange thing is, I made him a promise when he died. I swore I'd make a difference with the time I had, not waste my life. And I feel this…primal need…to keep my word. Maybe if I do, Declan will still look out for me."

Steven cleared his throat. *Force the words out, you fool.* "I hope Amy thought the same, even though I never came to rescue her."

CHAPTER TWELVE

The only things certain in life are death and taxes.
~ Benjamin Franklin

Declan brought Ian Kendall to Bonaventure Cemetery, where all Savannah orientations for the newly dead took place. Its remote location, away from historic downtown and adjacent to the Wilmington River, proved ideal for welcoming the newbies.

Statuesque headstones lined every curved row of graves, Spanish moss hung from oaks like a grand canopy, and the air smelled sweet like perfume.

Ian glanced around, confusion in his eyes. "I thought you said we were going to break some rules."

"After your orientation," Declan said. "I need to check in with my designated mentor."

"What? You're leaving me here?"

"Yes, but only for a few days."

Ian shrugged. "So you'll come back and get me once the orientation is over?"

"Yes. Be on the lookout."

He introduced Ian to the administrative group, a cluster of Southern ladies who dubbed themselves the DWW, Death's Welcome Wagon.

They'd fawn over the rookies, answer questions, point out things everyone had in common.

Declan chuckled. That was one thing about death. It united people. Republicans, Democrats—whatever cultural stances and arguments people clung to so much in life—in death they were all in the same situation. It leveled the playing field.

He turned away from the graves and stood under the arched granite entryway to Bonaventure. With closed eyes and a destination in mind, he waited. Seconds later, he stood miles away in Columbia Square, the designated meeting place with Connell, his mentor and supervisor.

Declan opened his eyes and admired the lush green grass of Columbia Square. A single-tiered fountain stood at the center, surrounded by oak trees in all directions. On one side of the square stood the Kehoe House, an ornate, red brick building with bow windows and a turret. Now one of the nicer inns of Savannah, the home had once been a funeral parlor. Guess that was why Connell liked this area for meetings.

Declan stepped forward and waited. Connell hovered over the fountain, placing himself above Declan and humanity. He took no notice of Declan or the young women scoping out the area for wedding photos. Connell had been around for a century or more. Back when he was alive, he'd been the commander of several military squadrons. Now that he was dead, he kept the same demeanor—that of Harry Hard-Ass. Admittedly,

Connell was fairer than many. He mentored groups of deceased, processed special requests, organized assignments, and ran interference if needed. The kind of ghost to get things done and cut through the red tape.

After a long moment, Connell stopped scribbling on his clipboard and looked down. "Declan? This is a surprise."

Declan tried to smile. "I need to talk to you. It's important."

"Oh?"

"It's about my sister, Brianna. She's in Savannah."

Connell didn't seem fazed. "I'm aware."

"You're aware? Why didn't you send for me? Why not tell me?"

Declan's anger turned his transparent body into knotted shadows that twisted and coiled across the ground. Emotions of the dead had that tendency.

Connell narrowed his hazel eyes. "You know how these things work. Family is off-limits."

"Can't you make an exception? I've worked my ass off to help the deceased. I spent five years in Pigsknuckle, Idaho. That's hell, my friend."

Connell's eyes crinkled. "True."

"I haven't asked for anything in return for my service. Please do this for me." Declan paced around the fountain, suspended amid the young women chatting up how beautiful the area would be with peach-colored roses. "I want privileges to talk to my sister, know she is safe."

"She is safe. You can't interfere."

Clearly, Connell was not going to grant a wish that could be deemed selfish. Declan racked his mind for another approach.

"Ian Kendall, my latest recruit, tells me she works at the funeral home. Just grant me inside privileges so I can talk to her. She's sensitive. She heard Ian, meaning she has the gift to hear us. Think of the good we could do with her help."

"I can't do that." Connell set down his clipboard and waved his hand to the birds in the surrounding oak trees. "Just as in nature, we have rules."

"Screw the rules," Declan said. He kicked a pinecone with all his might, but it didn't move.

Connell leaned forward, put one hand on his knee, and glared down at him. "Don't test me."

Declan swallowed hard. "We're allowed to haunt people when the situation warrants it. Please? Why can't I make contact with my own flesh and blood?"

"This time, it's not up to you alone," Connell said. He leaned back and scribbled something. "Granting your wish is up to her."

"What do you mean?"

Was there a way to contact Brianna without going through mentor channels? If there was any chance, he intended to find out. Maybe even break a few of the so-called regulations. What were they going to do to him? He was already dead. They'd only send him back to Idaho if he got caught—which he had no intention of letting happen.

"Brianna is unique," Connell said in a tone as cryptic as his answer. "She's different from the others. We can't interfere. Not yet."

Did that mean they could interfere at some point in the future?

"If not yet, then when?" Declan asked.

Connell took a long glance around Columbia Square. "In time."

"Fine," Declan said, turning to leave. "I'll find my own way."

"Declan." Connell's tone was low, a guttural growl between spirits. Declan turned back, required to look upward and give respect to his mentor.

Connell's eyes burned gold, with fury imprinted in those large pupils. "Don't cross me on this. Trust me."

Declan stiffened. Connell might be a hard-ass, but he didn't issue threats lightly. And yet, he'd granted exceptions in the past, provided they were earned. So why not offer a semblance of hope where Brianna was concerned?

"Please." Declan knelt on the ground. "I'm begging you. Let me talk to her. I'll work overtime the next one hundred years if you want."

Connell exhaled a resigned sigh. "You are correct. Brianna is special, but if you interfere right now, you'll only make things worse."

CHAPTER THIRTEEN

The soul that can speak through the eyes can also kiss with a gaze.
~ Gustavo Adolfo Becquer

By the time Steven walked Brianna home from drinks at the pub, the full moon had risen. Dark clouds dissolved into transparent shapes as they traveled across the illuminated sky.

Brianna paused on her front doorstep, shivering. Partly from the chilled air, partly from standing so close to Steven.

He removed his tan jacket and draped it across her shoulders. "Better?" he asked.

She smiled. "Yes, thanks."

Keep it cool. Don't be an idiot. He's a Southern gentleman. Doesn't mean he's going to kiss you good-night. She stole a glance at his lips. Not too thick, not too thin. Fantastic kissing potential.

Warnings of self-preservation weren't doing much good. Offering his jacket had been a simple gesture, but she couldn't help the gaping grin now covering her face. Even her cheek muscles ached. She didn't care.

"I had a great time." She met his moonlight-dappled gaze.

He curled his incredible lips into a smile. "Me, too."

Kiss me. Please kiss me.

As if he could read her mind, he traced his soft fingers along her cheek. The touch sent jolts of pleasure racing through her body. *This must be what flying feels like.*

Then he cupped her face in both his hands. Oh. My. Heaven. Was she shaking? Her face trembled at his touch. Try as she might, she couldn't control it.

"Are you still cold?" His soulful gaze met hers with a yearning she longed to answer.

"I…I don't know."

She didn't know? How lame. Her brain scrambled words and sounds. None sounded intelligent.

"My jacket looks nice on you," he whispered, his breath hot and heavy.

Was she imagining things, or was there a longing in his glance as well? Or was she misinterpreting the signals?

"Um, thanks—"

"Shh."

Seconds later, his lips were on hers. She hadn't been wrong. His mouth was strong, yet his touch held tenderness. She reciprocated and opened her mouth wider. Bliss. He flicked his tongue, exploring her mouth, playing her like an instrument—lyrical, sweet, and incredibly intense.

"Yankee woman? Are you French kissing on the first date?" Virginia quipped from inside.

Just what every woman wants to hear during her first kiss with a gorgeous man.

"Shh," Brianna said.

Steven pulled back and grinned. "Shushing me again, are you?"

Oops.

"I thought I heard Plato whine," she said.

Yeah, a weird excuse. But better than admitting Steven's mother thought Brianna was easy. Such a thing couldn't be explained, even if he knew Brianna could see and hear ghosts. Something he would never be privy to.

"Turnabout is fair play," Steven said.

"Oh?"

He winked at her, those piercing green eyes staring deep into her soul.

Be careful. Don't get too close. At this moment, she was ready to tell him everything. Such a move could only end in disaster.

"Yes," Steven said. "Shh."

He leaned in and pressed tiny kisses—flutters of affection—up and down her neck. Her body tingled with pleasure as he nuzzled her ear. He met her lips once more for a long, wet kiss good-night.

When he pulled back, he smiled. "Have dinner with me tomorrow?"

She blinked twice, fully expecting to wake up. But she didn't. This wasn't a dream. It was real.

"I'd love to."

"Good," he said. "There's something I may need your help with."

"Such as?"

"Let's talk tomorrow." He stroked his hand along her arm, down to her wrist, and squeezed her hand before letting go. "Good-night, Brianna."

"Night," she echoed. Good thing. No other words popped into her brain.

A few awkward seconds passed as they stared at each other. *You idiot. He's waiting for you to go inside. Southern gentlemen do things like that. Don't blow this.*

She smiled once more before shutting the door. Through the peephole, she watched his muscular form saunter off in the moonlight. Such a gentleman. Handsome, sweet, an incredible kisser, and—

"You Yankee slut."

And the son of a Southern crackpot living in her house. Back to reality.

"How dare you get so intimate on your first date with my son," Virginia said. Her chest was puffed out, her shoulders back. The woman looked ready to rumble with Sherman himself.

"Virginia, times are different now—"

“Maybe in your part of the world. Not in Savannah.”

Brianna rolled her eyes. Where were James and Amy? Had they elected Virginia to be their lookout?

“I’m not going to explain my actions to you. I like Steven. You raised a gentleman and I enjoyed his company. That’s all.”

James appeared from the back hallway. “What do you think he wants your help with?”

“James, please.” Virginia’s double chin clenched as she maintained her shocked appearance. “We’re discussing their date.”

“No, we’re not,” Brianna said. “James, I don’t know what Steven wants. But I’ll tell you one thing, I’d be a whole lot more inclined to help those who don’t call me names.”

James shot an angry look at Virginia. “Please excuse my wife’s comments. She gets rash sometimes.”

Virginia frowned. “Did I ask you to speak for me?”

“Enough,” Brianna said, throwing her arms up. “I’m tired. It’s late. I’m going to bed, and there’s nothing any of you can do about it.”

She stomped to the fridge, poured herself some water, and marched down the hallway. From behind her, she heard Virginia’s indignant tone.

“Humph. We’ll see about that. Hasn’t that damn Yankee learned anything yet?”

###

Shrill and off-tune singing woke Brianna out of the perfect REM cycle. What the hell? Who was singing at this hour? And more importantly, why? She rubbed her eyes. It was still dark. The clock lights flashed red at 2:08 a.m.

"Ninety-six bottles of beer on the wall, ninety-six bottles of beer…"

Damn it. Please don't let it be true. Virginia?

Virginia's uppity voice—which couldn't carry a tune to save her life—clanged through the house. "Take one down, pass it around, ninety-five bottles of beer on the wall…"

Most. Annoying. Song. Ever.

Ugh. Brianna tossed off the sheets and pattered down the hallway to the kitchen. No ghosts. The singing temporarily stopped and no sign of the Graysons. She thrust open closet and cabinet doors with a fervor she hadn't used since playing hide-and-seek as a kid.

Nothing.

"You'd better stay hidden," Brianna bellowed to the walls before storming back to bed.

"Ninety-four bottles of beer on the wall…"

Brianna pulled an extra pillow over her head to block out the noise. This was going to be a long night.

When the Monday morning sunlight crept into the master bedroom, Brianna groaned and rolled over. Last night had been the worst sleep of her life. Virginia's damn singing had lasted the entire night. Damn ghost got all the way down to one bottle of beer on the wall, then started over from ninety-nine. Virginia's stubbornness was clearly not to be reckoned with, not without a lifetime supply of earplugs anyway.

One thing was for certain: Brianna couldn't afford another night like last night. Maybe there was a way to find out about Begley without breaking any laws.

She strolled into the kitchen, turned on the coffeemaker, and took Plato outside. He poked his nose in and around flower beds, sniffing and snorting with delight.

"Hurry it up," she said.

Plato whined and stared up at her.

"You're right. I wouldn't want to be rushed either. Sorry."

He snuffled at her guilt-ridden apology but finally did his business. She brought him inside.

She opened the cabinet and went to grab her favorite mug—where was it? The blue one, the one she always kept on the bottom shelf. The cup she drank her morning coffee in because it held eight ounces more than the other cups.

She checked the dishwasher. Not there. "Where the hell did it go?" she asked Plato.

“Mama hid it,” Amy said, standing in the doorway between the hall and the kitchen. “Along with your white sandals.”

Brianna shook her head. “Why am I not surprised?”

“She means well.”

Brianna poured coffee into a small mug and added milk. “You think so?” She pulled out an oak dining chair and sat at her small breakfast table.

Amy nodded. “She can’t help herself. Trust me, what do you think it was like being her daughter?” She slipped into the chair opposite Brianna without pulling it out from the table.

“True. You deserve a medal. So does Steven.”

Amy’s eyes widened at Steven’s name. “He was lucky. He got out and had a life, made some rocking music with his band. Mama disapproved of the lyrics and the loud noise. She would’ve killed me if she’d known I bought all his CDs.”

A dull ache inched its way across Brianna’s chest. How could she explain that Steven seemed more damaged after the life he’d supposedly had? Which was better? To have a life cut short like Amy or Declan? Or to be the one left behind, the one forced to survive and face reality without loved ones?

“I know he was surprised to hear you and your parents died,” Brianna said.

Was she being too serious—or worse, too sappy—before coffee? She pulled the cup to her lips and let the warm liquid wake her up.

"I wish he could've come home sooner." Amy twirled her long hair between her fingers.

"Do you know why he didn't?" Brianna asked, hoping she hadn't sounded too intrusive. There was a fine line between talking to the man she liked and talking to the man while knowing the secrets of his family, complicated by the fact that they were ghosts living in her home.

Amy shrugged. "Steven never liked the pressure to conform in Savannah. People here conform—a lot. We're always worried about what the neighbors will think, what our actions say about who we are. And for what? Now I'm dead, and do you think the neighbors could care less?"

Brianna let the coffee seep its stimulant properties into her system. "Sounds like a lot of pressure while growing up."

"Definitely," Amy said. "So the minute Steven was able to leave and join a band, he split and never looked back." She stared out the window, her gaze stretching over the hydrangea and going somewhere far off, like she was searching for meaning.

"You must have missed him," Brianna said.

"He called me all the time, but he made me promise not to tell anyone where he was."

"A tall order to fill," Brianna said. By now, she'd had one cup of coffee and the brain cells were perking up. "It's a lot of guilt to be the one kid left behind with the parents."

Amy stopped twirling her hair and looked up. "That's right. You were in the same situation too."

Brianna poured another mug of java and sipped more coffee. "When my older brother died, I had to be the surviving kid. Trust me, filling those shoes was a lot of work and excess pressure I could've done without." Instead of sitting, she set her cup on the table and leaned her elbows on the back of the chair.

Amy smiled. "But you're doing so well now—"

"Not really." Where had that come from? Why be so honest?

"Sure you are," Amy said. "And if you help us out—"

"Did Virginia put you up to this?"

Damn it, why had she asked such an accusing question? Must be the lack of sleep.

Granted, Virginia *would* be the type to saddle her kid with championing a cause, but Amy didn't need the extra pressure. Brianna sure hadn't needed any after Declan died.

"I'm sorry," Brianna said. "I didn't mean to accuse."

Amy turned and studied Brianna's face. "Mama can be overbearing, but I'm not a puppet for her—"

"I know you're not."

"Check the pantry, third shelf, for your mug and other items. Mama is stubborn, but she lacks imagination when tormenting the living."

Brianna smiled. "I doubt that. I doubt that very much."

CHAPTER FOURTEEN

Death leaves a heartache no one can heal,
love leaves a memory no one can steal.
~ Headstone in Ireland

After witnessing Steven's grief over his family, Brianna's guilt took a strong choke hold. She called her parents the next day and invited them to visit for the weekend. They hadn't been down South before, so maybe the time together would be healing for everyone.

Maybe.

They'd opted to drive, having no trust in airplanes after Declan's crash so many years ago.

She scrubbed bathtubs and countertops Thursday night to prepare for their visit. She'd rather have been on a date with Steven. But he'd not called the entire week. She'd asked for a vacation day Friday. Edwin had been reluctant but she reminded him she'd worked on her day off.

Brianna sat on a kitchen barstool to catch her breath.

"What are you doing? The guest bedroom still needs vacuuming," Virginia prompted. The bossy ghost was in her element: micromanager of neatness. Brianna wondered if that job came with dental.

"They're not arriving until tomorrow. I'll do it later."

Virginia wrinkled her perky nose. "Come, now. You want your home to look better than usual, don't you?" She rubbed a finger along the tabletop and frowned, seeming upset her fingers could no longer hold dust to make her point. "My fingers may not show it, but this place is a mess."

Brianna rolled her eyes. A habit she'd developed since meeting Virginia. They'd been cooped up inside with some recent rainy days, and Virginia had quickly become an obnoxious second mother. And Brianna's real mother arrived tomorrow.

"Don't you go rolling your eyes at me," Virginia said. "In the South, we make things nice for our relatives. What do you plan to do for dinner? Lord knows you can't cook. How about I tell you how to bake one of my famous grit casseroles?"

Oh god. "Virginia?"

"Yes?"

"I don't mean to be rude, but I doubt Mom and Dad will like Southern cooking."

"Hogwash. I'm sure they'll give it a try."

Amy, sitting on the stool next to Brianna, tried to help with Brianna's point. "Mom, Brianna knows her own parents and what they like."

"I was always the proud cook in the family," Virginia began, her voice indignant.

"Yes, but you're ghosts. I don't know how my parents will feel…"

Virginia stood, mouth open, like someone had slapped her.

"You haven't told them about us, have you?" Virginia said.

Brianna grabbed a Guinness out of the fridge.

"Do they know you drink that stuff?"

After swallowing a long, chocolate-tasting swig, she responded to Virginia's madness. "Yes. We're Irish. They know I drink. So do they."

"So why haven't you mentioned us? Are you ashamed?"

Absolutely. The last time she admitted to chatting with ghosts, she wound up in a padded cell. She wasn't going to revisit the horrors of her past if she could help it.

"I just want a quiet weekend visit with them, Virginia."

"In other words, make ourselves scarce," Amy said, likely guessing her mother didn't get the hint.

Virginia's rotund cheeks turned hollow, like someone had let the air out of them.

"Fine," Brianna conceded. "You can help with the cooking. But no grits, please. I'm planning on making several stew recipes. We're going to relax and enjoy a visit. That's all."

James hadn't shown himself much. Perhaps because Virginia drove him crazy too.

"Please pass the word along to James. While my parents are in town, I'm begging the three of you to lay low," Brianna said.

"Better get to cleaning, then," Virginia said, circling back to her original point.

###

Brianna's parents always honked three times when they arrived anywhere. For the longest time, she presumed everyone did the same. Weird stares from friends had proved otherwise.

On Friday morning, three long honks announced their arrival. Brianna sprinted through her house to make sure everything was in order. All cookbooks with grits recipes were put away, the guest room was spotless, and Plato was bathed and brushed and handsome. Preventing him from absorbing outdoor smells and debris had been the hardest task.

Brianna ran outside and hugged her mom's neck. "Mom, thanks so much for coming."

"Good to be here, away from the snow." Her mother walked with a careful tread in her step. Even though she was only sixty, she looked ninety.

"Hello Brianna," her father said. She gasped for breath when she saw him. His hair had turned white, his eyes from cornflower to opaque blue, like clear water. In those eyes, she saw despair and emptiness, with no hope of anything new. He even still drove the old Chrysler LeBaron he'd bought two years before Declan had died.

"D—Dad." She held back the tears. "Glad y'all could come."

He picked up his suitcase, looking more like a random stranger than her father. "You doing okay?"

"Fine. Let me get you both settled in, then we'll catch up."

She helped them unpack in the back guest room. Upon returning to the kitchen to fix drinks, something caught her eye. On the glass table was a book: *The True South: Why We Should Have Won the Civil War.*

"Not funny, Virginia," Brianna whispered, tucking the book into the closet.

Muffled ghost giggles came from the bathroom. "Still not funny," Brianna repeated, though she couldn't help chuckling herself.

An hour later, Brianna poured Guinness into three frosted glasses.

"Here you go." She handed a beer to each of her parents.

"Humph," Virginia said, shooting a judgmental glare into the den.

Leave me alone with my parents.

"How are things in Boston?" Brianna asked.

Her mother sipped her drink, cradling it in her feeble hands. "Uncle Jack broke up with Candace."

Brianna situated herself on the recliner, offering them the couch. "How's he holding up?"

Her mother shrugged. Every movement was in slow motion, the weariness evidently from carrying the world on her shoulders.

"He's coping. It's sad for us too. With her mafia connections, we never had to wait for a table. Now those perks are gone."

Her father gulped down his pint. "Candace's name had power to get the best seats in the house." He said it proudly, like mob connections were an envied social status.

"I told you the damn Yankee was trouble," Virginia said.

Brianna choked on her beer and had to clear her throat. Damn ghosts. She needed them to lay low, leave her alone. Her parents thought she was insane once. She wouldn't put it past them to think the same again.

"What about the rest of the family?" Brianna asked, steering the conversation away from mafia princesses.

"Aunt Nadine is taking cooking classes, finally," her mother said. "That woman could burn water."

"You must take after her," Virginia quipped.

Brianna glared toward the kitchen. "Enough, damn it."

"Who are you talking to?" her mother asked.

Crap. Too much conversation with too many people.

"Nobody," Brianna said.

If her parents heard her cursing out ghosts, they'd drag her home to Boston—and right back to her last psychiatrist.

Her father looked around the room. "Your house is cozy, and Savannah seems nice. At least here, you don't have to shovel snow." He swallowed hard. "Declan always said Savannah was a beautiful place." Tears formed in her father's eyes.

Her mom shot him a dirty look. "You promised not to bring him up."

"I miss my son, Irene. Forgive me for having a broken heart, damn it."

"I loved my son, too. I certainly never wanted him to join the military."

Like a bad tennis match, Brianna watched them bicker over someone who'd been dead fifteen years.

"Let me get you another beer," Brianna suggested, grabbing their half-full glasses.

When she returned, her parents sat on opposite ends of the couch. The two feet of cushioned space between them spoke volumes.

"We can see some sights tomorrow and catch up. I've missed both of you."

She hoped her agenda would end their arguing, but it only brought an excruciating silence. Lifeless as the son they'd buried, her parents remained seated, saying nothing.

Hello? This was why she'd left Boston. She was alive, their daughter, and she was sitting right in front of them. A living, breathing person, though right now they never would have noticed.

"I'm going to put in a movie," Brianna said. She couldn't take the silence any longer. Two hours concentrating on an electronic box would ease the discomfort over the pink elephant sitting among them—Declan's memory.

“I’m tired, honey. I’m going to turn in,” her mother said.

Brianna breathed a sigh of relief. If one of her parents was in another room, that would dissipate the arguing. “Night, Mom. Thanks again for coming to visit.”

“Sean, are you coming?”

“I’ll stay up with Brianna,” her dad said. “Be there soon.”

“Okay,” her mother said and went to apply her face cream, a nightly ritual since Brianna was little. Brianna knew the cold cream was terrific at removing makeup, but it didn’t make a dent in the pain.

“Anything specific you want to watch, Dad?”

He sipped his beer, smiling at a moment’s peace. “Whatever you want is fine.”

Figuring he’d hate estrogen-filled chick flicks, she chose *National Treasure*. For the next two hours, they let television hues wash over them, an attempt to bond while looking in the same direction, deliberately avoiding the pain injected into their lives.

CHAPTER FIFTEEN

Grieving is a necessary passage... not a permanent rest stop.
~ Dodinsky

On Saturday morning, Brianna woke up her parents, something she hadn't done since Christmas when she was little. There were so many family traditions back then. Declan's death erased all that had gone before. Family activities for four shifted into confusing agendas for three.

Her mom tied a white terrycloth robe around her waist and walked into the kitchen. "Do you want me to help you with breakfast?"

Virginia hovered nearby, wanting attention. "I knew they'd expect you to cook. Why can't I fix grits for everyone?"

"I'm fine, Mom," Brianna said, ushering her into the den and away from Virginia. Even though her mother couldn't actually *see* the stubborn ghost in her kitchen, Brianna knew Virginia's presence took up all the hot air. Better to go into another room.

"We'll grab something to eat as we sight-see," Brianna said. "Why don't you go get dressed and we'll go in a few minutes?"

"Sure," her mother said with about as much enthusiasm as someone about to get a root canal.

Brianna hated seeing her parents so lifeless. She hoped to cheer up their spirits by showing them some of her favorite Savannah places, locations Declan would've loved.

Grabbing her car keys off the hook in the kitchen, she fiddled with them to ease her anxiety.

"For Yankees, they seem tolerable. Don't you want to cook grits or something from my Southern cookbook?" Virginia asked.

Brianna smiled at Virginia's tenacity. At least the Graysons hadn't abandoned their hopes and dreams, even if her parents already had. "Maybe later."

By midmorning, Brianna's parents seemed in better spirits, and they followed her with the implicit trust one gives a tour guide. They saw the many historic squares, sage and lavender Victorian homes, and Forsyth Park with its famous fountain. Its ornate, two-tiered structure stood in the center of the park, surrounded by a cast-iron circular fence. The main centerpiece sprayed water into an arch, and water droplets fell onto plaster white swans and cherub angels at the four corners. Each corner piece blew water from oval mouths, creating an elaborate dancing effect—individual pieces working as part of a whole.

Like family is supposed to do. Brianna stared at the nearest swan. *But that changes when one piece dies.*

Throughout the day, Brianna pointed out some of Declan's favorite places. Though her mom smiled, Brianna knew that one movement from her lips required concerted effort. Mom had frowned so often for the last fifteen years, reversing her lips into a smile must be like swimming against the current.

Later, after a full day of sight-seeing, they returned to the house.

Her dad walked into the kitchen for some crackers. "Um, Brianna?"

She winced when she heard his tone. What the hell had Virginia done now?

"Yes?"

"We supported your decision to move down South, but—"

Oh god. Virginia, I'm going to go Ghostbusters *on your ass.* "But what?"

"Are you becoming a grits connoisseur? These books weren't here before, were they?"

Brianna sprinted to the kitchen. On the counter, lined up in neat, alphabetical stacks, were dozens of cookbooks, all of them centered on grits and how the almighty grit came into being. The ghost even had one on specialty cheese grits. Did grits come in flavors? Geesh. She still had a lot to learn about the South.

Brianna racked her brain to explain the books to her dad. "I, well, I figured, why not try new recipes, now that I'm living in Savannah."

“Are you doing okay, here in…his favorite place?” her mother asked, not daring to mention Declan’s name.

Brianna choked back a tear. “Don’t worry about me or my life here. I’m doing just fine.”

They seemed satisfied with her answer, and in many ways, it was true. But seeing her parents again, seeing the spirit gone from their eyes, Brianna wondered if she’d ever be *just fine* again.

CHAPTER SIXTEEN

Never ask a favor of someone till they have had their dinner.
~ Old Saying

"Damn it." Steven examined his freshly cut index finger. He'd known the risks when he decided to investigate someone as corrupt as Begley, but who knew intense research would slice his hands with paper cuts?

"Occupational hazard," Dennis said, holding up his own scarred hands. "Want a Band-Aid?"

"Nah, but you could venture into this century and convert the data to a digital format. How have you kept up with all the paper files?"

"One step at a time," Dennis said, grinning. "Besides, even if I went digital, you'd complain about carpal tunnel."

Steven gave Dennis a sarcastic smirk. "If it isn't one thing, it's another."

"Amen, brother."

Man, it was great to be back in Dennis's place. Steven had missed many of the nuances between musicians, sayings like *brother.* Words people in the real world didn't say. Home was beginning to get on his good side. But Begley would always remain on the shit list.

"These files keep leading me to the same dead end," Steven said.

Dennis set down the folder he was reviewing. "At the property purchase, right?"

"Exactly. Each house burns down, faulty wiring is blamed, and Begley buys the land cheap. Then he restores or revamps the house to rent."

"And we both know there's more to it than simple real estate," Dennis said. "Begley doesn't do anything without intent."

"But what is the intent? The man has gotten away with arson, possibly murder. Where are the cremated remains from all these fires? The listing of people Begley supposedly called to inform next of kin?"

Dennis shrugged. "The eternal question. Begley has cops and city officials in his back pocket. I've been trying to make headway for years, but you know how life is here. Secret deals and handshakes go a long way in Savannah."

"I remember," Steven said, shaking his head at how things worked down South. Everything was about saving face, keeping up public appearances.

"What about the woman Begley's renting to? Didn't you say you met her?" Dennis asked.

"Brianna. I'm taking her to dinner tonight."

Dennis cracked a grin. "You always did have a way with the ladies. Think she'll help us? If we could get a look at her lease papers, we might be able to see if Begley's doing anything illegal on that front? It's a long shot but worth a try."

Steven set down the files, and against his macho persona, reached for a Band-Aid. "I think she'd be willing to help. I'd planned to ask her about her lease papers at dinner."

"Combining business and pleasure," Dennis said. "Feels like old times."

Steven's face turned hot. "She's not like the others."

"Oh?"

"Honest, man. She's different."

"Uh huh. If she'll help us take Begley down, then I'll believe you. Until then…"

Steven put on the Band-Aid. "Ever thought of going to the feds with any of this, especially since Begley owns cops?"

"Yeah, but we need more than circumstantial evidence," Dennis said. "That's why if this woman will help us, get us some concrete evidence Begley is doing illegally in his real estate business, maybe we have a shot. But of course, that means you need to charm her, like you have so many others."

Steven bit his lip. True, he'd been the wild child back in the day, but Dennis had Brianna all wrong. She wasn't like the others. Maybe because she knew what losing someone felt like, what losing a *sibling* felt like. Every day people could empathize, but *understanding* was another matter.

Besides, along with Brianna's understanding came amazing lips. He hadn't intended to kiss her that first date. He'd wanted to keep things casual, but the yearning desire practically burned from her eyes, so he'd obliged. He had no idea the kiss would affect him too.

He hadn't called her again until this week. He'd been busy hanging out with Dennis and with research that was going nowhere. But he liked this woman. If she'd be game for helping him take Begley down, he could see himself getting serious for the Irish beauty—even if she was living in the home that should be his. What he'd do with it if he owned it, he still hadn't figured out. It's not like he planned to stay in Savannah forever.

###

"Quite an interesting place," Brianna said. Her blue eyes sparkled as she glanced around the open-air patio.

"Glad you like my choice of restaurants. I figured you might want to experience something only the locals know about."

His intuition had been correct. Rather than take her to another River Street place, he'd driven her to an old favorite, Café Interpol. The place had once been a bus depot, but the owner had turned it into a French-Italian eatery. It was so far off the path, only the locals knew about it.

The waiter ushered them to a quaint table in the corner. Along the back wall, large canvases displayed rich-colored paintings: apple and pear still life, zombie-eyed self-portraits, the skyline of downtown Savannah.

"The paintings are done by SCAD students, Savannah College of Art and Design. If you like art, this city's the place to be."

Brianna's lips turned into a smile, like she'd been let in on a secret. He hoped she would respond to his request for help with as much enthusiasm. Tonight, she wore a bright-blue, low-cut blouse and a teardrop diamond necklace. Her dark hair curled sweetly at her shoulders. He didn't need beer—he'd drink in the sight of her.

"I've seen sketches hanging in the local coffeehouse. Someone mentioned SCAD."

The waiter took their drink order and set a rose in the center of the white-linen covered table.

Steven unfolded his napkin in his lap and offered his best smile. "It's a pretty sweet deal actually. Students get to put their pieces all over the city, expanding their portfolio. In return, residents get to see some talented artists. Savannah is one giant art gallery, if you think about it."

When she smiled, he found himself staring at her lips. The lipstick she'd chosen was a berry color. He wanted to taste them, see if they tasted like raspberries. Damn, she was beautiful.

"How'd you find this place?" she asked.

Focus. Keep things professional.

"My mother loved all the spots for locals. Our family ate here at least twice a month."

Brianna choked on her water.

"Are you okay?"

She coughed and nodded. Had his explanation startled her? Or was something else wrong?

"I'm fine," she said, her voice hoarse. She swallowed more water and the color in her face returned.

Steven motioned for the waiter to bring them another water pitcher. "You sure?"

"Yes." She cleared her throat. "So, what did you want to talk to me about?"

Wow, she did like to get right down to business. Good. If she kept things professional, he could keep his concentration.

Oh hell, who was he kidding?

He flashed a smile, hoping to make a good impression. She smiled back. A positive sign.

"I think Begley's corrupt," Steven whispered. "Not only for his lack of effort after my family died, but I've been investigating his property purchases. Things aren't adding up. Is there anything about him that you've noticed? Anything a little…off?"

Brianna took another sip of water. Was she pondering his question? She didn't smile or agree though. But she hadn't disagreed. If only he knew what she was thinking.

"If you prefer not to answer—"

"I'm fine," Brianna said. "Just feels like everyone wants to know about Begley these days."

Hmm, strange. "Who else would be asking you about Begley?"

Her cheeks flooded with color. "Never mind. What kind of information are you looking for? He's my landlord. Fairly decent, though he seemed blasé about a few concerns I had regarding the house."

"Would you mind if I took a peek at your lease agreement? It's none of my business what you pay in rent. I'm more concerned about Begley doing any kind of illegal setup with the houses he's renting."

"I'll let you look at my lease." She tilted her head and searched his face. "What do you expect to find?"

He leaned in. "I think Begley killed my family to get the house. I'm not sure what he did with the ashes though."

All color drained from her face, leaving her ghostly white.

"What's wrong?" he asked.

She closed her eyes and breathed in and out. Was she all right? Did she know something?

"Just let me breathe," she said. "Give me a second."

He felt like he should reach out to her, pat her hand, do something. But what? What was the protocol for something like this?

The next few moments stretched into infinity. She inhaled deeply, took a sip of water. After what seemed forever, she finally spoke.

"I have to tell you something. About ashes."

"What?"

"After I first moved in, I found black ash on the closet floor. Begley seemed really surprised when I contacted him about it."

Why would Begley be surprised about ash on the floor? Better yet, why had he rented a house with leftover ashes? Were those the cremated remains? Could it be possible?

"What happened?"

She shrugged. "When Begley came out to investigate, the ash had disappeared. He dismissed me like I was crazy."

"Can I take a look later?" Steven asked.

"Sure, but I doubt you'll see anything. I only saw the ash once."

Their food arrived, which provided a good diversion. They ate and drank for the next twenty minutes, exchanging basic conversation about work, life, and happenings in Savannah.

When the waiter brought cups of after-dinner coffee, Steven took the opportunity to return to his original intent.

"My buddy Dennis and I are investigating some of Begley's property deals. I know I can't ask you to spy on your landlord, but if you notice anything—"

"I'll let you know," she said.

Her jaw was clenched, like she'd just been coaxed into doing someone else's homework. Did she resent him for this?

"I intend to prove Begley set fire to the house," Steven said. "But until then, be careful around him. I'll look at your lease agreement. Maybe there's something illegal there that we can nail him with."

"You really think he is capable of murder? Of arson?"

Steven thought a moment before answering. "Yes, I do."

CHAPTER SEVENTEEN

Knowing is not enough; we must apply.
Willing is not enough; we must do.
~ Old Saying

Between the Graysons' antics, her parents recent visit, and Steven insisting Begley was a killer, Brianna needed something else to occupy her mind. Savannah may have been her brother's favorite place, but she'd experienced a little too much of it—and too fast.

There was nothing like a fatal bus crash to skyrocket her workload in one day's time. While she wouldn't wish death on anyone, the long hours helped take her mind off everything else. Careful steps had to be taken with each body and all things accounted for.

She liked this part—double-checking details and managing each task. The required precision offered a sense of routine and accomplishment, something she'd missed in recent weeks.

Of course, working in the mortuary arts had its oddities. Fifty people had died on the tour bus, all Elvis impersonators. Apparently, they'd been on their way to a conference when the driver ran off the road on Interstate 16. Thirty bodies were shipped back to their cities of origin, while twelve were from the Savannah area.

Car crashes often proved challenging in restoring a lifelike appearance. However, thanks to Margie's love of all things Southern, including Graceland, Brianna had her choice of Elvis prints to work from. Who knew that seminar Brianna took on sideburns would ever come in handy?

She started on Elvis number twelve, otherwise known as Bobby Ray Canters. Good lord, was there a more Southern-sounding name?

The skin toner bottle was almost empty, but maybe it could last until she finished Bobby Ray. Popping open the cap, she squeezed the bottle with all her might. Only a few drops dribbled out. Nope. This wouldn't do. She'd need a spare, and Edwin always kept more supplies in the racks.

She scanned the shelves, cabinets, and racks where all the creams and lotions should be. Nothing. Had Margie moved them for some reason?

Brianna pulled off her gloves and walked toward Edwin's office. Surely, he would know where the spares were kept. She hoped so. She didn't want to drive to the store this late at night.

When she approached the doorway, she heard male voices. Gruff, guttural sounds. Who would Edwin be talking to at this hour? Margie was the only other employee working this late.

Brianna tiptoed several steps and remained near the doorway, out of sight.

"We can't risk it," Edwin said.

“I’ll tell you what you’ll risk and what you won’t,” a Southern accent hissed. “He’s already dressed up like Elvis, thank you, thank you very much.”

Begley? What the hell would he be doing here? Her pulse raced and sent a sharp pain into her stomach. Something was wrong.

“How do we explain to the family?” Edwin asked, his voice trembling. “What am I supposed to say? We cremated the remains by mistake?”

Brianna swallowed hard. What were they talking about? Restful Oaks had an impeccable reputation. If Begley was making threats, and he owned the place, what secrets lurked behind the positive name?

“Tell the family anything, say the bus caught fire,” Begley said. “I don’t care how you do it, but cremate the body. He has no kids. Should be a walk in the park.”

“Won’t the cops find out the truth?”

She adjusted her stance enough to peek in without being seen.

Begley loomed over Edwin like a dark cloud. “Don’t worry about the cops. They’ll do what I tell them. Just cremate the damn body. Remember, we’re in this together.”

“I never wanted to get this deep.” Edwin clasped and unclasped his hands, his typical gesture when nervous. “Just keep the police away.”

With a carefree chuckle, Begley patted Edwin on the back. “No worries.”

Brianna gulped. What the hell was going on? How did Begley have any say-so over cremations? And why?

“I’ll give Brianna the instructions,” Edwin said.

Instructions? *Me?* She had no intention of becoming involved in Begley’s corruption.

Footsteps clicked against the floor. Shit. Begley was leaving. She tiptoed five feet down the hall and into a side room. Seconds later, she heard the hall door close.

Breathe. She checked her pulse. Beating like a hummingbird on speed. Relax. Walk into Edwin’s office and play dumb. Just ask for more toner cream and go back to Elvis number twelve.

After a deep breath, she entered Edwin’s office, where he sat with his back to her. Should she interrupt him or come back? No, better get the lotion and get the hell out of there.

“Hi, Edwin. Do we have any more toner cream?”

Edwin spun around in his chair, his pupils large and black like a scared cat. “What?”

“Toner cream. I’m working on Bobby Ray Canters and ran out. There aren’t any spare bottles in the racks.”

Edwin pressed his bony fingers to his temples and rubbed. "Um, about Bobby Ray…there's something we need to discuss."

She bit the inside of her lip to avoid showing any emotion. "Oh?"

"We've been unable to locate any of Mr. Ray's family, so we'll be cremating him."

"Excuse me?"

Edwin cocked an eyebrow at her abrupt tone. Oops. Guess her words *had* sounded like an accusation. Keep it together.

"I mean, when did we change the plan from burial to cremation? I've been working on him because you'd told me—"

"And I appreciate all your effort. You've stepped up when we were slammed. Thank you. And to show you how grateful I am, I'll be giving you the rest of the week off."

Huh? Normally, she'd be thrilled for some time to relax and see Savannah. But after the conversation she'd just witnessed, it seemed too much like coincidence. A terrible coincidence.

"I don't understand," she said. "I thought we had to finish up the bodies of the local Elvis impersonators because we have the Taylor family to start on tomorrow. I don't mind working long hours—"

"I know, but right now I need to get through all the cremation paperwork. Therefore, your cosmetology services won't be required.

Relax, enjoy, and spend some time getting settled in. I know you haven't had much time to unpack since moving here."

She stared at the stacks of papers on his desk, desperately trying to think of some way to stall the conversation, to figure out a way to learn more.

"I appreciate the gesture, but as I've mentioned, my goal is to run a funeral home someday. Meaning I need to learn the ins and outs of cremation, embalming, and other tasks. Perhaps I could stay around and watch, even if you don't need my cosmetology work?"

He frowned. "Not this time, I'm afraid."

Why not?

"I won't be any trouble. Perhaps I could help Margie with paperwork, learn the legalities of cremation documents—"

"No!"

She stepped back, alarmed by his harsh response. What was he hiding that she couldn't learn the cremation process? Such requests weren't unreasonable.

He cleared his throat and smiled at her over his spectacles. "I apologize for my outburst. I'm quite tired."

Tired? Perhaps he was tired of being Begley's puppet. She didn't dare ask. This time, she'd find out on her own.

"Don't worry about it," she said.

"You've done a good job here, Brianna. Take the rest of the week off. End of discussion."

Her mouth fell open, ready to object.

"That will be all," he said. "You are free to go."

"What about Bobby Ray Canters? His body is on my table."

Edwin let out a heavy sigh. "Put him in cold chamber number forty. Then start your vacation."

"Will do."

She returned to the preparation room, uncertainty flooding through her with every step. Why the sudden need to cremate Bobby Ray Canters when only an hour prior, Edwin had said all the Elvis bodies would be buried? And what did the mysterious conversation between Begley and Edwin mean?

For the first time, she *wanted* the dead to talk to her. In the silent preparation room, she stared at the Elvis look-alike on her table.

"Hello?"

No answer. Well, hell. When she didn't want to hear voices, they came out in full force. The one time she'd like to talk to the dead, they'd gone silent. Murphy's Law of the dead?

She opened the cold chamber halfway. No. This was wrong. Maybe Bobby Ray wasn't telling her in so many words, but her clenched gut was doing some heavy talking.

Didn't Restful Oaks have another set of chambers, one they only used for overflow? Margie had pointed them out once. Yes. The basement would be the perfect place to keep Bobby Ray for now.

Brianna gathered her things and wheeled him down the winding hallway and into the service elevator. When they reached the bottom level, the bell dinged and the doors opened. She maneuvered the table to the right, passed two side hallways, and curved around to the back basement doorway. Behind old boxes and furniture, there was a cold chamber with six slots. Edwin kept the unit active in case of overflow, but to her knowledge he hadn't used it in months.

The confusion of this new place would stall Bobby Ray's impending cremation long enough for her to figure out what the hell Edwin and Begley were plotting and how she could stop them.

CHAPTER EIGHTEEN

We stand at the crossroads, each minute, each hour, each day, making choices. We choose the thoughts we allow ourselves to think, the passions we allow ourselves to feel, and the actions we allow ourselves to perform.

~ Benjamin Franklin

Brianna didn't sleep worth a damn. Even after she went to bed with a sense of pride for saving Bobby Ray from cremation—temporarily—she'd tossed and turned all night. Virginia's soprano rendition of Civil War songs hadn't helped. The woman's voice left something to be desired. Left quite a lot, actually. Perhaps the Southern soldiers could've won if they'd had Virginia there to serenade the Union troops all night long.

No matter what, Brianna had to get a decent night's sleep. This couldn't go on. She needed to decide whether she would move forward and help the Grayson ghosts or not. With that lovely thought zigzagging in her mind, she dressed and snapped on Plato's leash.

"Let's go to the park, boy. I can get coffee on the way."

He spun around with glee, tangling the leash in his front legs. She smiled and untangled him. "C'mon. Let's go."

"Going out?" James asked, suddenly appearing in the front doorway.

Damn it, why did the dead always appear out of nowhere? Couldn't they learn to chime or something, first? The living knocked on doors before entering. She needed to find something similar for the deceased.

"Yes. I need some peace and quiet, time to think."

"I understand," he said, offering a gentle smile. "Have you thought any more about our plight?"

Plight? He made it sound like there were too many pickles on the sandwich they'd ordered. Three ghosts living in her house, needing her to spy on her landlord and her boss, not to mention risk her career, qualified as a hell of a lot more than a plight.

"I have, but I haven't made any firm decisions as to how much I'm willing to risk. That's one reason I wanted some time alone."

He immediately stepped aside. "Then I won't keep you. I hope you and Plato have a good walk."

She couldn't help but smile. James would've made a great politician. Always knew the right time to say things, always knew when to back away.

"Thanks," she said. "C'mon, Plato. Let's go."

Minutes later, coffee in hand, she and Plato started their trek in Forsyth Park, where he immediately set his nose to the ground and explored the bountiful smells.

She took a deep breath, the cold air tickling her nostrils. Far from the hustle and bustle of River Street, Forsyth Park was the epitome of serene. It was also the ideal place to think through concerns.

Immense blue, pink, and sage Victorian homes overlooked the park along with luxurious bed-and-breakfast inns. At this early hour, the birds chirped morning tunes and gathered seeds for their young. The only people nearby were a few dedicated joggers. For the first time since overhearing Begley and Edwin's mysterious conversation, Brianna began to relax.

"Guess vacation days aren't all bad, even if they're forced on me." She took a sip of coffee and enjoyed its warmth on her throat.

Plato pulled his nose out of the grass, glanced up at her with a doggy smile, and wagged his tail. He seemed to enjoy the quality time too.

She led him along a walking trail around the outskirts of the park. Overhead, a canopy of oaks provided shade. After they'd walked about a mile, she sat on a bench near the main fountain.

Plato rested one paw on her knee.

"Hi, boy."

He tapped at her knee and whimpered. Dog speak for "What's wrong?" How did dogs read human emotions with such ease?

"I'm fine, just a few things on my mind." More like a jillion.

Plato's eyes gleamed big and curious, or maybe he was just happy to be in the park.

"I don't know what I'm doing," she whispered. He tilted his head and made a snuffle sound.

"With this *gift* of mine," she said. "I made a promise to Declan to make a difference with what time I had left. Well, time is ticking by, and other than providing good skin care, what difference have I made, Plato? I don't like seeing ghosts, but it's my reality. It's sure as hell not going to change. Moving down South proved that."

He nuzzled her foot. Such a sweetie. Of course she made a difference in *his* day-to-day existence. She was the provider of all doggy meals, treats, and belly rubs. But what about in anyone else's life?

"I need to tell Steven about Begley and Edwin. He deserves to know what they're up to."

Plato eyed a squirrel looking for acorns. She gripped his leash tighter. The last thing she needed was for him to run off when she was deep in her thoughts.

The decision to tell Steven about the recent events—what she overheard from Begley and Edwin, the forced vacation, the cremation threat, everything—that would be easy. She couldn't mention she saw and talked to the dead, especially his family. Someday maybe. Perhaps she could offer a way for him to make the amends he kept speaking of, but not until she felt more secure in their relationship.

"Plato, what am I supposed to do? Am I supposed to protect the dead at all costs?"

He pawed at her foot, leaned his head against her knee, and nudged.

"Would that be a yes in dog language?"

He barked twice and spun around before sitting again.

"I guess so." She rubbed his ears and he snorted with contentment.

"What about the cost to me? Edwin forced vacation on me because I wanted to learn about cremation paperwork. What will he do when he learns I'm snooping on Begley's dealings?" A pang hit her stomach. "He'd fire me. That's what he'd do."

She pondered the thought. Getting fired would not be good, but she had references from Boston. Worst-case, she could eliminate Restful Oaks from her resume.

What would happen if she did nothing? If she remained neutral, didn't get involved? Like Switzerland. Things would keep going as they had been—ghosts tormenting her, voices haunting her, the Graysons never leaving.

The Graysons never leaving.

Holy crap. The Graysons never leaving.

No, she couldn't handle permanent ghosts in her home. Occasionally, and until she helped out to get things resolved, fine. It's not like she had much choice. But the Graysons living with her forever? No.

Besides, what if she and Steven worked out? She'd heard of living with the in-laws, but this would be too close for comfort, and then some.

Okay, she could take the risk. She could summon her courage and snoop on Begley. Trespassing, but not stealing.

Besides, if Edwin was involved in some kind of scheme, she needed to find out about it. Even if she did nothing, Edwin might get caught, and what if the cops closed down Restful Oaks after an investigation? She'd lose her job. Same risk. She may as well snoop and find out the truth, especially since she'd have help from Steven and his journalist friend.

"C'mon, Plato. Let's go home. I have some good news for the Graysons."

Plato spun around and barked three times. No amount of wine could equal the thrill of doggy approval.

As they walked, she plotted out what she would say. This could work. She could tell the Graysons she'd be willing to help them. Doing so would count as keeping her promise to Declan. It damn well better count, especially after all the serenading and haunting voices.

When they approached the house, another thought struck her. What if Begley found out she was investigating him? She might lose her house. There had to be legalities in place to protect tenants from landlords who simply didn't like their renters. But knowing Begley, he'd get around all legalities.

This was a true risk, but what was her alternative? Living with the Graysons forever. She couldn't do it. Human beings needed REM sleep.

Besides, if Begley evicted her, she could always find another home in Savannah.

She had no intention of getting caught by Begley or Edwin. Hopefully, things wouldn't reach the point of job termination or eviction.

If they did, she would jump off that bridge when she got there.

CHAPTER NINETEEN

Fashion is a form of ugliness so intolerable
that we have to alter it every six months.
~ Oscar Wilde

Brianna rummaged through her clothes, or lack thereof, in the master closet. Was breaking and entering a good idea, or just an intriguing concept when she'd had too many beers?

"Don't you have anything black to wear?" Virginia asked, looking over Brianna's shoulder. "Your closet is an ode to beige and pink. You can't sneak into Begley's office looking noticeable, not to mention bland."

Irritation prickled down Brianna's back. "I don't live in Hollywood and I work with the dead. Fashionable black outfits aren't my top priority."

"You're in the South now. Fashion and reputation are essential."

"Why?"

"Why what?" Virginia asked, obviously surprised anyone would question her wisdom.

"Why are those things so important? Look at your family. You're dead. Declan died when I was fifteen. Life's too short to focus on what others think. Clothes don't decide who you are."

Virginia wriggled her nose. "Heavens to Betsy, are all Yankees this dense, or is it just you?" She sat on the edge of the bed.

“Mama, stop,” Amy said. She settled across the queen-size bed on her stomach, her knees bent and ankles crossed.

“Presentation counts,” Virginia said. “You may think I’m full of myself, but we care about reputation. Even during the War of Northern Aggression—”

“The what?”

Amy laughed. “That’s her way of referring to the Civil War.”

“Oh.” How did Steven turn out normal with Virginia as a mother?

She wanted to sit on the bed herself and put her black tennies on. Virginia should certainly approve of wearing them. But the bed was too crowded, so she sat on the padded window seat.

“Don’t you get tired of catering to others’ opinions? What good has it done?” Brianna asked.

She’d tried to be the surviving child for her parents when Declan died. Keeping them happy, occupied, busy—in the end, nothing had worked. They lost part of who they were after Declan’s death. Understandable, yes. Ideal for the teenager left behind? No.

Virginia gave a blank stare. “Your point?”

Brianna shrugged. “In the end, life’s about who we are inside, not about the clothes on our backs.”

Amy frowned. “But don’t all Yankees wear dark colors? Dark leather jackets and black sunglasses, like in the movies?”

“Thank you,” Virginia added. “I thought so too. She can’t be inconspicuous if she doesn’t wear dark clothes.”

Brianna couldn’t think of what to say, but an uneasy feeling rose to the surface. Sure, she’d decided to help their cause. But did the Graysons wish they’d stumbled upon someone else who could see and hear them?

“Haven’t you ever needed a black outfit?” Amy asked.

For Declan’s funeral. I was fifteen.

“I’ll shop tomorrow. Begley will probably be at his country club Thursday night, so I’ll find a way into his office to look at his files. Besides, it’s not like I have to be at work. Let’s hope Edwin doesn’t figure out where I put Bobby Ray’s body.”

“Good. One more thing,” Virginia said.

Brianna waited with dread. “Yes?”

“Don’t shop near the historic district where you’ll be recognized. Go across the bridge to Tybee.”

Brianna raised one eyebrow. “Incognito cosmetologist in search of black wardrobe.”

Virginia chuckled, but her eyes held a sincere gratitude for Brianna’s help. “Exactly.”

###

The next day, Brianna drove out of the historic district and toward Thunderbolt, which would get her to Tybee Island, the local beach area.

Thunderbolt only comprised a few square miles, mostly watery swamps packed with cypress trees. In the afternoon fog, the knobby-kneed trees were eerie. Living spirits, sloughing around in the water, awaiting their next victim.

Oak trees lined the narrow roads, and decrepit homes with small, dimly lit windows stood in the distance. Why had Virginia recommended this route? Brianna couldn't imagine someone as upper-crust as Virginia going within fifteen feet of Thunderbolt.

She pressed on the gas, eager to reach the bridge to Tybee. On either side of the road, dormant kudzu, a southern ropelike vine that supposedly grew more than a foot per day, wrapped its wiry tongue around the oaks, trying to swallow them whole. Brianna locked her doors.

Ghosts were in her home. Ghosts seemed alive and well in Thunderbolt. This wasn't the life she envisioned when she moved down South.

Twenty minutes later, she'd escaped the fog and reached Tybee Island. Shops with tall windows displaying hot-pink bikinis, sunglasses, and Bugs Bunny beach towels flanked the streets. Visible from the highway, the Atlantic Ocean waves lapped up the shoreline.

While a tourist destination, Tybee provided an ideal beach getaway for Savannah locals. Those who avoided living in Savannah proper bought beach homes, even Begley.

Shit. Begley had bragged about having a Tybee beach house. What if she ran into him when shopping for dark clothes to break into his office?

Relax. Shopping wasn't illegal, regardless of intent. Besides, Edwin had forced vacation on her. What else was she supposed to do with free time? Most Savannah folks went to the beach. She was simply trying to fit in. Nothing suspicious.

Near the end of a so-far-unsuccessful shopping strip, she found consignment stores featuring eclectic attire. She parked in the back, keeping her sunglasses on as she entered. Better safe than sorry. She didn't want anyone to recognize her.

She browsed the clothing racks for any dark clothes. Unfortunately, most items in black were too ornate for breaking and entering. Smiling, she wondered if there was an ideal outfit for such things. Perhaps it could be the next hot-ticket item on QVC? Suitable B&E Clothing, now only $19.99.

Frustrated, she looked in the store's adjacent space. No black outfits in her size, so she settled for a pair of petite, striped pants. Time was running out and she needed something. She couldn't risk another Tybee trip. Edwin might find Bobby Ray's body before she had a chance to learn the truth.

With a resigned sigh, she selected a few darker-colored tops and brought them to the counter.

The desk clerk wore an array of teals, purples, and pinks—all mismatched—and resembled an exotic bird. "Will this be all, darlin'?"

"Yes, thanks."

"How do you want to pay for this, honey?"

Brianna looked up. "Cash. Absolutely, cash."

With her change in hand, Brianna strode to her car. As she traveled over the bridge back to Savannah, the sunset began to paint the sky with pink and purple swirls.

The nearer she drove to the historic district, the more doubt crept inside her mind, nesting there like squatter mice. She continued on Highway 80, exiting on Bay Street, the last road in the historic district before the land dipped to River Street. Upriver stood the Talmadge Bridge with its illuminated cables. Against the setting sun, the cable strands reminded her of two large harps. A twinge of homesickness washed through her. The Talmadge could be the twin to the Bunker Hill Bridge in Boston.

River Street would be too loud tonight. She stayed on Bay and drove to Churchill's, an authentic English pub. Once inside, she sat at the long mahogany bar with decorative carvings in the wood. Mugs of amber-colored ale twinkled beneath frothy heads. Liquor bottles of every shape and size sat against the back mirror, reflecting their colorful images across the walls.

"What can I get you?" the bartender asked. He had a British accent watered down by the Savannah South.

"Black and Tan, please."

"Coming right up."

He poured Harp Lager halfway into the glass before moving to the Guinness tap. With precision, he slowly poured Guinness over the back of a spoon until its dark color settled on top of the lighter ale.

She watched in awe. The classic Irish drink wasn't like pouring a simple beer. Black and Tans took skill to create. Many tried but mixed the Harp and Guinness together. She knew the trick was to keep them separate in one glass.

After two swallows of the thick, chocolate-flavored head of the Guinness, the dark bubbles cascaded into the pale ale like two weather systems colliding.

She would be colliding with Begley soon, but she had to see this through. *Move forward. Remaining stagnant is what kept you in Boston so long.*

Sipping the cold beer, she tried to prepare herself for tomorrow night. The dark outfit she'd purchased wasn't perfect. But if she got caught breaking into Begley's office, the real police would come for her, not the fashion police.

"Get you another one, miss?" the bartender asked while pouring a cognac for an older gentleman a few stools down.

"Yes, please."

As he mixed her drink, she pulled out her cell. Should she do this?

She pressed the numbers into the phone and hit enter.

"Hello?"

"Steven? Hi, it's Brianna. Listen, I need to tell you something."

CHAPTER TWENTY

Right actions in the future are the best apologies for bad actions in the past.
~ Tyron Edwards, Theologian

"Are you freaking kidding me?" Steven asked. He'd bolted to Churchill's Pub the minute Brianna called him.

"Shh," Brianna said, nodding her head toward the crowded place.

He scrutinized the bar and dining areas. She made a good point. All the booths were taken—who knew so many people wanted shepherd's pie and English ale tonight?—so their privacy was limited.

Lowering his voice, he smiled and said, "Ever notice that whenever we're together, one of us winds up shushing the other one?"

Rosy color spread from her neck to her cheeks, and her eyelids crinkled when she smiled. So damn cute.

"I suppose that's because one of us always needs shushing," she said.

He leaned in and kissed her, right then and there. To shush her on his own terms.

Her lips met his and didn't waver at his touch. Yet he sensed hesitancy. Was she nervous about kissing in public, or was she holding back for some other reason?

Best to stay on track and return to their discussion. The bartender slid him a bottle of Guinness.

"You actually heard Begley and Edwin discussing illegal cremations? Are you absolutely certain?"

She furrowed her brows and took a long sip of her beer. Was she stalling him? Or hurt he'd asked for clarification? Or thrown off guard by the kiss?

"I'm sure," she said. "I don't know exactly what Begley is up to, or how Edwin is involved, but I intend to find out."

She broke eye contact and traced her fingers along the mahogany bar top. Her mouth opened, like she was ready to say something more, but she stopped. Hesitation. There it was again.

Maybe she didn't realize how much he needed her? Needed her help, but also as someone by his side? Home hadn't been an easy reunion, and she made everything about Savannah better.

"I want us to work together," he said. "Share all info on Edwin and Begley. Dennis can help with any official investigation things, but you and I have the time to research. I'm going to nail that son of a bitch Begley if it's the last thing I do."

"I'll be frank," she said. "I'm nervous about snooping into Begley's affairs."

"Understandable."

"I won't let Begley take down Restful Oaks. This isn't a job for me. It's a career. I won't be part of a scheme to hurt the dead."

And there it was—passion. Steven had been trying to put his finger on the trait he liked the most. Passion—for her work, for how she sent the dead off, and the respect she offered for details that mattered. She didn't just dress up individuals, she honored them.

A deeper resolve surged through his veins. When the time came for him to die, he wanted to have lived a life worth honoring.

"Steven?" she asked, knocking him out of his thoughts. He'd apparently been gazing at her without saying anything.

"Sorry," he said. "Zoned out. I was just admiring your commitment to your career. Don't worry. We'll find a way to bring Begley down. The bastard has no checks and balances. Time for that shit to end."

"What do you want me to do?" she asked. "I can ask Edwin about the cremations and how Restful Oaks handles them, out of professional curiosity, but if he shuts me down—"

"Just keep digging. Get what info you can. Check the forms signed with each cremation. I'll tell Dennis where we are. He covered a few corruption scandals with burials in Atlanta a few years back. Maybe he still has contacts."

She gazed up at him, a hint of longing—or perhaps needing—in her blue eyes. "I'll ask Edwin next Monday when I'm back at work."

"Great." Steven took a long swig of beer. "Forgive me, but it seems you had something else you wanted to say?"

Don't scare her off, you fool. He couldn't help asking though. He'd seen that expression of holding back before. Usually in the mirror.

She smiled a little too quickly. "No. I'll share what I find out at work next week."

Steven paid the check. His unfinished beer remained on the counter. "Do you want to meet up tomorrow night? Dennis has tickets to some exclusive book signing. I can see if he can get you in too."

"Um, no thanks. I have plans tomorrow night." She bit her lip, as if she'd said too much.

Had he been blind this whole time? Was she seeing someone else? She didn't seem like the type to play the field, but maybe he'd misread the signals.

Firm up things for the weekend. At least get on her calendar.

"Okay, then let's touch base on Saturday. Maybe we can walk Plato in the park, or if Dennis and I make headway with any of the pubs, you're more than welcome to hear us play."

Her face practically glowed. He loved watching her lips curl into a wide grin. Took everything he had not to plant another intense kiss on her.

"I'd love to hear your music," she said. "What kind do you play?"

"You could say I'm between genres at the moment." He reached for his beer and took a sip, taking time to relish the flavor on his tongue.

"Back in California, I did the hard rock scene. But now, I want something different."

She gave him a knowing smile. "Like what?"

"Even in my band, I wanted to do a few ballads. Some slower tunes, leaning toward folk or coffeehouse type music."

Her fingers traced the side of her glass. "I love low-key music. Rock is okay, but after a while, it just doesn't have the same…"

"Substance," he said, hoping his word would be the sentence ending she sought.

"Exactly. Rock is great to dance and jam out to, but the ballads are what reach out and touch people's hearts. Don't you think?"

Offering her a flirtatious wink, he said, "Your enthusiasm is reassuring. Dennis and I are working on a set. Let's hope we can get a gig and you can hear us."

"That would be great." She glanced at her phone and her eyes widened. "I have to go. Sorry to leave so soon." She put her keys in her blazer pocket.

Why did she seem in such a hurry? He wanted to ask, but she acted eager to rush off.

"Sure. I'll give you a call on Saturday."

"Thanks." She stood and grabbed her purse.

"Let me walk you home."

Maybe she'd open up more, say whatever she was holding back, if they weren't in such a crowded place. Besides, he longed to kiss her again.

"I have my car," she said. "Besides, I need to stop by the Pink House for catering menus. Margie is doing a big shindig."

"Let me come with you. The Pink House has an amazing piano bar and jazz band."

"Not tonight." She reached for a napkin and ripped it into tiny strips. A nervous gesture?

He narrowed his eyes. What was she not telling him? She'd seemed so curious about his music only a few minutes ago. Was this the brush-off?

"Call me Saturday, okay? We'll figure out the next steps," she said.

He rubbed the ache in his chest. Was this a mistake, asking her to work together? She'd kept something from him—it was obvious—he just didn't know what it was.

With as much nonchalance as he could summon, he said, "Sure."

He walked her to the car and watched her drive away. Saturday, he'd see her again. Tomorrow was Thursday. Edwin had given her the rest of the week off.

So what the hell did she plan to do between Thursday and Saturday that she needed to be so secretive?

CHAPTER TWENTY-ONE

A man can't be too careful in the choice of his enemies.
~ Oscar Wilde

Brianna sped away from Churchill's, guilt seeping from every pore. Sure, she'd been honest and told Steven what she'd overheard at work. She'd just left out one key factor—her plan to break into Begley's office tomorrow night.

Why *had* she held back? Steven noticed her awkwardness. The hurt on his face was more than evident, especially when she told him she wouldn't see him until Saturday.

Maybe she wasn't sure if he'd break her heart, so why confess a crime she planned to commit? Or maybe because the Graysons—his dead family—had put her up to the idea in the first place?

She still could've mentioned her plans, leaving the Graysons out. Stop. Guilt wouldn't accomplish anything, not at this point. She needed to blast some music and forget the last hour.

At the next stoplight, she flipped through her CD case and pulled out the Dropkick Murphys. Cranking the volume, she fast-forwarded to their kick-ass rendition of *Amazing Grace*. Bagpipes and electric guitars, combined with the gruff male voices, let her escape into her own mini rock concert for the drive home. She'd love to see Steven perform ballads one day. But on some occasions, the hard rock was the perfect escape.

When she opened her front door, Willie Nelson's version of "Georgia on my Mind" reverberated through the house. Only she didn't own any Willie Nelson music, and her CD player at home had been on the blink.

The ghosts cooked grits. They sang a lot, off-key. Now they came with their own speaker system?

"Greetings, Yankee." Virginia offered a warm smile and returned to dusting the counters.

Ghosts housecleaned too?

"Um," Brianna said, a bit taken aback by Virginia's nicer side. "Thanks. You're cleaning?"

"Just doing our part, a thank you for agreeing to help us."

Ah, so Brianna's help was what sparked this nicer, nonsinging side of the woman whose Southern roots stretched deeper than the Earth's core.

"Thanks." Brianna set down her purse and relaxed on the couch in the den. James sat in the recliner, reading the paper with Plato at his feet. Amy said she'd straightened up the kitchen and put glasses away.

Wow. If Brianna had known her agreeing to help them came with free housework, she might've said yes sooner.

And yet, something besides satisfaction stirred in her soul. Appreciation, maybe? Not only for the chance to keep her promise to

Declan, but for the Graysons' faith she would succeed. James had told her so, long before she ever agreed to help.

Her parents didn't operate that way. Not only had they become empty shells since Declan's death, they stopped having faith at all unless something or someone proved successful. To see the Graysons believe in her, have faith even though she hadn't accomplished the goal yet, warmed her insides.

Was she feeling an appreciation for Southern life, that evocative custom that charmed so many?

She didn't know. Dare she admit it? As she relaxed, listening to Willie Nelson's melodic guitar—twangy though it was—she imagined herself strolling under cypress trees, soaking in warm sunshine, breathing in summertime's freshly cut grass.

A leisurely Southern day, one she wanted to spend with Steven without a care in the world. Such a wish might come true, but only after she helped the Graysons, kept her promise to Declan, and brought Begley and maybe Edwin to justice.

If she could succeed, she could face anything.

###

On Thursday evening, Brianna walked to Begley's office. Her new pants hugged her thighs, and she sucked in her stomach to ease the pressure. The shopping trip hadn't been what she'd hoped, and in the end she'd settled for a stretchy pair of horizontal black-and-white striped tights, in petite. At five foot nine, she looked like a rogue *Cat in the Hat* as she traipsed her way through dark Savannah squares.

She ducked around parked cars and trees, hiding from clusters of Savannah ghost tours. Offered on foot and by trolley, ghost tours fascinated tourists, who flocked to where hauntings were spotted, or at least imagined, at any given time. Brianna had no trouble not adding her ghost-invaded home to such a tour.

A boisterous trolley driver drove past, exclaiming to her passengers, "And y'all may not realize how many ghosts live here in Savannah..."

Yes, I do. They're squatting in my house.

Couples walked the main streets, holding plastic cups filled with beverages. Unlike the rest of Georgia, Savannah allowed people to walk around with open containers, provided they weren't made of glass. A cup of Guinness in her hand meant she blended in, and it made the neighborhood seem sweeter, though she wished the tourists would hurry up and move. She needed to break into Begley's office without witnesses.

When she reached Reynolds Square, she heard footsteps and ducked behind a live oak. Men with dark navy jackets and women in sequined tops strolled past, laughing and joking about their week. They were likely headed to the Pink House for dinner, one of Savannah's most delectable restaurants on the square.

Just thinking about food made her stomach growl. She should've eaten a granola bar or something before this venture. But preparing for criminal activity wasn't a skill on her resume. Live and learn.

Once the square cleared out a little, she sat on the park bench to prepare herself. In the center of Reynolds Square stood a large statue of John Wesley, founder of the Methodist church. It towered over her, seemingly judging what she planned to do.

"I'm doing the right thing here, John," she muttered. "Begley's corrupt. I'm only going to peek, not take anything."

The statue didn't reply. She didn't expect it to, but given all the paranormal things in her current life, anything was possible. Wait a second. Why was she explaining herself to a Methodist statue, anyway? She was Catholic.

Focus. She sprinted across the street and reached Johnson Square, the location of Begley's office. While most squares had homes, churches, or hotels on their corners, prestigious Johnson Square had banks, law firms, and corporate buildings. Wall Street wannabes.

Sneaking up to the building, she jimmied the back door lock. "Thanks, Uncle Jack," she whispered. Uncles who dated Irish mafia princesses and knew how to break into offices weren't such a bad thing. There's always something positive to say about family, right?

Once inside, she took a quick look around. His office conformed to every other executive suite she'd seen: filing cabinets against walls, overstuffed bookshelves, and an antique oak desk placed in the center. Its enormous legs must have killed ten trees. Way to go green, Begley.

She pulled on the desk drawer. Locked. Uncle Jack's criminal expertise couldn't help her on this massive beast. Surely, she hadn't done all this worrying and prep only to have no access to any files.

Glancing around, she noticed a scuffed file cabinet in the rear corner, with two dents in the side. Strange. Begley's Southern charm and vanity were key parts of his persona. Why have a crappy looking cabinet amid all the ornate décor?

Knowing his pompous attitude, if he wanted to hide something, the perfect place would be where no one would suspect. No one would ever think Begley would keep anything of use in such a cheap-looking piece of furniture.

A few whacks to the side, and she opened the top drawer. Thumbing through the files, mysteries became disturbingly clear. All the notations listed families who refused to sell, with their names, addresses, and comments. She suspected every case matched a house fire in the historic district. Steven would probably know. She'd have to tell him about her new criminal lifestyle.

Smith family, August 2011: refused to sell. No children, matter handled without issue.

Ballard family, January 2012: refused to sell. Four children, case closed.

Case closed? She wrote down the details and would research later. Did case closed mean he had killed—or arranged to kill—the four kids who would inherit the house?

When she picked up the next folder, her pulse beat loud in her ears.

Grayson family, January 2012: refused to sell. Difficult case. Must keep oldest son out of affairs.

She flipped through the other papers in the Grayson file. There was a dummy ad in the *Los Angeles Times* that looked more photoshopped than real. Had Begley lied about trying to find Steven? She wouldn't be surprised.

What else was in the file? She flipped through, searching for any other clues.

What the hell? A cremation permission form signed by James? He hadn't mentioned anything about allowing cremation. Knowing Virginia with her three-generations-spent-in-Savannah stance, she already had the perfect family plot picked out and ready. Doing so would assure her remains stayed south of the Mason-Dixon Line.

Oh shit. Brianna looked closer, analyzing the scribbled signature. She recognized the handwriting—and it wasn't James's. It was Edwin's.

So that's how Begley and Edwin work together? Anybody Begley wants to kill gets burned in a house fire, and Edwin authorizes the cremation slips after the fact? Holy shit. This mess went deeper than she thought.

She just hadn't wanted to believe it.

Sirens blared outside. Shit. She'd been so careful. Torn between the desire to get the hell out of there or pee in her fashionable pants, she froze. No doors busted open. No voices demanded she leave, that they had the place surrounded. Had she watched too much TV?

A few seconds passed. She couldn't stay still forever. Tiptoeing, she went to the window and peeked through the blinds. Two fire trucks sped by, the sirens drowning out all other sounds.

"Thank God." She exhaled the breath she'd been holding. Time to write down a few notes and run like hell.

There was another signature in the files, a Lt. Grainger. One of Begley's crooked cops, perhaps? She grabbed a purple Post-it on Begley's desk and jotted down the information.

Before leaving, she glanced through Begley's rolodex. There were numbers for developers, land surveyors, and funeral homes. What would the three have in common?

A strong wind blew outside, rustling through the oaks and carrying violin notes. Uh oh. Strange things happened when violins played in the wind. Last time, she'd met Anzhela. She wasn't about to stick around to see what other oddities would happen.

Gathering her notes, she replaced the files and slipped out the back door. Begley would never know she'd snooped around. Perfect. Time to go home and continue to keep her promise. Things were going to work out after all. Nothing could stop her.

CHAPTER TWENTY-TWO

A crust eaten in peace is better than a banquet partaken in anxiety.
~ Aesop

The cell phone's shrill ring woke Brianna out of a sound sleep. She'd wanted to sleep late Friday morning, especially after traipsing across town last night to get info from Begley's office. No such luck.

"Hello?"

"It's Edwin."

She bolted upright in bed. "Hi."

"Enjoying your vacation?"

Considering you forced it on me, I suppose I am.

Why had he called her? One thing she had learned about the South—no one ever got to the point without going through the greeting, the small talk, the warming-up part.

"I miss work," she said.

There was a long pause before he spoke. "How'd you like to work the phones this morning?"

Reception work wasn't her favorite, but it would get her back into the office. She'd wanted an excuse to check on Bobby Ray's body, and manning the phones would explain her presence in Restful Oaks.

"I'd be happy to, but I thought you said—"

“We are busy with the cremations, but Margie has the big shindig, so she’s unavailable. I can’t manage the phones and run the place, and I hate for callers to get voicemail as their first contact when a loved one dies.”

Brianna couldn’t help but smile. Somewhere, deep down, Edwin had the same respect for the dead that she did. So why was he in cahoots with someone like Begley?

“Give me forty-five minutes,” she said. “I’ll be there.”

“Excellent, thanks.”

She hung up with a newfound sense of excitement. Now she could research cremations, check on Bobby Ray, and get some paid work done.

Plato puttered into the room as she threw the quilt off her legs. “Things are looking up, boy. It’s like all the stars are aligning in my favor.”

###

Brianna carefully set Margie’s coffee mug aside and settled into the front-desk area. “Where’d Margie go, again? Some fancy party?”

Edwin clutched a folder to his chest. “She’s organizing a big blowout for all the Red Hat ladies.”

Margie would make the perfect Red Hat lady. The women all wore purple dresses and big red hats and regularly descended upon tearooms, dinner theatres, and lunch bistros.

Edwin glanced over the front desk. "Do you have everything you need? I have a meeting in a few minutes with the bank."

He was leaving? This could be her chance to check the basement for Bobby Ray.

"I'm good. You have your cell if anything major comes up?"

He nodded. "I should be back within an hour though."

"Sounds good." Brianna grabbed a pen and paper, looking the part of a good employee. In reality, she couldn't wait for him to leave so she could check on Bobby Ray.

Minutes later, Edwin left. Finally, this was her chance.

When she stood, the phone rang. It was as if the outside world knew he'd walked out the door. She spent ten minutes answering phones, taking messages, and forwarding callers to Edwin's voicemail.

In between calls, she leafed through the top file cabinet. A huge stack of cremation slips nearly burst out of a manila folder. Even in a funeral home, why the need for so many forms? Their bread and butter consisted of the expensive caskets, the flowers, all the extra services Restful Oaks provided. Cremations were economical. Why would he lose money in order to meet Begley's demands?

The phone stopped its incessant ringing. Great, now to check on Bobby Ray's body. She forwarded the lines to voicemail, locked the front door, and jogged to the service elevator. When it chimed and opened on the basement level, she closed her eyes for a moment. “Please, still be there.”

Twisting and turning through the hallways, she reached the cold chamber. This was it. She leaned down and opened Bobby Ray’s chamber—and gasped.

Empty?

Crap. How had the body been found? The alternate chamber was used only for overflow. Sharp pain lodged in her stomach, like she’d been sucker-punched.

Damn you, Edwin. You deserve to rot in hell for what you’ve done.

She opened every enclosure. Maybe Bobby Ray had been moved to another rack? A miniscule chance, but possible. She couldn’t give up.

Every slot was vacant. Edwin had cremated Bobby Ray before she could save him. She slammed each chamber into place. “Shit!”

What now? Wasn’t the whole point in this to help the dead? Keep the oath that Edwin had long since betrayed? Obviously Edwin or Margie had found Bobby Ray’s body and proceeded with the cremation.

What should her next step be?

Damn, the phones. She couldn’t leave them forwarded to voicemail for long. Particularly because Edwin was the type who’d call to make sure the phones were being manned properly.

In a wandering daze, she returned to the main floor and heard loud banging on glass.

When she approached the reception area, her heart plummeted into her stomach. On the other side of the glass doorway stood Begley—and he was pissed.

Focus. Don't let him get the upper hand.

She opened the latch. Begley pushed hard to get inside, knocking her a few steps backward.

"Since when does Restful Oaks close in the middle of the day?"

"I…I had to attend to something in the back. Edwin always keeps the front area secure when no one is at reception."

She stumbled to the reception desk and sat in the office chair.

He cocked an eyebrow, studying her for a minute. "Where is Edwin?"

The awkward lump in her throat grew exponentially. "At the bank for a meeting. He'll be back within the hour."

Shit. All alone with Begley. She clasped her hands together under the desk so he wouldn't notice her anxiety.

"Can I have him call you?" she asked, attempting a leisurely Southern accent.

He picked up a brochure on the desk, unfolded it, and stood for several long seconds—like he owned the place and the people inside it.

According to Edwin, Begley *did* own everything. Judging by Bobby Ray's empty chamber, Begley controlled all Restful Oaks employees.

But not her. Never.

"I guess you're playing Margie today?" he said.

"Yes."

She organized a few pencils, straightened her notepad, anything to keep busy while he made polite chitchat. No way had he stopped by on a whim. The shiftiness in his glance gave him away.

"Admin duties must be quite a change from prepping bodies," he said, his fake smile inviting further conversation.

Talking to him was the last thing she wanted to do. She certainly didn't want to extend the conversation.

"Yes, but I like variety." She glanced at the phone and moved her stapler. "Listen, we're expecting the phones to be busy in the next few minutes, so if I can help you with something—"

"You can tell me why you broke into my office last night."

Crap. He knows. How? Think. Come up with something to say. Couldn't they go back to the chitchat part?

One look at his menacing glare answered her question. He was the hunter; she was the deer in his crosshairs.

"I wanted some additional information on my house," she said.

"What are you talking about?"

Apparently her answer threw him for a loop, which had been the intention. Now she had to think of something else to say. Lord knows she couldn't tell him the truth, or say anything that would implicate Steven.

Think—Realtors, homes, moving down South, ghosts… That's it! She had her excuse. She'd read an article in the paper just last week.

"Savannah's law," she said, finally able to breathe.

Begley arched one eyebrow. "What law?"

He seemed interested rather than angry. Good.

"The one about haunted houses," she said, as calm and authoritative as she could. Beneath the desk, her knees wobbled. But Begley didn't know that.

"Meaning?" Begley asked.

"Residents can sue the landlord if he rents out a property known to be haunted. The law is specific to Savannah, since there are so many haunted claims. I learned that not only can people get their rent money back but can also sue for damages."

His mouth twitched downward into a frown. "You're saying your house is haunted?"

"I've noticed strange things for a while now. You told me it was mice."

He closed his eyes for a second, seeming deep in thought. "Why not contact me? Why break into my office?"

Good question. Think of a good answer. To stall, she paper clipped a few blank sheets together. He wouldn't be the wiser.

"I'm in a rent-to-own situation," she said. "True, I could've asked you about any suspicious hauntings. But how would I know you were telling the truth? I apologize for my method. However, as a businessman, I'm sure you understand the need to guard my financial assets."

He gawked at her for five long seconds. Was he buying anything she said?

"What proof do you have the place is haunted?" he asked.

Brianna leaned back in her chair. "Things go missing, kitchen utensils clatter on the floor without reason. Stuff like that."

Begley's lips tightened into a cunning smile. "I know you're new in town. And I appreciate your concern about the property. Really."

Hmm. He's going with the charming and patronizing approach. Typical.

"But remember," Begley began. "You work with dead bodies all day. If it were me, my mind would be playing tricks too."

She glanced at her watch. Edwin would be back eventually. No sense arguing with Begley now.

"You're probably right," she said. "Sorry for breaking in, but look at the bright side. Now you know you should get the back door fixed." She held her stance, hoping he didn't notice that her legs were trembling below the desk. Legally, he could press charges for trespassing. But she *could* create a stink for him with Savannah's law about haunted properties. She guessed—more like hoped—that profit outranked pride in Begley's world.

Sixty long seconds ticked by. Begley leaned his arms across the desk, almost like staking out his territory.

"Thanks for the tip, girlie."

Girlie? She swallowed hard and hoped he didn't hear it.

"Now let me offer you a little tip," he said. "You best stay out of my affairs. If I catch you snooping in my business or anywhere near my office again, I'll make sure you regret it."

Panic twisted in the pit of her stomach. "I didn't mean to offend you. But my house…"

He leaned in further, invading what remained of her personal space. She rolled the chair back a few inches.

"I'm a self-reliant man," he said. "Do you know what that means?"

She narrowed her eyes. Where was he going with this? "Um—"

"I could have you arrested right now for breaking and entering. But being self-reliant means when I have an issue, I don't like going to the cops. I prefer to handle things on my own. I've done it before. Don't think I won't do it again. Especially if you dare cross me or come anywhere close to my office again."

A knot formed in the back of her throat, but she refused to flinch. Damn, Begley was smooth. While evil fury danced in his eyes, he'd done the two-step shuffle with his words. No direct confession for killing those who stood in his way. No clear threat to her life. Just stating with authoritative clarity that she'd better not interfere again. Considering she'd committed a crime, it was a perfectly legal request to make.

She wiped her sweaty palms on her pants, where Begley couldn't see. "What do you mean, exactly?"

He leaned in closer. "You're a smart Yankee. Figure it out."

You son of a bitch. "I think—"

"Begley?" Edwin said, standing in the open doorway.

Brianna bit the inside of her lip but refused to break eye contact.

"Hello, Edwin," Begley said, his Southern-sweet tone back in play. He wouldn't let on that he'd just shown his evil side. "I was just chatting with Brianna."

"How can I help you?" Edwin hung up his jacket and shook Begley's hand.

"Just dropped by to discuss a few formalities. I can come back if this is a bad time—"

"Nonsense, come on back." Edwin walked toward his office.

"Great, one sec," Begley said.

He flashed Brianna a wicked grin. “Good to chat with you, Brianna.” Then, tapping his gold ring twice on the desk—inches from her face—he said in that sweet tone, “You have yourself a good day now.”

CHAPTER TWENTY-THREE

Wisdom begins in wonder.
~ Socrates

Once Begley and Edwin were behind closed doors, Brianna set the phones to voicemail and raced to the bathroom. And promptly threw up.

Damn her nerves. At least she hadn't given Begley the satisfaction of seeing her panic. What the hell had he meant by he'd handled things—handled people—before? And he had no problem doing it again?

It meant he will kill you if you get in his way.

Crap. She couldn't go to the cops without incriminating herself. Standing her ground had been the right choice, but she needed to be more careful going forward. Begley's dangerous streak could explode at any moment, and she had no intention of letting him harm her.

What the hell was up with that whole wishing her a nice day thing? Menacing intent laced inside politeness. Was this the Southern way? It was Begley's way, at least.

She splashed cold water on her face and grabbed a breath mint from her pocket.

Yet Steven was different, and he'd been born and bred here. The Graysons, except for Virginia's awful singing, were good people. So was Begley just an imposter, only pretending to do good by Savannah?

She didn't know. But she intended to stop him.

Time to return to reception before Edwin thought she was goofing off. Begley had won this round, cremating Bobby Ray before she could stop him. She would win the war.

###

After work, Brianna went home and let Plato outside. She called Steven while her dog sniffed the beautyberry shrubs in the back yard.

"Hello?"

"It's Brianna."

"Hi," he said with no trace of his usual warmth. Instead, there was a distinct lack of emotion.

"Are you mad at me?"

She wouldn't blame him, after she'd given him the brush-off at Churchill's the other night.

Long pause. "I'm just a little confused."

"I know," she said. "I don't blame you. Can you meet me somewhere to talk?"

"Where?"

"I'm not taking you away from any gigs?"

"Not exactly. I have a few things to tell you about that disaster."

Hmm, wonder what happened? But after the crappy day she'd had, she'd welcome the chance to hear his story. Misery did love company, right?

"I'd love to see you," she said. "But I need a break from Savannah."

"Where do you want to go?"

She kicked around a couple of ideas. Tybee was too close, and she had no desire to run into Begley. Knowing her luck, she would.

"What happens if we go across the Talmadge Bridge? Where will it take us?"

"South Carolina. Hilton Head, to be precise, about forty-five minutes from here. Want to go? They have great beachfront restaurants and pubs."

"Perfect."

"Then I'll pick you up in thirty minutes. And Brianna?"

"Yes?" *Ask me anything. I will say yes.*

"I look forward to talking with you."

Warmth fluttered around her heart and into her abdomen. He had a way of making her feel like she was the most important jewel in the world.

Just don't break my heart, she prayed.

###

He drove his red classic Mustang across the Talmadge Bridge at sunset. "Take a look back," he said. "And enjoy the most fantastic view of Savannah."

She turned around in the passenger seat. Wow. He wasn't kidding. Feathery pink clouds hovered over the historic district skyline with its jagged steeples, gold-plated government buildings, and the River Street bars. The crimson sun cast a deep glow on the pubs and waterfront buildings, and their wiggly reflections in the Savannah River looked like an exquisite Impressionist painting.

"Beautiful," she whispered.

He reached for her hand and squeezed. "So are you."

Giddiness bubbled inside her. No man had ever been so in tune with her before, knowing what she wanted to hear—words that tickled her spirit.

"You're quite the charmer, Steven. Anyone ever tell you that?"

"Occasionally," he said, giving her a coy smile. "But they don't go all mysterious on me."

"I am sorry—"

"Want to tell me what all that was about?"

She flexed her hands and rested them on her lap. "I did something I'm not proud of. I wasn't sure I could trust you with the information."

"Why not?" he asked. "I am trustworthy, you know." His gaze flickered briefly on her before turning back to the highway. Those green eyes, so open and trusting, made it difficult for her to answer.

“You don’t know this about me,” she said, “but I’ve never had luck with men.”

His fingers tightened around the wheel, even though they were on a deserted highway flanked with pampas grass. “Hard to believe.”

“It’s true.” For reasons she couldn’t tell him yet. Like hearing and seeing ghosts.

“Even so, I hoped you could trust me. What were you holding back the other night?”

She sighed. Be honest. Just don’t mention the ghosts.

“I broke into Begley’s office to look at his files.”

Steven cocked his head around. “You did what?”

“I told you, I’m not proud—”

“You broke into his office? Do you know what could’ve happened if he’d caught you?”

She clenched and unclenched her fists. Where were those stress balls when she needed one?

“Actually, he found out.”

Wide-eyed, he gawked at her for a short moment. “What happened?”

For the remaining thirty minutes of the drive, she told him about the files she’d found, her *Cat in the Hat* pants, Bobby Ray being cremated, and about the threats Begley made with the guise of Southern charm.

Silence rang loud between them when they passed the Welcome to Hilton Head Island sign. He appeared to mull the facts as he drove.

"Please say something," she whispered, ending the agonizing quiet.

"We need to talk."

Nothing good ever came of such words. She held her breath and braced herself.

"Are you starving, or can you wait an hour or so until dinner?"

Huh? She'd expected the dreaded "You aren't who I thought you were, so let's part ways" sentence. Instead, he was mentioning food?

"I'm fine. Why?"

He looped the car through the roundabout and took a right. "Let's get some privacy by the beach first. The place I had in mind for dinner has music and a lively atmosphere."

"Sure," she said. Not the typical guy, not even close.

Minutes later, he parked along a stretch of Atlantic Ocean shoreline. He opened her car door and extended his hand. She took it, and he pulled her into his arms. Behind them, the white surf crashed against the sand, trickling in seashells and other jewels from the high tide.

"I like this position," he said, keeping his arms around her as his lips spread into a smile. "We should do this more often. Maybe it'll keep you from backing away so much."

The salt air chilled her arms, but Steven's touch made her flush with heat. "I…"

"What, cat got your tongue?" he asked.

Nope, you do. My tongue and everything else.

His eyes gleamed as though he'd read her mind. She held her hands to her cheeks to offset the warmth.

"I think you might, kind sir," she said with the best Southern accent she could muster.

He laughed out loud—beautiful, gut-belly sounds of amusement. "We need to work on your accent."

"Shh," she said, smiling wide.

He cupped her face in his hands. "You just shushed me."

She trembled at his touch. "Well, one of us was bound to go there, sooner or later."

"I want you to trust me, Brianna. Trust me enough to tell me anything."

"You don't think I did a rash and foolish thing? Most people would." With trembling fingers, she reached up and enclosed her hands around his, bringing them down to her waist. Better.

He eyed her for a long moment, the ocean reflected in his gaze. "Let's just say, you're my kind of criminal. I only wish you'd told me, taken me with you."

"I won't keep you in the dark anymore," she said, meaning every word with each fiber of her being. Someday—not now, but eventually—she would tell him about his family, about her *gift*. But in the meantime, she wouldn't keep her plans to thwart Begley a secret.

"That a promise?" Steven asked.

She coughed. A promise? She couldn't afford to break any more promises, nor did she want to where Steven was concerned.

"I promise to tell you everything about Begley and any efforts to stop him."

Steven tilted his head, analyzing her last sentence. "What about never holding back, anything, again?"

She couldn't go there. She couldn't make another oath she intended to break.

Stroking his cheek, she said, "I'm enjoying getting to know you. Please be patient, as there are things about me I don't know you'll like. So yes, some parts of me may remain hidden, temporarily. But I'll do my best to open up. Good enough?"

"For now," he said. "C'mon, let's walk along the beach. Forget Begley and corruption for a few minutes."

She breathed a sigh of relief. One day, she'd open up completely. Tell him everything without hesitation. For now, she'd made a promise she knew she could keep.

They meandered along the shore. Seagulls tracked across the sand, leaving tiny footprints as they chased after crabs and other moving creatures. The ocean lapped onto the sand with rhythmic patterns. Steven clasped her hand in his. For the first time, the silence between them wasn't threatening, but pleasurable.

She didn't know how much time had passed. The next thing she knew, the moon began to rise. "Time seems to vanish in a place like this."

He nodded and pulled her to him, wrapping his strong arms around her waist. She put her hands around his neck and met his kiss.

"Sit with me for a minute," he said.

She sat next to him on the sand, and he put his arm around her. How did such simple gestures make her entire body tingle?

The moonlight reflected across the tips of the waves, creating sparkles of white across the dark water. She leaned in to meet his lips once more. His tongue gave tiny flicks, exploring at first, then slightly more intense before a deluge of passion.

She ran her fingers through his hair. The length was perfect. She loved being able to grip the ends tight. He groaned and lifted a hand to stroke her breast. The ocean sounds, salt air, and cawing of gulls only made the heat flare with more intensity. A surge that coiled into all her nerve endings, places she'd long ignored.

She traced her fingers across his chest. She wanted more, but it had been so long since she'd been intimate…and how could she make love when she'd kept her gift a secret?

"I don't want to push you," he said, arranging a few inches of distance between them before planting tiny kisses along her neck. "You're not ready to be open yet, but when you are—"

"Shh."

He smiled at their secret joke. "When you're ready to trust me, I'm here for you. I'm willing to wait."

"Okay," she said with a mix of relief and sadness. Part of her wanted him to hold her, caress her, and make love in the sand dunes. The surroundings were too perfect.

But wasn't it wrong to become so intimate with someone while holding back something so big? She hadn't just talked with everyday kind of ghosts—she'd talked with his family, who lived in her house.

Take things slow. Get to know him better. Soon, she'd be ready to take things further with the handsome Steven.

As if sensing her need, he pulled back. "We should go to dinner."

"Um, hmm," she said, wanting to enjoy the salt-air breeze for a few more seconds before leaving.

"C'mon. We have lots to talk about."

CHAPTER TWENTY-FOUR

We know what we are, but know not what we may be.
~ William Shakespeare

Steven pushed away his frustration while he drove them to Bijou's for dinner. Think of things nonsexual. Folding laundry. Taking out the garbage. Muppets.

Muppets? Where had that random thought come from?

He'd wanted to take her on the sand, but she needed more time. Truthfully, he did too. He wanted Brianna to trust him, to know he wasn't going anywhere. Even though his track record wasn't the greatest. For her, he would stick around.

He could see things working between them. Besides, he didn't need another woman who kept secrets. When Brianna could open up to him, be completely honest, the time would be right. And what a night that will be…

Stop. Keep focused. Tell her about Hilton Head. Talk.

With a determined breath, he eased the car around the two large roundabouts. Clumps of trees were planted in the center, making it look like he was circling Gilligan's Island instead of an intersection.

"You'll notice Hilton Head doesn't have many four-way stops," he said.

Brianna looked out the window. “Why not?”

“No idea. They love roundabouts. Seems like a traffic nightmare waiting to happen, if you ask me.”

She smiled at him, those freshly kissed lips turning upward. “One of those classic Southern things, like cow tipping or grits?”

He laughed. “Wow, you’re up on your culture. Ever been cow tipping?”

“You’re kidding, right? I don’t even understand the point. Tipping over a cow in the middle of the night for fun?”

Shrugging, he drove the car into Bijou’s lot and parked. “It’s a college thing.”

“Must be,” she smirked. “Did you ever do it?”

“Nope, but Dennis has. I finished high school and got the hell out of Savannah.” He strode around the Mustang, opened her door, and pulled her to him. “I do like grits though.”

She gave him a quick kiss on the lips. “C’mon, I’m hungry.”

So was he, but not for food.

The hostess led them out to a corner table overlooking a pond with big green lily pads. “Your server’s name is John and he’ll be right with you.”

“Thanks,” Steven said as he pulled out Brianna’s chair.

Her eyes gleamed at the gesture. The woman was so easy to please. Had no one shown her gentlemanly manners before? No matter what culture she lived in?

Once seated, they reviewed the menus. “Anything Lowcountry is going to be amazing,” he said. “You’re in the heart of Lowcountry right now.”

Their server approached, took their drink orders, and left them to their privacy.

“Tell me what happened with your gig,” she said. “I’d hoped to be able to hear you play sometime.”

Bam. Back to reality in one fell swoop.

“I suppose at some point, we can’t avoid discussing Begley, can we?”

Her eyes narrowed. “What do you mean? What does he have to do with your music?”

“Dennis and I talked to a few riverfront places to see if we could get on their calendar. Weekends are booked with scheduled entertainment, but we figured weeknights would be a good opportunity.”

“Right,” she said.

John, their server, returned with their beers, some bread, and olive oil. “Have we decided, or do you need a few more minutes?”

They may as well go ahead and order. Steven wanted some uninterrupted conversation with her. Brianna took his advice and ordered the Lowcountry shrimp and grits, and he ordered the fresh catch of fish.

"Good, now we have some time alone."

"So you were trying to get a weeknight gig," she prompted.

"Yes. The Brick Tavern was our top choice. They were ready to sign us, give us three nights a week doing ballads and folk."

"That's great," she said, her blue eyes beaming. "So what's wrong?"

He loved her enthusiasm. It offset his occasional cynicism.

"The manager got our names and made a phone call to the owner, kind of a silent partner of the place. We figured it was routine. We were all ready to sign." He took a swig of beer. "Guess who owns the Brick Tavern?"

Her jaw fell open as the news registered. "No. Begley owns the place?"

"Yep, Mr. Lying Bastard himself. When he learned it was me wanting to play in his club, he shut us down. So Dennis and I are back to square one."

"You'll find something else," she said. "I know it. I have faith in you, Steven."

How did she affect him so much? Those little things, her confidence, her faith, her optimism. All he needed was her trust. If he had that, he could see himself sticking around Savannah and seeing how things turned out.

"Steven?" she asked, jolting him out of his thoughts.

"Sorry, I spaced out," he said. "But I'm touched by your confidence. We'll get a gig somewhere. Just takes time. At least Dennis is letting me crash at his place."

Her face turned solemn. "It's good to have friends."

"Do you miss Boston?"

"I miss my brother, but I like seeing the things he would've liked here in Savannah. Thanks for all the tour-guide excursions."

"My pleasure," he said.

Their food arrived, and they took a few minutes to settle in and dish up condiments.

She took a bite of her grilled shrimp and closed her eyes. He knew that look. Ecstasy. Lowcountry food had that effect.

Somewhere between the tilapia and the grilled asparagus, he spoke up. "I know you need a break from talking about Begley, but the man did threaten you. I think we should stick together over the next few days. Let me protect you."

You fool. You couldn't protect Amy. Or Kate, the only other woman you came close to loving. Both died. If you get Brianna killed, you'll be a three-time loser.

He clenched his jaw and waited for her answer. Would she think he was rushing her? He didn't want to invite himself to stay in her house—his family's house—but who knew what kind of stunts Begley would pull?

"During the days," she said, "I'm at work. But between work and nighttime, if you want to hang out, that's fine."

"I do. Until Begley is locked up, neither one of us is safe."

CHAPTER TWENTY-FIVE

The Irish...
Be they kings, or poets, or farmers,
They're a people of great worth,
They keep company with the angels,
And bring a bit of heaven here to earth.
~ Irish Saying

Brianna woke up early on Monday morning, eager to return to work. She could research more about the cremations, find out exactly what went wrong with Bobby Ray—why would anyone need to get rid of an Elvis impersonator?—and gather what evidence she could, all while taking care of the dead.

Without the funeral home's day-to-day tasks, she hadn't known what to do with herself. Spending time with Steven had been incredible and she certainly couldn't complain. Salt air still lingered in her nostrils when she remembered their intimacy on the beach. Soon, they could become more intimate. When she could be honest with him, she'd tell him things she hadn't told anyone since the psych ward.

An hour later, she entered Restful Oaks and saw an empty front desk. Edwin approached her, a large folder under his arm. More cremation slips? Or was she paranoid?

"Where's Margie?" she asked.

Edwin rolled his eyes. "She has some ladies' league meeting this morning. Of course, she didn't mention it until dinner last night. I'm sorry,

Brianna, but I have a chamber of commerce meeting this morning. I need you to watch the phones. Just for the morning, then prep the bodies. We have two women in the cold chambers."

"No problem. Are we expecting any body deliveries today?"

Edwin adjusted his spectacles. "No, so the morning should be easy. I appreciate your help."

"I don't mind," she said. The statement was true. This would give her a chance to snoop some more.

"I'll be back after lunch." Edwin grabbed his jacket and walked out the front door.

After pouring a cup of coffee, Brianna settled into Margie's chair once more. She flipped through papers in the in-box to make sure nothing needed immediate attention.

Wait—what was this? A cremation form in the in-box? She searched for the name. Riordan O'Shea. About as Irish as one could get. Why hadn't Edwin mentioned him? Edwin specifically said the two bodies ready to prep were female. So who was Riordan? Another victim of Begley's?

She opened the Internet and ran a Google search on Riordan O'Shea. A giant lump formed in the back of her throat. She coughed and continued to read the article. It was a death announcement, stating Riordan O'Shea had been killed in a hit-and-run accident on Bull Street yesterday. Foul play suspected but no one had been caught.

How could Edwin have the cremation form this soon, if Riordan died yesterday? The cops should be doing an investigation.

She set the phones to voicemail and sprinted to the main cold chambers. Nope, no male bodies. Only two women, like Edwin had said.

When she returned to reception, she double-checked the authorized signature. Yep. Edwin's handwriting. To an outside eye, it looked like a standard signature, but she'd seen enough forms to know the way Edwin looped his *e's* and *p's*.

So not only had Edwin and Begley cremated Bobby Ray for whatever reason, they planned to cremate this Riordan O'Shea.

Just one question. Where the hell was Riordan's body?

###

Two hours and another cup of coffee later, a black van pulled up to the receiving door. Brianna narrowed her eyes. A delivery? Edwin had said they wouldn't be receiving any bodies this morning.

Behind her, a man dressed in gray wheeled in the body bag, stepped into reception, and plopped the file on the desk. He handed her the acceptance sheet. "Sign here."

"We weren't expecting any bodies today." This guy in gray was new. Usually, Keith brought the bodies. Maybe he'd called in sick?

"I don't know, lady. Just heard I was to bring the body here. That's what Edwin said."

Edwin? Could this be Riordan's body?

"What's the name?" she asked, signing the acceptance form and opening the file.

He already had his hand on the door, ready to leave. "I don't know. Some Irish name I can't pronounce. Killed yesterday in a car accident."

"Wait—"

"What? I need to get going. Three other funeral homes are waiting for deliveries."

Ignoring his impatience, she checked the file. "Shouldn't the body have gone to autopsy first? That's a given in hit-and-runs, any kind of open investigation."

"I'm new, lady. I have no idea. Edwin told me to bring this body here. He was pretty stubborn about it too. Made me miss lunch with my grandma to get it here by noon. Maybe they don't do autopsies right away?"

"But it's standard practice to—"

"I don't question Edwin. Not only could I lose my job, but I'd wind up in a body bag. I deliver the body. That's it." He tipped his hat and exited the door.

At least now she knew where Riordan's body was. Had Edwin been mistaken about body deliveries today? Or had he flat-out lied?

Resilience churned inside her. Another chance. She'd been unable to protect Bobby Ray, but she could prevent Riordan from cremation—at least long enough so an autopsy could be performed.

Only one problem. She had to hide Riordan before Edwin returned. Knowing her prying boss, Edwin would hover near the main chambers all afternoon to make sure the two women were prepped for the wake. She couldn't keep his body in the main area.

Her stomach clenched. She had to save the guy—Begley likely had been the instigator of the auto accident. She hated the idea of hiding Riordan in the basement, but she didn't have a choice. Maybe if she returned tonight, she could save Riordan, and Edwin wouldn't be the wiser.

Convinced her plan would work, she wheeled Riordan to the basement chamber. Once at the desk again, she grabbed the forged cremation slip and stuck it in her purse. To make its disappearance seem more like an accident, she spread out papers and forms on Margie's desk. This way, it would appear lost.

She could make a difference. No longer was the promise to Declan a burden, but a challenge. She wanted to do it. Besides, Steven had said he'd be willing to help. Whether he would go along with her latest plan remained to be seen.

CHAPTER TWENTY-SIX

Hell, there are no rules here—
we're trying to accomplish something.
~ Thomas A. Edison

Declan fixed his eyes on the funeral home's front door, waiting for Brianna to arrive.

"When she walks out," he reminded Ian, "make sure she sees you. Then give her the news, understand?"

"Yeah, and I'm supposed to tell her to be careful around Begley?"

"Right, and that I'm watching out for her. I never had the chance to tell her good-bye."

Ian fiddled with the silver stud on his tongue. Gross. "So, your mentor was cool with this?"

"Sure," Declan said. A little white lie never hurt anyone, did it?

"Bullshit," Ian said.

"Don't cuss in the afterlife. It's frowned upon."

"Whatever. I have no problem breaking the rules, but at least tell me if we're about to piss someone off," Ian said.

Ian was smart, Declan would give him that.

"Fine, we're about to piss off my boss something fierce, but I don't care. Brianna's my little sister. I promised to protect her. It's worth the risk."

"I told you I liked her. Your plan works for me," Ian said.

A second later, Brianna walked out the front door. "Now," Declan said. "Make contact."

Ian approached her. "Brianna?"

She kept walking.

"Hello?" Ian said, and he zigzagged in front of her.

She walked through him, unable to see or hear anything.

An ache throbbed in Declan's gut. "Why isn't it working? You said she could see and talk to you inside the funeral home."

Ian turned back to him. "I don't know. Why don't you try?"

"Because family is off-limits. Even if I wanted to talk to her, yell at her, hurl something at her to get her attention, I can't." Declan watched her walk, oblivious to their presence. "But I figured you could."

Ian's semitransparent form began to fade. Staring at his hands, he asked, "What's happening?"

Declan lifted his arm, only to see it fading too. "Aw, c'mon. Not now."

"What?" Ian asked.

"We're being summoned."

###

Declan opened his eyes. Damn it. The woodsy atmosphere, arrays of flora and fauna, and the ornate Wormsloe Fountain with its trickling water gave away their location. Both he and Ian had been sent to Columbia Square, where they'd be forced to explain their actions.

Connell, boss man and mentor, tapped his fingers on the top of the fountain—and did not appear happy.

"Connell," Declan said, giving a feeble smile from behind the bricks surrounding the fountain. He thought it a good idea to keep some distance between him and his accuser.

Fury radiated from his mentor's controlling stare. "What do you think you're doing? I told you to stay away from Brianna."

"Technically, I did. I didn't say anything to her."

Connell cocked an eyebrow and waited.

"Okay, I admit, that was a childish response—"

"You think?"

Declan shuffled his weight from foot to foot. "I had to, Connell. I know my sister. She has a good heart, but she always loses her faith in people, in herself sometimes. I only wanted to encourage her, give her something to hold onto so she doesn't give up."

Connell narrowed his eyes, studying Declan for a series of long seconds. Seconds stretched longer in Connell's presence. They always had.

"The truth becomes you more than infantile excuses."

"Thank you, sir," Declan said.

Proper respect in the military often helped him in sticky situations. Perhaps it would help him now.

"However, this time you've corrupted a new soul. You've engaged this boy to do your bidding without warning him of the consequences—"

"Boy?" Ian said, frowning.

Declan shot Ian a glare. *Don't ever interrupt the boss.*

Connell walked closer and studied Ian's face, lingering at his Mohawk. "Boy, young man, punk rocker, whatever term you like. Labels don't mean much in the afterlife."

"I prefer man or artist," Ian said, grinning.

Kiss-ass. The kid looked like he'd just convinced the government to release who really shot JFK, when all he'd done was irritated Connell more. Newbies.

"Fine, artist it is," Connell said. "Did Declan tell you about the rules, about the penalty for breaking them?"

"I broke the rules when I was alive," Ian said. "It was the only way I could survive."

Connell stroked his chin and creases formed across his brow. Uh oh.

"Sir," Declan said. "Don't hold Ian responsible. I initiated this. It's my doing."

"I'm aware of that."

Please don't send me to Idaho. Please don't send me to Idaho.

Connell turned to Ian. "You will spend the next two months helping the newbies, particularly the punk crowd. Perhaps your…ability to relate to them will help. Any privileges you gain will be delayed by two months, and I'm going to reassign you to Jake."

Ian turned to Declan, bewildered. The kid had no idea how much horror he'd been spared. Though reporting to another hard-ass like Jake would be no picnic.

"It's a good deal," Declan said. *Say thanks and be quiet.*

"Thank you," Ian muttered.

Connell shifted his gaze to Declan. The intensity of anger flashing behind those eyes made one thing abundantly clear: he had no mercy left to give.

"Sir, please—"

"Quiet."

Declan bit his lip. Yes, he'd broken a rule. Never disobey your mentor. But he hadn't done it on a whim. He'd done it to help his sister. Besides, she could have conversations with ghosts. Couldn't she become part of things, a means to help everyone? Why would Connell be against such a good thing?

"Perhaps Brianna could use some encouragement," Connell said.

Holy hell, was Connell serious? Declan had broken the rules and Connell understood? Would allow him to help Brianna?

"I'm aware she has gone above and beyond for several spirits, and her intentions are pure," Connell said. "In return for her service, I shall appoint someone who can offer her encouraging messages, perhaps—if you behave—send her information from you."

From him? Connell was going to pick someone else? Not him?

"I don't understand, sir," Declan said. "Could I not be the one who talks to her?"

Connell laughed, and the trees rustled overhead. "You expect to be rewarded for breaking the rules? You know me better than that, Declan."

He clenched his fists and glared at the mentor he was forced to respect. "She's my sister."

"And I'm your boss," Connell said, unyielding tenacity in his clipped tone.

Declan took a deep breath. "Please. Delay my privileges, put me on whatever duty you want, but I should be the one who gets to talk to her."

"No."

Disappointment churned through him. He should've known Connell would enforce the rules.

"You mentioned I might be able to send a personal message to her?" he asked. May as well cling to whatever good thing he could.

"Yes," Connell said. "Provided you don't break any more rules."

Now Ian stared at Declan with the same look Declan had given him moments ago. *Say thank you and be quiet.*

"Thanks," Declan said, his tongue forcing out the word.

"That is all," Connell said. "You're dismissed."

They stepped away and began to walk across the square.

"Oh, Declan?" Connell said.

He turned around. "Yes?"

"Pull any more stunts, and I'll send you to places worse than Idaho."

CHAPTER TWENTY-SEVEN

Three can keep a secret, if two of them are dead.
~ Benjamin Franklin

"You want me to do what?"

Steven hollered through the phone, too loudly in her opinion.

"Help me steal a dead body," she whispered, holding the phone close to her ear in case Edwin walked in. "Begley's having him cremated, maybe to cover up a murder. I can't go to the cops. Someone there might be in Begley's pocket."

"If you're not taking it to the cops, what do you plan to do with it?"

"Give him a proper burial. Prepare him with the old customs my grandmother taught me."

She took a deep breath. How could she possibly explain this? "Riordan is Irish, part of my heritage. I feel like I need to do this, send him off in the right way. No one deserves to be murdered and then cremated to hide the evidence. I've arranged for Riordan to have a burial at Bonaventure at dawn tomorrow."

"Was this another house fire?" he asked.

"Hit-and-run. I know I'm asking a lot, but please? You said you wanted to be involved in my plans. I didn't tell you about snooping in

Begley's office and you got mad at me. Well, now's your chance to help me with something I intend to do."

Steven let out a long sigh. "And you make fun of the South for cow tipping."

"Please? I won't blame you if say no, but having two people will help."

"I can't believe I'm agreeing to this, but okay."

"Thanks. Just pretend we're Lily Tomlin in that movie *9 to 5,* sneaking a body out to the trunk of the car."

"She gets caught," Steven reminded her. "The cops pull her over."

"Okay, so it's not the best example." Brianna sat up straighter when she saw Edwin's car pull into the parking lot. "I need to go, but meet me at the house at six o'clock. We'll figure out details for tonight."

"You got it."

She hung up, but the smile wouldn't leave her face. Steven would help her. This time, she wouldn't fail. She might get arrested, but she wouldn't fail in her effort.

Edwin entered with a leisurely spring in his step. "Any messages?"

"No, it's been very quiet. How was your meeting?"

"Fine, but I didn't expect it to run as long. I need you to start on the two sisters' bodies. Go ahead and turn the phones to voicemail. It'll be fine for a few hours."

"No problem." She gathered her purse and phone, made sure Riordan's cremation slip was tucked away in her purse, and went to the preparation room.

Three hours later, she'd completed the makeup and hair for both Rosie and Ruthann Wilson. Brianna returned to reception and checked for Edwin. He was in his office and on another call. Good.

She unlocked her cell and dialed the nonemergency number for the police. She wouldn't give her name but would just ask some general questions.

"Downtown Precinct," the voice said.

"Yes, I had a quick question," Brianna said. "When there's been a hit-and-run accident and someone is killed, isn't an autopsy performed to collect any evidence?"

"That's standard procedure, ma'am."

"Why would a body not be autopsied? Any reason?"

"Maybe the family objected, for any kind of religious or personal reason? Sometimes the relatives don't want an autopsy performed."

Through the phone, she heard a stern voice in the background. "Who are you talking to?"

"Just a second, Lieutenant Grainger…"

Grainger? Brianna remembered his name on the cremation slips. A dirty cop?

“Ma’am, can I get your name?” the officer asked.

“I have to go,” she said, disconnecting the call. Crap. She’d used her cell to call the precinct. Maybe they wouldn’t look at the caller ID. The cop she’d talked to seemed decent, but Lt. Grainger was likely one of Begley’s goons.

Did the man own everything and everyone? She couldn’t afford to bring Riordan’s body to the cops. If she approached the wrong officer, her chance to save someone could destroy him. And her. But she wouldn’t let him be cremated. Begley ran enough of Savannah. Time to do things her way. She’d move forward with her Bonaventure burial plans.

For her next call, she used the switchboard phone. Even if someone scrutinized the phone records, this number wouldn’t appear suspicious.

###

Brianna snapped on Plato’s leash and took him into the backyard. His tail wagged nonstop, a sure sign he liked the quality togetherness. She hadn’t spent as much time with him as she’d wanted to lately, but the Graysons had spoiled him rotten with dog treats and praising voices.

He sniffed and snorted, happy as ever. “Steven’s coming by tonight,” she said. Plato barked and spun around with glee. Maybe she could take him to the park this weekend and have Steven come along too.

When she led him back inside and opened the fridge to grab a beer, Virginia gave her the evil eye. “Did you say Steven was coming by?” Of course, she kept her form close to Brianna. The better to distract her from Steven.

"Yes. We need to discuss getting Riordan's body."

"Is Riordan that good-looking guy, the one who played the mandolin?" Amy asked. She kept her distance from her mother—smart girl. But the teenage ghost was lying on the counter on her stomach, resting her head in cupped palms.

Did the Graysons know Riordan?

"I don't know. I had to hide his body quickly, and the file wasn't detailed."

Virginia drifted to the breakfast table.

"How'd he die?" James asked, leaning against the doorway.

"Hit-and-run."

James choked on his own pipe smoke.

"Are you okay?" Brianna asked.

He cleared his throat. "Riordan lived up the street in one of the bigger corner properties."

"So my suspicions are right. Begley had him killed."

James and Virginia exchanged glances.

"Well, I can't take Riordan's body to the cops. I'm going to do the next best thing—give him a proper burial."

"And you're enlisting the help of my son to steal the body from the funeral home?" Virginia asked, her nose twitching at the idea.

"Yes. I want his help, and he wanted me to be honest with him." She stood by the fridge. She really wanted to sit on a barstool and guzzle her beer, but with Amy occupying the counter…

"We should have a talk about proper decorum," Virginia said. "After all, he is my son."

Brianna couldn't forget that fact, even if she tried.

James puffed on his pipe, sending smoke tendrils through the air for several seconds. "When do you plan to tell him about us?"

"Good question."

###

Brianna straightened up the living room, set out two water glasses, and turned the thermostat down to fifty degrees. If she had to store Riordan's body in her house overnight, it needed to be cold. At least it was chilly outside. Summer in Savannah was muggy and humid and would have been a terrible time to hide a dead body.

At 6:00 p.m. precisely, Steven knocked. He was punctual, she'd give him that.

She opened the door and let him in. "Hey there."

"Hi yourself," he said.

Plato trotted over and put his front paws on Steven's knees. "Hey, boy. You miss me? Huh?"

Judging by Plato lying on his back with his tummy exposed for petting, she guessed yes. Such the ham for attention.

"Are you hanging beef in here?" Steven asked, hugging Plato's furry coat.

"I've arranged for Riordan to be buried at Bonaventure at dawn tomorrow, but I need to keep his body in my house tonight."

Steven stared at her for a second. "I never thought I'd hear a woman say that."

"Believe me, I didn't think I would either, but this is my chance—"

"I know," he said. He took her hand in his. "Your chance to make a difference, like you promised your brother."

"Don't you dare lock lips with my son in front of me," Virginia said. She stood right beside them.

On the other side, James put his hands in his pockets. "Give them some space. She has great taste, at least."

Brianna had the odd feeling she was the guest star on *Mystery Science Theater*. Lots of commentary, only with her actions center stage. And Steven couldn't see or hear a thing.

"Let's go outside," she suggested.

"Please stay," James said. "We'll behave."

“No you won’t,” Brianna whispered.

“What?” Steven backed away, and his eyes darkened to a hunter green.

Uh oh. “I’m sorry, what were you saying?”

He crossed his arms over his chest. “I said I’d be there for you, no matter what. And apparently you think I won’t.”

Damn it! She needed to get all these ghosts out of her home.

“I’m sorry. Please, come outside with me. It’ll be quieter.”

He glanced around her empty house, at Plato resting comfortably on the dog bed—not making a sound. “It’s quiet in here.”

Not really. “Please? It would mean a great deal to me.”

She glared at Virginia’s half-open mouth ready to speak. *Don’t say a word.*

For once in her ghostly existence, Virginia did as Brianna wanted. Good thing.

“Fine, let’s go outside.” Steven walked ahead, tension in his shoulders, not the easygoing demeanor he’d had only moments earlier.

She followed. How the hell was she going to explain her way out of this one?

“Listen, Steven—”

“I want to know why you have a problem with me.”

"I don't." *I have a problem with ghosts*. She led him to a bench under the arch of a live oak.

"So why do you constantly back away, not wanting to trust or believe me?"

"It's not you," she said. "Honest." She reached for his hand but pulled back.

He shook his head. "When you think about it, I have pretty damn good reason not to trust you."

"What are you talking about?"

"I return home, and you're living in my parents' house. The difference is, I'm willing to give you a chance. I like you, Brianna. But why the disbelief when I open up and tell you?"

She bit her lip. This was hurting him. She never meant to hurt him. He'd been the first person she felt comfortable around in years.

"I'm scared, but I believe you," she said.

Steven gave a sarcastic laugh. "Hell, I'm even ready to steal a body. I could be out with Dennis right now trying to salvage my music career, but I'm here with you. Doesn't that prove anything?"

"Yes." She reached out and put her hands around his. "It does."

His eyes flickered with suspicion. "I want you to trust me. Can you do that? Can you believe me when I say I want to help you, not only to bring justice to my family but for us to work together?"

"I believe you," she whispered. "Honest."

"Then why did you say you didn't?"

Because your bickering parents were annoying me.

Wait. Could she go there? Explain a little without telling him everything? Worth a shot, especially since she wanted him to understand. She didn't want to lose him.

"Sometimes, I hear things."

"Things?"

"Voices. You said it yourself. Working in a funeral home can be…creepy. While I like my job, I can't help but hear the dead bodies talking to me on occasion, saying things about how they want their hair styled or face done."

She studied his face. Was he angry? Did he think she was crazy?

"Go on," he said. The darkness in his eyes dissipated, and some of the seafoam green returned.

"Sometimes, there's so much in my head that I can't focus on conversations well. What do they call it in children? ADD?"

"You mean, you hear voices? Voices in your head? And that's why you sometimes can't hear what I am saying?"

"In a way. Look, can we change the subject? Usually when I mention this, friends go running in the opposite direction. Rest assured, this isn't about you. It's me."

His chin twitched, and he stared at her. The worry and concern in his expression was apparent. The man thought she was the CEO of a macadamia ranch.

"One condition," he said.

"Anything."

"I'll help you with the body, go with you to the burial tomorrow at dawn. But after that, if there's more, you tell me the truth. Whatever secrets you've been hiding."

The knot in her stomach tangled even more. The truth? Everything? She couldn't get away with her secrecy forever, but she hadn't wanted things to end this soon. Maybe if she could get Riordan buried without incident, and continue keeping her promise, she could move forward without a relationship. If Steven ended theirs.

"Agreed," she said.

The warmth in his gaze returned. "Good. Now, what's the plan for stealing a body? Is it anything like tipping a cow?"

CHAPTER TWENTY-EIGHT

There is no great genius without a mixture of madness.
~ Aristotle

Old Parisian-style streetlamps illuminated Warren Square, shifting a modern-day Savannah back two hundred years. While Boston had its share of revolutionary war history, Brianna loved the history of Savannah, too. Tales of pirates shanghaiing locals, getting them soused on River Street, and inducting innocents into their way of life. Stories of swashbuckling heroes who rescued women and escaped to the South from all over the world made her feel more welcome. So many had embraced these shores, and she was part of such a tidal force.

As with all tall tales, the adventures grew bigger, the heroes grew taller, and the drinks tasted better with each retelling. In the last two hundred years, Savannah's myths gave the city a powerful presence. The many ghosts roaming the streets—and homes—only added to it.

"How are we supposed to get inside?" Steven whispered. "You never told me that part, Lily Tomlin."

"Shh," Brianna said. "I have a key. It's my work, remember?"

Steven gawked at her. "Then why are we whispering? It's legal for you to enter your place of employment."

He had a point. "Because it sounds better," she said.

Steven's face lit up in a smile. "Well, all righty then."

She had enough difficulty concentrating as was. He'd worn black jeans, a black T-shirt, and boots. If they weren't about to steal a body, she'd be tempted to jump him right on the front lawn of the funeral home.

"Let's go." She inserted the key and turned the lock. Presto. It worked.

He followed her and shut the door behind him. "You're sure no one is around tonight?"

"Positive. Begley and Edwin are at some council meeting. Margie's doing her lady league thing."

They raced downstairs to the basement, where she stopped short.

"What is it?" Steven asked.

She swallowed the lump in her throat. "The last time I entered this room, Bobby Ray had been cremated. What if we're too late with Riordan, too?"

"Then we'll deal with it. Have a little faith."

His words clanged in her ears. "You sound like Declan. He always told me the same thing."

"You're the one who said he was wise," Steven said.

True. Why had she forgotten all those conversations on the couch after school? Declan continually telling her she had to trust people, open up. Now she was thirty and still trying to learn the things Declan tried to teach her at ten.

"Open it," Steven said. "And let's get the hell out of here."

She inhaled and held her breath a moment before exhaling all her doubt in one breath. This was it. She pulled open the chamber door.

"Thank God," she said. "He's still here."

"Where's the table you mentioned? The one with wheels?"

She pointed to the adjacent room. "Bring it in."

He did and set it up alongside the chamber drawer.

"It's going to be tight, but if we both lift him at the same time, we can move him onto the table. It's not really lifting. It's moving from one table to another, both similar heights. Like in a hospital."

"Gotcha."

"On three?" she said.

"Ready."

"One, two, three!"

They shifted Riordan from the chamber rack to the table. The wheels shifted right and spun it back a few inches. She grabbed the bottom of the bag, near Riordan's feet, and pulled him onto the table.

"Great," she said. "Now we just need to get it to the trunk and back to the house."

“The easiest part,” Steven said with a hint of amusement in his voice. Or perhaps his way of dealing with boggling situations? This definitely couldn’t classify as a third date.

“C’mon.”

She wheeled the body out the back entrance. With Steven as lookout, she popped open her trunk and they rolled the body bag in.

Steven shut the trunk for her. “You’re a talented little lawbreaker, Brianna McNeil.”

Blushing, she gave him a high five. “You’re not so bad, yourself.”

###

When they returned to the house, she stopped and idled before reaching the driveway.

“What’s wrong?” Steven asked.

She pointed. “The black car in my driveway. I don’t recognize it.”

He frowned. “Is someone inside the car, or am I seeing things?”

She peered as far as she could in the dark night. Great, now she needed glasses? No time at the moment.

“I see a shadow in the driver’s seat.” Her heart pounded in her chest, with the pulse booming in her ears. Why was someone hanging out in her driveway? Who was it? Should she call the cops? And tell them…there’s a strange car?

“I’m going with you. Whatever you do, don’t open your trunk,” Steven said.

She grimaced. In the last few seconds, she’d completely forgotten they had a dead body in the back.

“Fine. Let’s go.” She pulled into the driveway but left enough room for the unknown car to depart.

Steven opened her car door before stepping toward the other vehicle. When its car door latch opened, she held her breath. Begley stood, grinning wide at the two of them.

“Wh—what are you doing here?” she asked. Terror pulsed through her, shooting adrenaline into her mouth.

“Good evening, y’all,” Begley said, his words syrupy sweet.

Sweet as a poison fruit, she’d be willing to bet.

“Hello,” Brianna said, still waiting for an explanation. “It’s after nine, Begley. Is there a reason you’re here? All inspections of rental property require twenty-four hours’ notice from a landlord.”

Steven squeezed her hand and whispered, “Don’t put him on the defensive.”

She squeezed back. What the hell was she supposed to do? Offer him a hot beverage and cookies?

“You had me so upset the other day,” Begley began. “Mentioning all that hoo-hah about haunted houses. I felt terrible, truly I did.”

Yeah. Right.

"Okay. That still doesn't explain why you're here," she said.

Begley stroked his chin and stared intently at both of them. "Well, to make amends, of course."

"What kind of amends?" Steven asked, his tone flat and nonaccusatory. How did he control his emotions so well?

"Easy, Mr. Grayson. I'm just speaking with my tenant here. And to answer your question, since it would be rude not to, I brought out a bunch of new soil and mulch to redo the front yard."

"Mr. Grayson is my father," Steven said. "I'm Steven."

Begley nodded and smiled. Not sincerely, though.

Brianna narrowed her eyes. "I don't understand." Who makes amends with gardening supplies?

Begley opened up his trunk. "Look. Mulch, fertilizer, dark soil. I'm even going to bring some new crepe myrtles to plant when the time is right."

"Thank you," she muttered. How was she supposed to react? Couldn't Begley have come by earlier in the day? He knew exactly what he was doing to arrive this late at night.

"Now why don't you make yourself useful," Begley said to Steven, "and help me unload these?"

With trepidation, Steven helped Begley stack fifty-pound bags of mulch on the side of the driveway. There were still ten bags remaining.

"Oh, looks like we have ourselves a little problem," Begley said. "Ten bags left, and this is my wife's car. She'll have a hissy fit if I leave soil and supplies in here." He glanced to Brianna's car. "How about we put the extras in your trunk? Just for a day or two until I can get the gardeners out here."

Trunk?

Steven swore under his breath. Brianna bit her tongue to prevent herself from swearing out loud. Come up with something. Don't act suspicious.

"Sorry, Begley, but we've just been to Costco and my trunk's completely full."

Begley smiled that flashy, wicked grin he so often used. "Oh, heavens. Where are my manners? Let me help you unload."

This was getting creepy. "No thanks, but I appreciate the offer." Now go away.

"You're sure?" he asked.

Time to bring out the heavy-hitting excuse so Begley wouldn't insist. How did he get her to resort to new lows and excuses, even for her?

"Positive. I have some…well, feminine supplies in the trunk. It's personal. You understand, of course?" She offered a sweet smile.

"Absolutely," Begley said, but suspicion remained glazed across his face.

"Thanks, and I do appreciate the effort." Now leave.

Begley had a stare-down contest with Steven for a few seconds. He slid into his BMW, slammed the heavy door, and drove away.

Whew. Brianna ran her hands through her hair and attempted to calm her nerves. "That was close."

"Feminine supplies?" Steven asked, grinning. "Women have men beat on that one."

"Shh," she said playfully and socked him in the arm. "Desperate times call for desperate measures. C'mon, help me get Riordan's body inside."

After they carried Riordan's body into the back room, Brianna gathered any lotions she could find. The cold temps and skin care would have to be enough until he could be buried tomorrow.

Steven watched as she collected lotions and skin toner. "The burial is early tomorrow, right? What time should I be here to go with you?"

Butterflies danced in her stomach once more. She liked having someone else living to help her with the dead. Not as lonely, and she never could've swiped Riordan's body and wheeled him out on her own.

"Be here at six? The burial is at six thirty, in Bonaventure."

He nodded. "I'll be here. Keep your door locked and bolted tonight. I don't trust that son of a bitch Begley for two seconds."

“Me, neither. Thanks.” She walked with Steven to the front door.

“Remember our deal,” he said. “After the burial, I’ll take you to a special spot and we can talk. You tell me whatever else is lurking around in your mind.”

Right. The deal they’d made. He’d help her steal the body; she’d open up to him. Damn.

“I guess I’ll see you tomorrow, bright and early, then,” she said.

“Yep.” He leaned over and kissed her. The kiss wasn’t long or intense, but her lips still tingled. Right now, a quick kiss was better anyway, especially since his parents and sister could see and hear everything.

“Night,” she said and locked the door.

Plato padded to her and she knelt to pet him. “Let’s hope that wasn’t my last kiss, Plato. Because when I tell him the truth tomorrow, he might want nothing more to do with me.”

CHAPTER TWENTY-NINE

Bonaventure is so beautiful that almost
any sensible person would choose to dwell here.
~ John Muir

"The real question is," Brianna said, "who are you, Riordan O'Shea?"

Riordan didn't answer, which was strangely comforting. She had enough ghosts in her house and had requested some privacy from the Graysons as she prepped the body for tomorrow.

With soft sponges and water, she began to wipe down Riordan's face. Don't think about Begley or his eerie appearance at her house. The Irish body on the table, like any of her own family or ancestors, deserved better. Deserved her full attention.

A few seconds later, she'd entered her zone. That miraculous place where the outside world vanished, where every ounce of mental energy focused on caring for the body in front of her.

Thin, black cords hung around Riordan's neck. Dangling from them were an Irish family crest, an ankh, and a Celtic cross. Scrapes and bruises covered his chest and forehead, probably from the hit-and-run. The back of his skull was crushed, but his long hair could be adjusted to give him a decent burial.

Further examination revealed calluses on his hands. While his right hand had mild abrasions, his left fingertips were rubbed raw.

Fingertips? She stepped back, collecting herself. She'd seen those callus patterns before, when her dad forced Declan into guitar lessons. Based on Riordan's hands, he'd spent a lifetime playing and not just a few hours after school.

"Riordan O'Shea," she whispered, reverence in her tone. "I'll bet the trees and stars danced when you performed."

She brushed his long, curly hair. "I never lived in Ireland. My brother did, but my family moved to Boston before I was born."

Even though Brianna's parents had abandoned the old Irish ways, her grandmother had not. Gram passed along the old legends, stories, and the care given to those Irish souls who passed on. As Brianna stood there, staring down at Riordan's Irish features, she knew what she had to do.

She stepped to the small window in the room and opened it—but only a few inches. "Allow the body's spirit to leave in peace, move to the next world," Gram had said.

Next, a deck of cards. She dug through a box marked *miscellaneous* until she found a pack of cards, so old and worn the four different suits had faded. On the small corner table, Brianna dealt two hands of cards and left the stack in the middle. "Set the spirit's mind to playful things. Allow for an easier transition of the dead," Gram told her.

Good. Now Brianna needed string. She rummaged through the box until she found a wad of maroon thread. That would do. She tied it around each of Riordan's big toes, so they clung together like a set. She could hear Gram's thick accent even now. "Keep the feet together in death, just like life, so the devil doesn't know you're dead."

Leaves rustled outside but silence filled the room. "I don't know any other rituals," Brianna said. "Except to wish you well. Play your guitar for new audiences, Riordan O'Shea. When I hear the leaves rustle, I'll know you're rocking on a heavenly stage."

She looked at his angular chin, the determined eyes, and the jewelry he wore for his heritage. "I'm sure your music thundered the heavens, even when you were alive."

A brief chill swept across the room, and Brianna knew his spirit had left. She closed the window, following what Gram had taught her. "Never leave the window open too long lest the spirit try returning to the body, its safety net."

"Good-bye, Riordan," Brianna whispered.

###

Steven arrived at 6:00 a.m. as promised. Brianna handed him a cup of coffee and looked outside. The only sight visible was a ghostly tree silhouette framed against the full moon.

"Ready to put Riordan in the trunk?"

Yawning, Steven nodded. "What about a casket, something to bury him besides the bag?"

“I arranged everything with Father Flannigan. He’ll bring a wooden coffin. It’s not glitzy or expensive, but it’s better than cremation.”

Steven yawned again and gulped the coffee. Brianna smiled inwardly. He had walked to her house, but apparently the morning stroll hadn’t woken him up.

They placed Riordan’s body in the trunk, keeping boxes around it so it wouldn’t shift during the drive. Twenty minutes later, they arrived at Bonaventure Cemetery and drove toward the back corner, next to the Wilmington River.

Bonaventure contained more scraggly oak trees swathed in Spanish moss than anywhere else in the Lowcountry. Historic tours of this haunted, serene spot attracted tourists year-round, but thankfully, not at this early hour.

The full moon’s beams illuminated the angelic statues and rows of oaks. Some trees stood proud and distant, almost like lookouts for danger. Someone had tossed wind chimes on the mimosa tree branches, creating a tinkling harmony when the wind blew. Other trees seemed to beckon, giggle, and cry for those souls who’d been buried here.

“Legend says Savannah ghosts gather in Bonaventure and walk around on lazy afternoons,” Steven said, pointing to the gravestones and walking pathways as he drove toward the meeting spot.

"Really?" she asked, pretending surprise. *Buddy, you have no idea. They also hang out in my house, a fact I need to tell you. Eventually.*

"There's Johnny Mercer's grave, the famous musician," Steven said, motioning to the large headstone.

She glanced out the window, but instead of seeing the gravestone, she saw Johnny himself. He gave a little wave and toasted a martini glass toward her.

Oh lord. Steven said the ghosts didn't come out until the afternoon. Were they like humans—some morning types and evening types?

"I didn't realize there were so many graves here," she said. Along with the ghosts attached to them.

"Oh yeah," Steven said. "We can tour the place sometime, if you like."

"Maybe," she said. "For now, let's get Riordan safe and buried."

They reached the back of the cemetery where the land tipped down to the water. Father Flannigan stood by a tree, waiting. "Morning, Brianna. Are we ready to begin?"

"Yes, Father. Thank you so much for doing this, and at this early hour, too."

"You're welcome. I think it's most generous you've arranged for his burial."

They placed Riordan in the casket, and the grave diggers had already prepared a plot for Riordan's burial.

"Let's begin with a prayer," Father Flannigan said.

Brianna reached for Steven's hand. She'd done it. She hadn't been able to take the body to the police, but she'd stopped the cremation.

She peeked while Father Flannigan prayed. The sun's early light glowed on the cypress trees in the water, their knobby stumps brushing against the waves like children wading knee-deep in the ocean. Everything would work out—including her upcoming talk with Steven.

CHAPTER THIRTY

Love is composed of a single soul inhabiting two bodies.
~ Aristotle

Steven shifted the gear in reverse and turned Brianna's Jetta around. Slowly, he drove away, the tires making a crunching noise on the pebbled pathway. In the rearview mirror, the gravediggers shoveled soil and silt to cover Riordan's grave.

"That was a pretty incredible thing you did back there," he said. "Not many people would go to such lengths to help someone else. Especially someone who was already dead."

Her eyes lit up at the compliment. "Thanks, but I enjoy helping out. It's why I went into the mortuary business. One of these days, I'd like to run a funeral home, not just do makeup. But run it correctly. Not like Edwin appears to be doing with Begley."

"A lofty aspiration," he said. "So, what drive-thru food are you craving?"

She frowned. "Drive-thru? I thought you were going to take me out to breakfast, to talk?"

"Don't pout yet," he teased. "I am buying you breakfast, but I wanted to take you to see something cool while we eat."

Her lips twitched. "Okay. Then how about Sonic?"

"Good choice. A woman after my own heart."

They ordered breakfast sandwiches at the drive-thru and ten minutes later, they parked on Bay Street. "This way," he said, leading her down the cobblestone slope to River Street.

"River Street is the something cool?"

"Nope," he said, giving her a coy grin. She'd teased him enough by keeping secrets, and now it was his turn. Turnabout was fair play, right?

###

Where was Steven taking her? Brianna glanced up and down River Street, admiring the sun's morning rays warming the red brick buildings.

He took her hand and led her to a waterfront bench. "Let's eat."

"Here?" she asked, staring at him.

What was he up to? True, she would enjoy his company anywhere. But sitting on a bench was something cool? The sunrise was pretty, but his mysterious demeanor led her to think he had something else planned.

"Don't worry. You won't be disappointed." He winked at her. Yep, he was up to something. She just didn't know what.

She sat and opened the crinkled wrapper around her breakfast sandwich. "Whatever you say."

"Really?" he asked, flirtation oozing from those tempting lips. "You'll do whatever I say?" He bit into his Texas Toast sausage and egg sandwich. Sonic Special.

"Not so fast, smart guy."

"Because if so, I'd tell you to share whatever secret you've been hiding."

Wow, he'd shifted from coy to serious within seconds. To stall on her confession, she took a large bite of her sausage, egg, and cheese croissant. Then she chewed it thirty-two times until it turned to mulch.

"Well?" he prompted.

She looked out, staring at the rising sun's reflection in the Savannah River. *Just do it. Get the truth out.*

"I talk to the dead," she said.

He didn't flinch, didn't blink. So far, so good?

"But what I haven't told you is…"

"Is what?" He took another bite of his sandwich.

Say it! Force the words off the tip of your tongue.

"They talk back."

He blinked once in slow motion. Then he arched both eyebrows. She couldn't tell if disbelief, concern, or fear lurked in his stare.

"They what?" he asked. "Are you saying—?"

"I'm saying I can hear the dead speak. And since arriving in Savannah, I can also see them." She paused to allow the information to sink in.

“I know I sound crazy,” she said, laying her sandwich in its wrapper, which was on her lap. “If you must know, I spent a year in a psych ward when I was a sixteen because my parents thought the same thing.”

“Your parents committed you?” The apprehension in those gorgeous green eyes made her entire body tingle. She was telling him something unbelievable, something bizarre—and his first reaction was her own welfare.

“Yes. It was a horrible place, a time I don’t like to remember or talk about.” She bit her lip. “I only mention it now to tell you, with all sincerity, that I’m not crazy.”

He studied her, an intense stare that made her feel like a bug under a microscope.

“Say something, Steven. I can’t take the silence.”

He lifted the sandwich to his mouth and took a bite.

“Stalling, are you?” she joked and took the opportunity to take a few swallows herself.

He nodded and finished his bite. “I don’t know what to say. Things like ghosts, voices, I’ve never believed in them. Even growing up here, I always thought of ghost tours and tall tales as exactly that…something to tell the tourists.”

My life is not a tourist attraction, but it may as well be.

He rubbed his eyes and took a swig of coffee. “But you’re saying it’s real. I…I don’t know how to respond.”

She reached for his hand. He smiled at her but didn’t yank it away. Progress.

“I don’t expect you to believe in something you’ve never thought was true,” she said. “I just need you to understand that it’s real for me. I’m not nuts.”

His patient glance held kindness and a hint of curiosity. “I don’t think you’re nuts.”

She smiled and sighed with relief. “One of the spirits told me hearing and seeing the dead was a gift, something I needed to use to help whoever I could. That’s why I arranged Riordan’s burial. Protecting the dead, and knowing their wishes, is a way for me to help.”

She took a tiny bite of her sandwich but swallowed it whole. She needed to get the remaining words out. Looking into his sweet face, she said, “This is a way for me to make a difference.”

He inched closer and draped his arm around her shoulder. “Thanks for opening up to me. Anything else?”

Else? Her head throbbed and she rubbed her temples. She’d had enough honesty for a decade, telling him she saw ghosts, confessing that she’d been in a psych ward.

She would tell him about his family—just not yet. Not with sharp pain grating into her skull.

"Not right now," she said.

Change the subject before he asks for more truth. Steer the conversation away from opening up.

"So, what's this cool thing you wanted to show me?" she asked. "The sunrise is beautiful, but—"

"Shh."

"You're shushing me?" she asked.

He cupped her face in his hands and brushed her hair off her cheeks and tucked it behind her ears. "I am."

It worked. She didn't want to talk anymore. She wanted his lips on hers. Now. "Kiss me."

He leaned in, pulling her lips to his own. Wet, intense kisses that ignited every cell in her body.

"Looks like my technique worked," he whispered, sexy and hot breath blowing on her ear. Goose bumps spread down her neck and across her arms.

"Your touch makes me shiver with pleasure," she said, and she ran her fingers through his hair, bringing his lips closer to hers for more.

He grinned through the kiss, and her lips joined his in their simultaneous smile. "Good to hear," he said. "I love kissing you, but this isn't the cool thing I told you about."

It wasn't? Necking with him as the crimson sun rose over the river was pretty damn cool.

He released her lips. "Nope. Check it out." He pointed toward the Talmadge Bridge. "Watch the river."

She glanced at the water and its fast-moving current. "What am I watching for?"

He squinted and kept watching. "There," he said.

She looked. "No way! Dolphins?"

"Yep. They come out every morning to hunt for fish. Get here early enough, you can see several of them playing in the water."

As a morning breeze blew across her face, she watched with awe. She'd never seen dolphins this close before, let alone so many. Their triangular fins appeared, followed by their tails, up and down, over and over in the water.

"I thought dolphins lived in the ocean," she said.

"They do, but all the water's connected. It's not far for them to swim in, get themselves a good breakfast, and swim back out again."

"You're right," she said, her cheek muscles aching from smiling so wide. "This is cool."

He leaned over and kissed her once more. “So are you, Brianna. So are you.”

CHAPTER THIRTY-ONE

Nothing in life is to be feared. It is only to be understood.
~ Marie Curie

After dropping Brianna and her car off at home, Steven took his time walking back to Dennis's place. He needed to think before diving back into the research stacks.

The last twelve hours had been more bizarre than he'd been accustomed to. Stealing a body from the funeral home, helping set up a secret burial, and hearing Brianna tell him she had conversations with the dead—and they talked back.

She'd certainly thrown him for a loop. He'd presumed she was seeing someone else, not the dead. Or maybe she had some dark secret crime in her past that prevented her from opening up to people? But the big secrecy was talking to ghosts and seeing them? Every person had quirks and oddities.

If he worked in a funeral home, he'd probably be convinced he saw and spoke with dead people, too. Especially since she'd grown up with a family who ran a mortuary.

At least she didn't act emotionally unstable or burst into tears at dinner because she'd gone thirty calories over her daily limit. Talking to the dead and maybe hearing them? He could handle this.

Cars whizzed past as he walked down Drayton Street toward Dennis's house. When he reached the Oglethorpe red light, he waited for the walk signal and entered the crosswalk.

He took two steps. A navy BMW slammed its brakes, stopping inches from his thigh. The car's wheels shrieked to a stop and left skid marks smoking on the pavement. What the hell?

"The light's red, dumb ass!" Steven patted his legs, arms, chest, and other areas to make sure all body parts remained where they should. What kind of idiot speeds down the historic district streets, anyhow? Unless the driver had a sudden seizure, the jerk had no excuse being behind the wheel of a car.

Slowly, the BMW's tinted window slid down. Holy shit. It was Begley.

"Morning, Steven. You're not hurt, are you?"

Steven clenched his fists and stormed over to Begley's car door. "Not a chance. Did you not see the crosswalk? Savannah pedestrians have the right-of-way, as I'm sure you know." Asshole.

"Yes, and as I'm sure you're aware, helping Brianna perform illegal acts is also a crime."

Steven's shoulders tensed. To not let on, he leaned into the window. "I haven't done anything illegal, but if you don't watch where you're driving, you'll be the one having to answer to the cops."

Begley let out a low, rumbling chuckle—an eerie sound from such a corrupt man. "You let me worry about the cops. You just take care of yourself, and have a good day now."

Before Steven could come up with some classic retort, the light turned green and Begley sped away. Damn it. The man was now trying to run him down on public Savannah streets?

Steven's heartbeat still raced. This had to end. He needed to step up his game, find a way to contact the feds, or maybe the press in another city. Somehow, Begley had to be stopped. How did the bastard even know—or did he—about them stealing the body? Or was Begley just fishing for some kind of information? Would he go after Brianna next?

Steven pulled out his cell and dialed Brianna's number. No answer, just voicemail. "Hey, it's me. Be on the lookout for Begley. The bastard just tried to run me over. I know you're at work, so you're safe, but let's meet up later."

He snapped the phone shut. At least she would be safe at work. He hoped.

When Steven crossed Chippewa Square, right around the corner from Dennis's place, he decided some fresh air without Begley around would do him good. He sat on the square's bench, under the rustling oaks and memorial statues, and took a deep breath.

Home wasn't as bad as he remembered, with the exception of people like Begley. Steven liked the grid layout, the lush green squares, each with individual history and landmarks.

Even this place, Chippewa Square, was famous. He traced his fingers across the wooden bench seat. Locals and tourists alike came to see the place where Tom Hanks told his stories in the movie *Forrest Gump*. After filming wrapped, the official bench had been moved to the museum, but people still walked the square to see its location.

When Steven thought about it, *Forrest Gump* footage was spliced and edited to make an entertaining film, but none of those 1950's clips really included Forrest. It wasn't real, but it didn't hurt anyone.

Brianna talked to ghosts, and she claimed they talked back. But she wasn't crazy, and she wasn't harming anyone. And considering she'd spent a year in a psych ward when she was sixteen, she'd turned out more normal than expected. He couldn't imagine what all those needles, doctors, beige rooms, and padded walls would do to someone, especially a teenage girl.

She's a survivor.

He was determined to survive too.

Together, they had a better chance.

###

At nine that morning, Brianna arrived at work. This was going to be a long day. She'd been awake and functioning since 5:00 a.m.

Begley's BMW was parked outside, but he wasn't in his car. Why would he be here? Another meeting with Edwin to discuss illegal operations, perhaps?

When she went inside, she stopped short and almost fumbled forward. Begley sat at the front desk examining several files.

"Excuse me? What are you doing?" she asked. He had no business being here, much less going through Margie's desk.

His fingers touched the file folder tabs, and he stroked them like petting a cat. "Checking on some paperwork. Don't worry. Edwin and I have an understanding about when I'm permitted to be here."

What kind of understanding? Begley checking the files to ensure anyone he'd killed wound up with the proper—meaning forged—cremation authorizations? Begley sure wasn't hiding his intentions. Did he think she was stupid?

"Begley, I'm not so sure you should be going through Margie's desk."

He slicked his hair back with his hands. In the dim reception area, he resembled a used-car salesman. He'd fit the part perfectly if he'd kept his sunglasses on inside.

"Don't you worry your Yankee head about anything. Edwin and I go way back."

Of his connection to Edwin, Brianna had no doubt. She rested her arms on the reception desk, pretending to be social but paying attention to which files he looked through.

Begley fidgeted for a few minutes. He obviously knew she was analyzing his every move. Finally, he shut the drawer. "I'll leave you to your work. Any bodies in today?"

You already know the answer. Why are you asking me?

"No, things are slow. I've been catching up on paperwork."

He nodded. "Can I ask you something off-the-cuff?"

She crossed her arms in front of her chest. "Sure." *As long as you leave after my answer.*

"Do you like working with the dead? How does one choose this profession?"

She shrugged. It wasn't an unusual question. She'd heard it numerous times throughout her career. "I saw how helpful the mortuary arts could be."

"I'm sure you're quite the expert," he said. "But why a cosmetologist? Why not a funeral director? Edwin can't run this place forever, you know."

In Begley's sick and twisted way, he was feeling her out, wondering if she would become part of their illegal scheme. Nausea swirled in her stomach. She had to force out the words without throwing up.

“I’ve enjoyed learning the ins and outs of the business, but I like cosmetology. I get to see the immediate fruits of my labor.”

Begley nodded. “Makes sense.” He chuckled—she hated his muddled laughter—and said, “And I suppose you’ve always got job security. People do keep dying. It can’t be avoided.”

If you keep killing them, that’s true.

“The stability in my work isn’t as important as the chance to help others, sending the dead off in a respectful fashion.”

How anyone could think the funeral home business was only about profit and not about helping humanity was beyond her comprehension. Sure, every business needed to make a profit, but most of the time, those who entered the business had a desire to comfort others.

“I like my job,” she said. “I guess I should get to work.” Besides, she didn’t want to talk with him any longer than she had to, for professionalism’s sake.

Begley strode to the door. “Well, you have yourself a good day now.”

His stupid farewell line always felt like a warning. Laced inside a polite voice, decorated by a charming smile with bleached teeth, his words chilled her down to her bones. She felt something ominous, as if waiting for the other shoe to drop. He was the queasy-green sky before the tornado.

###

After guzzling two cups of coffee at lunch, Brianna returned to Restful Oaks for the afternoon stretch. One more body to go before she could go home and sleep.

Setting her purse down, she checked her cell for any messages or texts. Damn, the battery had died. She'd been too preoccupied last night with Riordan's body to think of charging it. Oh well, she'd check messages later.

Back in the preparation room, she massaged skin foundation onto Martha McCauley, an endearing old lady who'd collected hundreds of clocks in her lifetime. Not many people plan their burial—most don't want to think about morbid things, other than maybe buying a plot.

Martha had been one of the few who organized everything in advance. When Brianna arrived in Savannah, Edwin had taken her to Martha's house to sign the final paperwork. That had been Brianna's first taste of the South—funeral homes making house calls when the client couldn't make it to the office.

"I'm sorry to see your time ended, Martha," she said. "But I'll take great care of you, like you wanted."

"Thank you, dear."

Brianna's stomach clenched, and she jumped inches off the floor before finally catching her breath. Martha's semitransparent form moved about the room, smiling and watching Brianna's handiwork.

“Will I ever get used to the way the dead suddenly appear?”

“Of course,” Martha said. “One can get used to anything.”

“True.” She finished the lipstick, the final touch. “What’s going to happen to all those clocks in your house? You had at least forty—”

“Sixty-three, dear,” Martha said with absolute pride and certainty. “My grandson will inherit them. You liked all my clocks?”

“Yes.” Brianna wouldn’t forget the moment every clock went off at the top of the hour. With at least ten in each room—cuckoo clocks, mantel clocks, and a dozen other kinds—the chimes created a one-of-a-kind sound.

“Time is life,” Martha said. “My house was a living testament of that.”

The little old lady was the sweetest Brianna had ever encountered. She didn’t want to overstep her bounds by asking questions, but she had to ask at least one.

“What if you spend all your time trying to help something, or someone, and you fail anyway?”

Martha’s hazel eyes sparkled. “Goals can be hard to reach, but don’t ever lose hope, dear.” She pointed to the clock and smiled. “Minutes are going to pass regardless of what we do. With a little faith, you can do great things.”

Brianna swallowed hard. “That’s what Declan always told me, to have more faith.”

“I know, dear. Quite a charmer, he is.”

Wait. What?

“Have you…did you see my brother?”

Martha’s form faded until there was no substance left, only the sweet smell of talcum powder. “Please, come back. Tell me—”

“Who on Earth are you talking to?” Edwin asked.

How long had he been standing there? She tucked her hair behind her ears, composing herself. Crap.

“I…um…”

“Never mind. Come to my office when you’re done here. We need to have a little chat.”

She narrowed her eyes. A little chat? Edwin had made a career out of speaking formerly to families, grieving widows, and young children. He never spoke in slang. What could he possibly want to have a little chat about?

“Give me a few minutes here.”

“Fine, just make it soon.” He left, and the room fell silent—except for the panic storming through her brain.

CHAPTER THIRTY-TWO

Our greatest weakness lies in giving up. The most certain way to succeed is always to try just one more time.
~ Thomas A. Edison

"Exactly what do you think your job description entails?" Edwin demanded.

His calming tone, the one she'd grown so used to, had vanished. In its place were irritation, abrasiveness, and impatience. Fortunately, she'd closed his door behind her when she'd entered his office, so Margie couldn't hear anything.

Brianna shifted her sitting position. Behind the large desk, Edwin's threatening glare blazed through his gold spectacles.

"I don't know what you mean," she said. "I do my job, prepping the dead for the funeral."

Edwin cocked an eyebrow at her. He'd grown more aggressive in recent days.

"Does your job include stealing the property of Restful Oaks?"

She dug her nails into the chair's arm. How could he know about Riordan so quickly? Play dumb. Just play dumb.

"You've brought me into your office to talk about needing an extra stapler? I'm sorry. I forgot to put yours back and Margie's was on the blink."

Edwin studied her with narrowed eyes. "I'm not referring to office supplies. I'm talking about a dead body, one you signed for. Mr. Riordan O'Shea?"

She coughed, almost choking on the lump in the back of her throat. "I don't know what you mean."

"Bullshit doesn't become us, Brianna."

She stared at the brown carpet. He knew. What now? Her only option was to stand her ground.

"You told me no bodies were to be delivered that day," she said.

"Margie should've worked that shift. She didn't tell me about her commitment until the night before. Things became busy, and I forgot you were manning the front desk on the day he was to arrive."

Edwin paused, wiped the sweat off his brow, and said, "Trust me, I regret letting you sign for the body."

Was there a scar on his forehead? Brianna sat up in her chair and tried to look without seeming too obvious.

"What do you want, Edwin?"

"I need Riordan's body. Where is it?"

"I can't do that," she said. *Even if you fire me.*

Martha's mention of Declan, of keeping the faith, had been the shot of hope she needed to see her efforts through. Brianna was doing the right thing. She would not back down now, not for some greedy corrupt set of good ole boys out to screw over the dead.

"Tell me," Edwin said, his stare dark and sinister.

"No."

He pounded his fist on the desk like a crazed monkey. "Tell me!"

"Why don't you tell me why you're cremating bodies when they should be going to autopsy?"

His eyes widened—a frightening sight behind his tiny, rimmed glasses.

"I run a decent funeral home," he said, his voice quaking.

Maybe the gentler approach would work? He seemed…conflicted.

"Edwin, don't you see that by doing as Begley says, you're only hurting your business, the dead, their families? It's negating any of the good you're doing."

"If I don't do as Begley demands," he said, "I won't have a business to run. He's the primary investor, the one who manages all the accounts."

Brianna widened her eyes. "I thought Margie took care of the admin side."

Edwin rolled his eyes. "Margie is a front. It's something to get her out of the house all day and she likes working with me."

Hmm. "How can Begley shut you down? Even he said the mortuary business has job security. Why do you need him at all?"

The next words off her tongue even surprised her. “Have a little faith.”

Wow. Where had that come from?

Edwin sat there, speechless. Unable to keep eye contact, he stared out the window. For the first time, she saw how long and drawn his chin had become, how hollow his cheeks were, and the dark bags under his eyes. Edwin wasn’t a leader in corruption. He was a victim of Begley’s stranglehold. Begley was like kudzu, the vine that grew by leaps and bounds each day, constricting the life force out of anything it wrapped its ropelike strands around.

Finally, after moments of silence, Edwin’s poker face returned. “I need Riordan’s body, Brianna.”

Nothing she said had mattered. Edwin would always work for Begley, a sad truth.

But she would never become like Edwin. Begley wouldn’t own her—ever.

“I’m sorry, Edwin. I can’t give you Riordan’s body.”

“Then I’m sorry, Brianna,” he said. “But you’re fired.”

CHAPTER THIRTY-THREE

Right is right, even if everyone is against it,
and wrong is wrong, even if everyone is for it.
~ William Penn

Brianna sprinted home. Most days, she meandered. Not today.

Fired? Freaking fired? Edwin and Begley were the criminals, and she'd been the one to get axed? Really?

Her clenched fists made the dash home more aerodynamic, and she made it to her front door in record time. Plato greeted her with licks and nuzzles and a happy dance. At least some things in life remained consistent.

Virginia peeked out from the kitchen. "You look terrible, Yankee. What happened?"

"Edwin fucking fired me."

"Please don't use such language—"

"Really? I tell you I got fired and all you care about is whether I use genteel language? I don't need this right now, Virginia, especially not from you."

Virginia crinkled her nose and returned to whatever the hell she'd been doing. James and Amy—the normal ghosts—approached Brianna with empathic faces.

“I’m sorry,” James said. “This is our fault for talking you into this—”

“No, it was my decision in the end. I just can’t believe he had the gall to fire me.”

She strode into the kitchen, avoiding eye contact with Virginia, and grabbed a Smithwick’s ale from the fridge before returning to the den and flopping on the couch.

“What can we do?” Amy asked. She paced and twirled her hair.

“I don’t know yet.” Brianna took a big swig. “I’ll tell you one thing. If Edwin and Begley think that getting me out of Restful Oaks will keep me out of their way, they’re dead wrong.”

James’s eyes beamed with pride. “That’s the spirit. Don’t give up.”

“I had my doubts, but this isn’t a half-ass effort for me anymore. Those good ole boys have awakened a sleeping mama bear.”

“We know Begley owns cops,” James said. “Do you think contacting the feds or someone in internal affairs might help?”

She shrugged. “I don’t know. Internal affairs would take months to investigate, and I don’t have that long. Steven’s friend Dennis was supposed to get in touch with his contacts in Atlanta, though. Maybe we can talk to the press there.”

James nodded. “Begley’s a big fish in a small pond here in Savannah. But in the big metro Atlanta, he’s a nobody.”

“Exactly,” she said. “Oh, that reminds me. I need to charge my phone. It’s completely dead.”

She plugged the cord in and her phone beeped. A message?

Dialing voicemail, she entered her password and listened to Steven’s message. “What the hell?”

All three ghosts lifted their heads in response to her shocked voice.

She tried to call him back, but no answer. She would try again later.

“What’s wrong?” James asked.

“Begley tried to run down Steven with his car.”

“That dirty bastard.” James hurtled out of the recliner and to the front door, ramming his body into the hard wood.

Slam. Slam. Slam.

James stretched his hand over the doorknob and reached for it, but his transparent form only passed through the physical object. He could grip a pipe, Virginia could make grits using actual pots and pans, but he couldn’t grasp anything that would let him leave.

Deep in Brianna’s heart, a sharp pain formed. They’d told her they couldn’t escape, but she’d never seen their desperation in trying to do so.

“James, don’t worry. I’m going to make sure Begley pays for this.”

Tears shimmered in James’s light blue eyes. “If he kills my son—”

“He won’t.”

Protectiveness surged through her. She had to help, had to find a way for James to eventually talk to Steven.

Reaching for James's arm but unable to grasp him, she said, "C'mon. Let's sit back down."

Reluctantly, he obliged. "You don't understand, Brianna. Steven and I haven't spoken in so many years. I know I made mistakes, said things I shouldn't have, things that haunt me to this day—"

"We all have," she said. "Don't worry. I'm in this mess until the end. Begley and Edwin are going to rue the day they decided to fire my ass. That's a promise."

###

Brianna tried to sleep, but the rustling leaves kept whispering, nudging her awake. She looked out at the full moon illuminating dozens of stars that seemed to float across the sky.

Was a meteor shower predicted for tonight? Strange timing, given it wasn't summer.

Go take a peek, the wind seemed to say. Until recent months, Brianna would have dismissed the words. But lately, ghosts and voices knew more than she did. She tugged on faded jeans, a black Saw Doctors T-shirt, and a nylon jacket. November had arrived, and the last few days had been chilly.

For safety, she brought Plato along. In reality, he would herd or lick a mugger to death, but no one else needed to know. His fierce bark would keep the questionable element away.

She followed the direction of the stars to Whitefield Square on the southeastern end of the historic district. Plato didn't care which way they walked. He was too busy poking his nose into all sorts of smelly places: under wet leaves, in dirt piles, behind pebbles and rocks.

"C'mon, boy," she said, tugging him along. They walked, the quiet night surrounding them. Plato barked at the large scraggly trees seeming to urge them forward.

"Let's keep going." She was determined to fight her comfort zone and begin to listen more to her instincts. They'd gotten her this far. Besides, even though she and Plato were walking late at night, the historic area was safe. She knew not to venture a block or two outside the grid unless Plato suddenly transformed into a Rottweiler.

When a soft breeze blew, the sound of melancholy violins floated in the air, and the wind was warm on her skin, like opening an oven filled with baked bread. Strange weather for November.

Plato barked at the tiny fireflies dancing and flitting in circular patterns. Hmm, yet another strange occurrence. Fireflies—or lightning bugs, as the Southerners called them—usually appeared in summer, hovering near front porches at dusk, catching wind of gossip, and carrying it through the town. But tonight, the fireflies skipped in the moonbeams and lit up the gazebo in the center of Whitefield Square.

Then she saw him. Riordan? The body she'd buried?

Inside the gazebo, he played a violin and sang a tune as familiar as childhood. Violins? Had ghosts in Savannah been playing violins and that's why she'd heard them? It seemed too coincidental.

Plato, usually a bark-fest champion around strangers, immediately sat down, transfixed. Completely out of character for a sheltie.

Riordan glanced up and smiled. "Well, if it isn't the lady who saved me from the fire." His Irish accent swathed and draped every syllable, adorning his words with centuries of legends and folklore. She hadn't heard anything close to authentic Irish since she'd left Boston.

Plato barked twice and tugged her forward with the leash.

Riordan chuckled. "I think your dog wants to hear an upbeat tune."

Did ghosts have the ability to read animals' minds? There were so many things she wondered.

He shifted to an upbeat tempo, rapidly changing the notes while stomping one foot in tune. She reached down to pet an admiring Plato and listened to the familiar Irish songs from her past.

In this magical pocket of woods, the wind blew in a fiery circle, hugging this tiny place on the planet. Fireflies, dragonflies, and squirrels remained still, listening to this ghost play the violin. She'd wanted to stop a crime being committed, but maybe there was another reason she'd been so insistent on saving Riordan from cremation.

"You have a great voice," she said when he finished.

"Thanks. I've been expecting you."

Expecting her? To show up late at night in Whitefield Square?

"I don't understand."

"You're doing well in your efforts, Brianna, but I have a message for you."

His cryptic tone made the back of her neck tingle. "What kind of message?"

Riordan glanced upward to the night sky. "Declan is proud of the work you're doing. He wants you to not lose hope, not give up, especially for this upcoming fight with Begley."

"Declan? You saw him? Talked to him? My brother?"

Her head pounded, half from excitement, half from never seeming to get enough information. Couldn't there be some kind of guidebook for people like her, an explanation as to how to manage talking with the dead? It would make things a whole lot simpler.

"Aye, Declan is a good man."

"Why can't I see him? I see every other ghost in Savannah—"

"I can't give you all the answers," Riordan said. "I'm new to this myself. But my boss told me to pass along that message."

She racked her brain. Was this real? Was she dreaming? She pinched herself. Guess not.

"A woman I worked on at Restful Oaks said she'd met Declan too. I tried asking for more details, but she faded away."

Riordan nodded. "Yes. She's moved on to her new residence. You, on the other hand, need to be prepared for anything. Begley is evil, as I'm sure you know."

A trace of doubt flashed through her mind. What if this was a setup? A trick of some sort? Begley owned cops. Maybe he had means to corrupt the afterlife? Doubtful. She really needed some sleep, but she best be sure the message had come from Declan.

"How do I know the message came from Declan, or that you really talked to him?"

Riordan let out a deep belly laugh, one filled with melodic chuckling sounds. When he did, a breeze blew gusts of wind around them.

"What's so funny?" she asked.

"I just lost a bet."

"A bet?" Ghosts in the afterlife placed wagers?

"Aye, Declan told me you'd need proof."

Prickling jolts shot through her and crawled down her spine. Now *that* sounded like the Declan she knew.

"Well, give me some proof, then," she said.

"You're lucky I'm Irish and know how to pronounce this," Riordan began. "Bí mar ghuth chan mar mhacalla."

The lump in her throat plummeted to her stomach. She remembered those words. "Be a voice, not an echo."

"You know your Gaelic."

"Only a few phrases. That was one of Declan's favorites."

"So you believe me now?"

She nodded as fat tears dribbled down her face. "Yes, even though I don't understand how anything in my life is possible."

"You help the dead, those who no longer have a voice. Be their voice, our voice," Riordan said.

When she looked into his intent stare, she saw an old soul, someone who'd lived a thousand lifetimes. Was that the way it worked? Had he helped others before and assisted those who were frightened of their gift, as Anzhela had done for her?

"Why am I seeing and hearing ghosts, Riordan? Can you answer me that question?"

He tilted his head quizzically. "You talked to us first. Why are you so surprised we're talking back?"

Holy hell. He was right. She'd started talking to the embalmed bodies in her family's mortuary when she was four years old.

"Tell Declan I won't let him down. Tell him I love and miss him."

“I will,” Riordan said. “Now relax and enjoy the music. You’ll need your strength in the coming days.”

She hugged Plato and got comfortable. Riordan began to play sweet and haunting notes. As he wielded the violin under starry skies, her fears were brushed away as the music lulled her into sleep, and the fireflies danced until the dawn.

CHAPTER THIRTY-FOUR

Put silk on a goat and it is still a goat.
~ Irish Saying

Brianna awoke to Plato's animated face licking her nose. With twinkling eyes, he gave two greeting barks right above her ears. Ouch.

She sat up in her own bed. Wait, how had she gotten home last night? She'd fallen asleep listening to Riordan play. Yet here she was, back at home. Had it been a dream after all?

Surely, it had been. She stretched her legs, lifted her arms above her head, and yawned. Her muscles felt relaxed, every part of her reeling with energy—as if Mother Nature had cradled her through the night.

"Morning, Plato." She rubbed his ears and noticed something white dangled from his collar. A note? She pulled it open and held her breath. In ornate script were the words: "Bí mar ghuth chan mar mhacalla."

"Be a voice, not an echo," she whispered. Last night hadn't been a dream.

Thumping noises echoed from the kitchen. What was going on?

She sat up to get dressed, but she already was. She still had on the clothes from last night.

When she reached the kitchen, Brianna saw Virginia. "What's going on?"

"Someone's at your door," Virginia whispered.

Had they been banging on the door loud enough to wake Brianna up? She looked through the peephole. Holy shit. Begley?

She turned around. James's kind face contorted and glowered. He was ready to rumble. "Stay calm," she whispered. "I'm going to set up my phone recorder." She turned on the app and hid her smart phone behind a lamp before she opened the door.

"Begley, what are you doing here?"

"Well, good morning to you, too."

The jerk wanted to lecture her on manners? After everything? Before she'd had her morning coffee?

"Morning," she said, deliberately omitting the "good" from her reply. "What can I do for you?"

He pushed his way into the living room. "I came by with several rose bushes, ready to plant."

He owned the place, but if he was so manners conscious, why not wait to be invited in?

He stood in the center of the living room. Behind him, Virginia clutched a large pot of grits, ready and aimed at his head. Brianna shook her head, needing Virginia to calm down. "Assault by grits" was not how she wanted to get kicked out of her rental agreement. Besides, she doubted it would work.

After being fired from her job, Brianna wanted to get something incriminating—on tape—of Begley's corruption. The best way to achieve that was to play his manners game.

"Roses would be nice," she said. "I have some work to do in here, however. Why don't I get you a soda since you'll remain outside?"

The question wasn't meant to be an inquiry. It was a hint for him to get the hell out of her house. Or the house she rented from him.

"I have a right to inspect my properties, inside and out," he said, glaring at her.

"And I have tenants' rights. You have to give notice."

Begley scowled. "Tell me what you did with Riordan's body. I know you tried to get Bobby Ray Canters's body too."

"I don't work at the funeral home anymore. Edwin fired me. Perhaps you should talk to him."

Begley's cool eyes held a restrained anger, a talent he'd obviously harnessed over the years. "Don't test me, girlie. You know exactly where that body is."

She didn't shrink back. She refused to give Begley the satisfaction. "I don't know what you're talking about."

"You broke into my office, and I never called the cops. Don't get any ideas."

“I was wrong,” she said. “But I didn’t steal anything. I only looked at your files because I wanted to confirm what I suspected. You’ve been having people killed for their property.”

“How ludicrous,” Begley said with arrogance.

“Why wasn’t there an autopsy done on Riordan’s body?”

Begley smirked. “Because I own the cops. Have more secrets on them than J. Edgar Hoover had on everyone.”

Please let the recorder still be working. She couldn’t go to the local cops, but perhaps she could go to the feds or the press. Or E. F. Hutton. When he talked, people listened, right? Or someone who could expose Begley for the greedy coward he was.

“So you bribed the cops, Lieutenant Grainger, to cover up Riordan’s death, bypassing the autopsy?”

Begley smiled, his arrogant eyes scorching her. “You’re not so dumb, for a damn Yankee.”

Knowing his stupidity was being recorded, she smiled and used her best Southern accent. “Why, thank you.”

Virginia lurked in the corner. “Keep your day job,” she mouthed. Brianna grinned. She’d never perfect the accent for Virginia, but that was okay. She’d help them get justice.

“I’m going to give you three seconds to tell me where that body is,” Begley said.

"Kids pull pranks in this town," she said. "Anyone could've taken it. I need you to leave. Now."

"Hold on a damn minute—"

Plato leapt out of his crated area—thanks to Amy—and plopped his furry self between her and Begley. While shelties only grew to knee height, in that moment, Plato could've been a Great Dane. He ripped out brief, sharp barks easily heard by neighbors.

Brianna stepped closer, eyeing Begley. "Good point, Plato. I believe he needs to leave."

Begley didn't flinch. Plato jumped, his front paws thumping into Begley's bad knee. "Ow! Damn it, stupid dog!"

"Leave Plato alone. It's bad manners for such a Southern gentleman. Perhaps your family lied about their heritage? Maybe you're related to Sherman?"

"Bitch," he mumbled under his breath.

"Get out." She ushered him to the front door without another word.

In the open doorway, Begley said, "You sure you don't have something to tell me?"

"Actually, yes I do. I hope you never, ever find Riordan O'Shea's body, considering you had him killed."

"What the—"

“And you have yourself a good day now,” she said in her best Southern tone, the kind Begley always used for his exiting quote.

She slammed the door and went to check the recording. If it had picked up their conversation, she could nail Begley to the wall.

CHAPTER THIRTY-FIVE

The World is a book, and those who do not travel read only a page.
~ Saint Augustine

Brianna pressed her hands against her blazer pocket for the tenth time in twenty minutes. She couldn't help herself. Her fingers had to make sure her cell remained there. The recorder had picked up every word, crisp and clear, that Begley had said.

She'd played the conversation over the phone for Steven and arranged to meet him for a drink so he could sync the recording to his phone.

She walked inside the 45 Bistro bar and scanned the place. He sat near the back end of the U-shaped bar, drinking a glass of red wine. Strands of dark hair framed his face as he lifted the glass of wine to his lips—how could he appear more attractive every time she saw him? Silly observations like those only happened in fairy tales, didn't they?

She crept up behind him. "Hi, stranger."

His body jumped for a second, and then his gaze met hers. "Hi, yourself. Have a seat. Tell me about the look on that jerk's face when you shut the door on him."

She sat down and rested her purse at her feet. "Best moment ever."

Steven leaned toward her, his breath warm against her hair. "I always liked a woman who could stand up to someone like Begley."

Heat coursed through her. She loved his breath on her and couldn't wait to feel his touch in other spots on her body.

"I'm just glad the recorder picked up the conversation." Once again, her hands wandered to her pocket.

"What can I get you?" asked the bartender, a distinguished looking man with salt-and-pepper hair.

She glanced at Steven's red wine. "Is it good?"

"Delicious," Steven said.

"One of our best sellers," the bartender said. "Ramspeck Pinot Noir, coming right up."

The bartender poured her drink, then walked to the other end of the bar to ring up other customers.

"Dennis is talking to his contacts in Atlanta now," Steven said. "If he can get a few days off, we're going to go meet them in person, see about putting a story together. Your recording will help a lot."

"Glad I could help."

He was going away for a few days? Even the short amount of time would seem long, given how much they'd seen each other in the last few weeks.

"I'll miss you when you're away," she said. Part of her longed to take back the words, not open up and stay safe, but she'd spent a lifetime practicing those bad habits.

Steven brushed a strand of hair behind her ear. "Would you—?"

"Would I what?"

Damn, why had she blurted that out and not let him finish? Was he asking her to go to Atlanta with him? She hoped but didn't want to assume. A trip out of town, hours from Begley and ghosts and Savannah, would be the chance of a lifetime. Besides, she'd told Steven over the phone that Edwin had fired her. She didn't have any other time commitments.

"Want to come along? I'm sure Dennis wouldn't mind. Hell, you've gotten further with that recording and your work than he has in months."

Her lips grinned wide, even though she willed herself to stay casual. "Sure, a road trip sounds great."

"Perfect," he said and took a long sip of wine.

"Perfect," she whispered, hoping from the very core part of her heart that it would be.

###

Brianna's Jetta was elected as the road-trip choice, seeing as how there had been enough room in the trunk to hold a dead body. Only now, it would hold all of Dennis's files on Begley along with their luggage.

Besides, the only other car choices were Dennis's Smart car, which barely held one person, and Steven's Mustang, which while sporty, wouldn't be comfortable either.

They left in midmorning. After twenty minutes, she discovered what prior travelers knew: Interstate 16, the connector between Savannah and Macon, won the award for Most Boring Road Ever. Pine trees and asphalt stretched into endless oblivion. The only interesting sight was the railroad-crossing barricades at each exit. According to Dennis, those formed the emergency hurricane evacuation system, should Savannah ever need a mass exodus.

At least she'd chosen to live in a place down South with a plan. A positive note, something she was trying to see more of.

The plan was to have lunch in Macon, get on Interstate 75, and take it into Atlanta. They'd check into their hotel and meet Dennis's journalist contact, Piper, in midtown for an early dinner.

Steven and Dennis reminisced about jamming together in old days, and Brianna's eyes glazed over as the trees blurred past her window. So much had happened in the last three weeks, she hadn't had a second's time to stop and rest. Well, not without ghosts at her side, commenting on her every move. Despite Virginia's abrasive personality, Brianna had grown to appreciate her. The judgmental attitude faded—at least somewhat—once Brianna said she would join their cause for justice.

Helping them had been the right choice, not only for their sake, but for hers. Knowing Declan wanted her to continue, would be proud of her, made every risk worthwhile. Besides, what else could she do? Crawl back to Boston, her head hung low, saying she'd failed? Never.

The car's droning engine channeled her into a vast sea of memories, things she'd not thought about since Declan's funeral.

"We're the February children," Declan had told her. "I'm twenty today, you're ten. We're going to celebrate our birthdays in style, not just today, but for the rest of our lives."

Her mother had insisted Brianna go to school, even though it was field day and all classes were cancelled. "How can balancing an egg on a spoon and crossing the finish line help me to do anything?" Brianna asked.

Her mother didn't have an answer and shooed Brianna off to school, reciting words like '"tradition" and "expectation." Fortunately for Brianna, Declan wasn't so provincial.

Sometime during the three-legged race and the egg toss, an announcement came over the gymnasium loudspeaker: "Brianna McNeil, please come to the office."

When she arrived, the school secretary smiled at her. "Your brother is here to bring you to your doctor appointment. He's waiting in the adjoining office."

Doctor appointment? Mom hadn't mentioned anything, but Brianna wasn't about to complain about leaving early.

"Thanks, Mrs. Soto," Declan said as they left. "I'll make sure she gets her homework done."

Once off the school grounds, Brianna slugged him in the arm. "How come Mom didn't tell me I had a doctor appointment? I'm glad you picked me up, though."

"You don't," he said, and he flashed a smile. "I've got a surprise for you. Our secret, so don't tell Mom."

God, she'd loved him.

They left all responsibilities behind and went to see the new aquarium, which had just opened. Dark rectangular rooms held floor-to-ceiling fish tanks illuminated with blue water. Sharks, red and yellow neon fish, and electric eels darted about.

"Pretty cool, aren't they?" Declan said. "Since they stick together, they have a better chance of survival."

She pressed her hands against the cool glass. "Like us?"

"Exactly. C'mon, I want to see the stingrays."

They wandered room to room. Being a weekday, the place wasn't crowded, making every second with him and away from school more precious.

After the aquarium, he took her to lunch along the waterfront. They split a sandwich and threw napkins at each other in fun.

But like a pending rainstorm, his mood changed.

“What’s wrong?” she asked.

He’d looked at her, unable to keep eye contact for more than a few seconds. “I have something I need to tell you.”

“What?”

“As you know, today I turned twenty.”

“Duh,” she said. “Wasn’t that why you got me out of school? To celebrate?”

He frowned. “I’m joining the air force, Brianna. I leave next week for training.”

She couldn’t speak for several moments. When she finally did, her voice cracked. “No. Please. Why would you do it?”

“Dad wants me to serve, and I’d rather fly airplanes than join the army.”

Stubborn tears trickled down her cheeks. She wiped them away. “Why now?”

He put his arm around her and squeezed her into a hug. “I admit the timing sucks. I didn’t want to spoil your birthday, but I wanted to tell you the news before you heard it from Dad.”

“But…you’ll be gone.”

“I’ll write you all the time, I promise. I wanted to sneak you out of class today to have some time with you. I’ll be flying airplanes, Bree. Airplanes!”

His eyes sparkled when he mentioned flying, but his sagging shoulders made her wonder. Whose decision was this, for him to go away?

"I repeat, why now?" She wiped her face. Stupid tears.

"Because I need to do something with my life, and the military is a good option. As much as I'd love to return to Savannah and bartend there for the rest of my days, I can't."

She knew his real reason. She was only ten, but she knew.

"Are you doing this for Dad or you?"

He pursed his lips, and when his gaze met hers, she knew the truth. "Declan, you can't do this to please Dad."

Staring at his feet, he muttered, "It's not only for Dad. It's the right thing for me."

Her chin began to quiver and she wrapped her arms around his neck, knowing she couldn't change his mind but wishing she could.

"Will you stay in touch? Promise?" she asked.

He unhooked her from around his neck, held her hands together, and stared into her eyes. "I'm your big brother. We will always stay in touch. I promise." He tightened his grip on her hands. "Understand?"

"Yes."

Those blue eyes never broke contact with hers. "There's a Gaelic phrase I want you to memorize."

She groaned. "More Gaelic?"

"It's a beautiful language," he said. "Don't groan at me."

"Okay. What is it?"

"Bí mar ghuth chan mar mhacalla."

She repeated it several times to get the pronunciation correct. "What's it mean?"

"Be a voice, not an echo. Always listen and find your own voice, Bree."

"I will. Thanks for today."

"Day's not over yet," he said, flashing a big smile. "I have a gift for you."

She blushed. "Getting me out of school and spending time with you was the best present ever. You didn't have to get me anything else."

He fumbled in his pocket. "It's something to remember me by, a means of knowing that I'm always watching out for you, and I'll always protect you."

She opened the jewelry case to find a silver Celtic cross.

"Declan—"

"Shh. Not another word," he had said, wrapping his arms around her. "Happy birthday, little sister."

"Brianna?"

She watched the trees continue to pass by.

"Brianna?" Steven repeated, bringing her back to the present.

"Sorry. Yes?"

"We're going to stop in Macon for lunch, and Dennis will take the next driving shift since he knows Atlanta traffic. Okay with you?"

"Yeah, sure," she said, leaving memories of Declan back along an endless stretch of highway.

###

Two hours later, they reached Atlanta's city limits just in time for bumper-to-bumper traffic. Dennis had warned them about Atlanta. The metro area didn't have a single rush hour, but rather, traffic crawled most of the day, with the rush hour lasting three hours.

Still, she wasn't going to complain. The elaborate skyline sparkled in the afternoon sun, and there were no ghosts nearby. Nobody bothering her. The perfect getaway.

"Where are we staying again?" she asked.

"The Peachtree Plaza," Dennis said.

"Ritzy," Steven said. "How'd you swing that for less than two hundred per night?"

"Our paper uses Westin for its conventions and other travel needs. They gave us a great deal."

"Sweet," Steven said.

After driving at five miles an hour for about fifty feet, Dennis pressed on the brake. "You're in for a treat, Brianna. They have a restaurant on the top that slowly rotates. Best view of the city. Maybe you and Steven can go up there for a drink after we see Piper. I plan to turn in early."

Turn in early? That would give her and Steven some alone time without constant Grayson ghosts in the background.

"Sounds good. I'm fine with whatever."

Steven had done the unimaginable—stuck around after she'd told him she exchanged conversations with the dead. She wanted to tell him about his family. Maybe later, after they gave Piper the files and the recording, she and Steven could spend some time talking—and other things. The thought turned her cheeks pink, and she ran her hands over her face to keep a cool head.

Twenty minutes later, they parked at the entry to the Peachtree Plaza. The building was cylindrical, all glass, and looked like a giant silo. Dennis checked them in—he and Steven in one room, her in the other.

The exquisite woodwork in the lobby, glass elevators, and ultramodern décor made her feel underdressed. She had no idea they'd be staying at someplace so nice. When Dennis handed her the room key, she was grateful for the chance to go settle in and change.

"Everyone meet here in the lobby in an hour? We'll go meet Piper," Dennis said.

"Sure," Brianna said and smiled at Steven. He gave a telling smile. Was he thinking the same thing as her, that spending some time alone in this romantic hotel would be a great item to add to their agenda?

An hour later, they went to the Midtown Plaza shopping center. They were scheduled to meet Piper at Après Diem, a local bistro in the back of the plaza. After parking, they walked past the open patio and into the darkened restaurant.

"Dennis, hi." The woman was young, blonde, and everything about her was sleek. Hair, red dress, Jimmy Choo pumps. She looked like someone who spent a lot of time in front of the camera.

"Piper," he said and gave her a polite hug. "Thanks again for meeting with us."

"I'm interested in this story. Let's have a seat and talk details."

Forty-five minutes later, Piper covered her ears. "I almost don't want to listen anymore. This guy Begley sounds like a real piece of work."

"He is," Dennis said. "He also tried to run Steven over."

Piper arched an eyebrow. "Tell me more."

They told her about Begley's recent stunts, his showing up at random hours in order to intimidate, and Brianna getting fired.

But the cremation slips Brianna had found at work, along with the Riordan hit-and-run story, was what really put a smile on Piper's face.

"I ran a story of a corrupt funeral home north of Atlanta several years ago," Piper said. "Greedy bastard was taking money to cremate bodies and instead left them in shallow graves on the property, left to rot. Terrible. The guy's in jail now."

"Do you think we have enough to expose Begley?" Dennis asked. "I've been working on this in my free time for years. The man needs to be taken off his pedestal."

Piper took a sip of her iced tea. "How come you're just coming to me now? Why not sooner? We've known each other for a while, met at the same industry events." She winked at him, seeming to say she'd be willing to be more than friends, if Dennis was interested.

Dennis remained so focused, he never got the hint. "I never had a source inside the funeral home before, didn't make that connection, until Brianna started telling us about the things going on. She also has a recording of Begley—"

"Right, the recording. Do you have it with you?" Piper asked. She'd reverted to her casual smile. She looked like she could get any guy she wanted, and if he didn't want to join her for some fun, she'd be just fine moving on with her life.

"Yes." Dennis, a tech junkie, had transferred the conversation to his computer and copied it to a pricey handheld digital recorder. He took the device out of his jacket pocket and handed it to her.

She pressed play and listened to the exchange. Brianna ate a bite of hummus on pita bread and watched the eclectic groups of hippies, yuppies, and youngsters walk across the patio and into the local cinema next door. She didn't need to relive that conversation with Begley again.

When Piper clicked stop, Brianna refocused her attention back to the table.

"A few things," Piper began. "Cases like this tend to elicit death threats, and it sounds like your Begley guy isn't above killing people for what he wants, so be careful."

"We already are doing that," Steven said, with Dennis nodding in agreement.

"Second, there's mention on the tape that Brianna broke into his office. Is that true?"

Damn, Brianna knew that decision would come back to haunt her. "Yes, but I didn't take anything. I jimmied the lock, looked at his files, put them back, and left."

"If charges are filed, we can likely get you to testify and tell your story. But we'll need to ensure you get immunity for the break-in."

"Okay." The conversation had turned surreal.

"What else?" Dennis asked, pen in hand. Ever the dedicated journalist.

“I have a feeling the feds will get Edwin to turn on Begley, testify against him for murder in return for a reduced sentence as an accessory. That’s the way the associate did it with that cremation case I told you about.”

“Edwin used to have a decent heart,” Brianna said. “He’s just stuck under Begley’s thumb.”

“Fair enough,” Piper said. “I’ll need to talk to my editor about this, the timing of the story. When we’re ready to run it, I’ll give you notice. However, no matter the timing, the situation won’t be pretty. All of you should think of an alternative place to stay until we get Begley behind bars.”

Alternative place to stay? Like where? The South Pole?

“We’ll figure something out,” Steven said. “Don’t worry.”

Brianna smiled. Learn to have a little faith. She needed that to become her mantra. Whatever happened in the weeks to follow, she and Steven could handle it—together.

CHAPTER THIRTY-SIX

Soul meets soul on lover's lips.
~ Percy Bysshe Shelly

Back in the hotel lobby, Dennis said, "I'm going to get out of y'alls hair and turn in early."

"You sure?" Steven asked. He didn't want Dennis to feel like a third wheel, not when he'd been such a huge help. "I wanted to show Brianna the rotating restaurant with the amazing city views. You're welcome to join us."

Dennis patted him once on the back, a gesture Steven understood. Steven wanted some time alone with Brianna, and Dennis wasn't going to stand in the way. All was right with the world.

"Nah, I'm good." Steven figured Dennis said it mainly for Brianna's benefit. "Y'all have fun."

"Thanks." Steven winked at Brianna. "Guess it's just the two of us."

Her neck blushed pink. He loved how her body responded to him, even when they remained fully clothed. How would she respond without clothes? If she was willing, he was more than ready to find out.

"I need a few minutes to wash my face," she said. "Why don't you come by my room in twenty?"

“Will do.” He followed her into the elevator, where they were alone, and pressed the button.

Once the doors shut, he cornered her, putting one arm on either side of her body. “You know, Aerosmith has this great song—”

“Love in an Elevator,” she said, her blue eyes practically begging for him to kiss her.

“Right,” he said, grinning wide. “You know your music.”

The doors opened and he held her hand as they walked down the hallway to their rooms. With Dennis crashing in their room early, maybe he could—at least for a while—stay in Brianna’s? He didn’t want to assume. Wait and see how the night goes. If she was up for it, he was.

“See you in twenty.” He brushed his lips to hers, leaving her with a brief kiss for now. There would be more on the menu later.

She’d opened up, told him her secrets, and trusted him completely. He hadn’t sensed any distance or backing away on her part since that day. Yes, now that he thought about it, the feeling stirring inside him had risen to his heart. He’d fallen for this beautiful Irish lass and wanted to make love to her.

###

Brianna applied a bit more lavender eye shadow to her brow arch and curled her eyelashes. She’d chosen a dark-blue cocktail dress, something she’d ordered online that, miraculously, had fit.

Rarely did she go all out with the hair, makeup, lipstick, and jewelry. But tonight wouldn't be spent with the dead. She'd spend it with Steven, wonderfully alive and caring Steven.

First, she'd have to tell her one last secret—that his family remained in her house, and she talked to them. A lot.

Steven wanted to show her the rotating restaurant upstairs. She could tell him then. Hmm, maybe not in a public place. He could freak out. Maybe she should wait until they were alone. Yes. Better plan.

Twenty minutes later, she opened the door to find his eyes flickering. His gaze roamed from her head to her toes and back again. Exactly the reaction she'd hoped for.

"You look beautiful," he said.

Her cheeks went hot. "Thanks. You look great too."

He did, with a dark-green shirt that brought out the seafoam green in his eyes.

"C'mon," he said, reaching to clasp her hand in his. "You're going to love the view of the Atlanta skyline."

###

Steven brushed his fingers into the small of her back as they walked to a table for two. The rotating restaurant with 360-degree views of Atlanta had tables set against the floor-to-ceiling windows.

"Can I offer you something to drink?" the hostess asked.

Brianna paused a moment, seeming unsure what to order. He leapt at the opportunity.

"Do you like champagne?" he asked.

Those ruby lips of hers curled into a smile. "Yes, though I haven't had it in a long time."

"Good. This one," Steven said, pointing to the drink selection.

"I'll be right back," the hostess said, taking the menus out of their way.

"Champagne, a beautiful view…holy cow, an amazing view," Brianna said, her face fixated on the glittering buildings at sunset.

He glanced out the window briefly but returned his gaze to her. "I agree. Beautiful and amazing."

It took her a few seconds to get his double-meaning, and when she did, she folded her hands in her lap and blushed. So damn cute and sexy at the same time.

"I figured we should celebrate," he said. "If things go as planned, Begley will soon be behind bars. Dennis and I might get our gig at the Brickhouse Tavern, I can return to my music. You can get reinstated or even run Restful Oaks if you wanted."

Brianna's eyes widened. "I hope all those things happen, and running Restful Oaks would be a dream, even if I had to hire someone until I get my license as funeral director."

The hostess brought a silver bucket with champagne on ice and two flutes. She popped the cork—how did they do that without it flying everywhere?—and poured their champagne.

"To a new start," Steven said. *Be brave, man. Say the words*. "To us."

She touched her glass to his. "To us."

###

Brianna fidgeted with her room card, but when Steven put his arms around her waist from behind and kissed her earlobe, she almost dropped it. The signal flashed red instead of green. She missed the simplicity and speed of regular keys. There wasn't time to argue with a sliding card. The connection between her and Steven had only grown stronger over champagne, and she wanted to be alone with him—now.

Steven's breath blew hot and musky on her neck. "Just slide it slowly."

In her stomach, butterflies swirled and fluttered, sending heat between her legs. She wanted him to slide into *her* slowly.

Finally, the light on the door lock turned green. They tumbled inside, his lips on hers.

Her purse fell to the carpet at her feet. His woodsy aftershave smelled new and erotic, like they were outdoors in a forest instead of in a high-rise hotel. In seconds, they stood at the foot of the bed, with the night's twinkling skyline as a backdrop.

He released her lips for a second, slowing the pace. With the tender hands he used to make music, he traced the sides of her cheeks, her neck, her breasts. Her nipples hardened instantly, and he took one between his thumb and forefinger, massaging it and sending wet pleasure between her legs. His touch was like electricity and flowed to parts of her body she hadn't awakened in a long, long time.

He cupped her flushed face in his hands. The passion in his glance, the light touch of his fingers, sent quivers of desire hurtling through her entire body. Even her toes curled, and she kicked off her shoes.

Bliss. This is what true bliss felt like.

"Thank you for trusting me and being honest," he whispered.

His breath smelled like cool peppermint, and she wanted to taste him.

"I know you haven't been ready until recently," he said.

Shit. She'd meant to tell him about his family, but she'd been…distracted.

"Steven, I need to tell you something—"

He wrapped his hands around her waist. "Don't worry. I'm okay with who you are, and I'm not going anywhere. Now kiss me."

"But—"

"Shh," he said, grinning as he planted his lips on hers. "Kiss me."

Okay. She could always tell him first thing in the morning. For now, she'd kiss every inch of his body, revel in his touch, and share a beautiful night.

"Lift your arms," he whispered, and he slowly slid her dress off and set it on a chair. He ran his finger along the sweetheart neckline of her black lace bra and unhooked it with expert skill, the dexterity of a man who'd coaxed beautiful melodies from a guitar. Damn, she loved musicians.

She unbuttoned his shirt, releasing each button one by one. When she'd pulled his shirt away from his well-muscled chest, he leaned in and took one of her nipples into his mouth, sucking it. His tongue was firm, circling the nipple clockwise, then in reverse, until she began to moan.

"I think you should get off your feet," he said. "You're trembling."

She nodded, unable to formulate a response. He kicked off his slacks, revealing the magnificent attraction he felt for her, and followed her onto the bed.

On top of her, he looked deep into her eyes and brushed a few hairs off her face. The weight of his body on top of hers felt amazing.

"You're beautiful, Brianna. My beautiful Irish lass."

Holy moly. She was in for the ride of her life.

Steven couldn't believe how responsive Brianna was. The woman blushed and trembled at his slightest touch. He'd never known anyone to do that before—or to moan precisely when she liked something. Sweet muffled noises when he tickled her, long groans coming from deep inside when he excited her.

The trust in her eyes only amplified his desire. He reached for her breast and massaged it while offering tiny kisses to her neck.

"Steven, my sweet incredible Steven," she murmured.

"Like that?"

"Hmm…"

He reached for her other breast to give it its due attention. Heaven forbid he ignore any part of Brianna's responsive body. He had to give equal time and didn't mind one bit.

Kissing her neck and down to her stomach, he could smell jasmine after a summer rain. This was a woman he wanted to lay naked next to her for many rainstorms to come.

He let his fingers graze down her stomach and between her eager legs. She moaned, and he continued to stroke her, tease her, and make music with this incredible woman's body.

He wanted her. Now.

When he arched his body away from hers for a split second, she whimpered. God, she was adorable even when she whimpered.

“Shh, just getting protection in place,” he said.

Her mouth curled into a sweet smile. With her head on the pillow, she looked up at him with eager eyes, trusting eyes. He could swim in those baby blues forever.

“Please? I want you inside me,” she said.

Hot damn. He pressed his body on top of hers, and when he slowly entered her, she moaned with pleasure.

Brianna gripped Steven’s hair as she pulled him deeper into her. Oh my heaven. She’d missed how sensual making love could be. His hot arousal thrusting deep into her made every worry, every care she had in the world, fade from sight. Every inch of her skin tingled with desire ignited by his touch.

He’d brought her senses back to life, revived them like old sheet music found in a drawer. And boy, did he ever know how to play her body—better than any instrument, she was absolutely certain. Hard, rhythmic, and satisfying every part of her soul.

As they both reached the height of their passion, she moaned his name and wrapped her arms around him, this man of her dreams.

CHAPTER THIRTY-SEVEN

The only reason for time is so that everything doesn't happen at once.
~ Albert Einstein

Brianna yawned and glanced out at the latest exit sign. They were almost to Savannah, almost home. The road trip to Atlanta had been fantastic. Last night with Steven, especially.

She'd planned to tell him about his family first thing, but they'd overslept. The drive back to Atlanta hadn't worked either. When musicians got together, all they talked about were amps, strings, chords, and lyrics. She'd slept in the back for most of the ride.

Her cell phone chirped. "Hello?"

No one was there, only harsh static.

"Hello?"

Click.

"Who was it?" Steven asked.

"Nobody. Just static and a hang up."

Steven's brows furrowed. "Maybe it's a coincidence, but we all need to be on our guard the next few days. Who knows what kind of spies Begley has on us. Hell, he knew where I'd be walking when he almost hit me."

"Agreed, brother," Dennis said. "Piper's supposed to call me today or tomorrow with an update." He pulled off at the Martin Luther King Jr. exit to head to the historic district.

As they drove down Bay, back home amid oak trees instead of pines, Brianna tried to figure out the best way to get Steven alone. After their intimacy last night, she couldn't keep the truth to herself any longer.

Dennis's cell phone rang in the center console.

"Caller ID says Piper," Steven said. "Pull over in front of Churchill's. You'll need your full concentration."

Dennis parked the car. "Yeah, Piper, what's up?"

Brianna and Steven listened and waited.

"Really? Great news," Dennis said, giving them a thumbs-up. "Oh, so soon? Yes, I'll let them know…right…I understand…yes, e-mail me…thanks…bye."

"Well?" Steven asked. "What'd she say?"

"She reached her GBI contact and they're going to question Edwin and Margie tomorrow."

"That soon?" Brianna asked. "Aren't cases like these supposed to take time?" She hadn't expected the Georgia Bureau of Investigation to jump on board immediately.

"Apparently the GBI friend owes her a favor from the previous cremation case they worked on. The GBI will build a case, with a promise for Piper to release the story. Your recording with Begley bragging about his crimes kicked this into motion, Brianna. That's the one thing I never had for all these years."

Steven's admiring glance sent warmth into her cheeks. "See, you are making a difference," he said.

His words were like music, a beautiful song meant for her heart alone. Her cheek muscles began to ache from the smile she couldn't wipe off her face. She'd kept her promise. Nothing could stop her now.

CHAPTER THIRTY-EIGHT

We love to dance, especially that new one called the Civil War Twist.
The Northern part of you stands still while the Southern part tries to secede.
~ Dick Gregory

After unpacking and settling back into her house, she proceeded with the next important mission: giving Plato numerous belly rubs. Snuffling sounds filled the den as he wiggled under her hands. Silly dog was ticklish but adored belly rubs. Go figure.

"How'd the trip go?" James asked. He relaxed in the recliner, of course.

"Things are moving along. I think you'll be free from this house before you know it."

She filled in the Graysons about the trip, omitting the part about her romantic night with Steven. Some things were best left unsaid.

"Steven remains…safe?"

"Yes, but we're being careful. We're meeting for a walk along River Street tonight. It'll be crowded enough with the tourists, so we'll be fine. Thanks for your concern though."

Virginia appeared, her nose wriggling. Probably a nervous habit she didn't even realize she had. "There's a lot of 'we' talk in that sentence."

"We talk?"

“We this, we that. What are your intentions with my son?” Naturally, she sat right next to Brianna on the sofa.

“Virginia,” James said. “This isn’t our business.”

“Yes it is,” Virginia said. “I appreciate your help, Brianna, but a serious relationship with my son—”

“You have a problem with me?” Brianna asked.

What the hell did this woman want? For Brianna to crawl back into the womb and be born south of the Mason-Dixon Line?

Virginia sighed. “Despite the obvious culture differences, which I’m willing to overlook, I don’t like how you’ve been withholding from Steven. You need to tell him about us.”

A jagged pain gripped her insides. She hated to admit it, but Virginia was right. Brianna hadn’t been fully honest—not even after they’d made love in Atlanta.

“You’re right. I’ll tell him.”

“When?”

“Tonight. I need to leave now, but I’ll invite him back after dinner. I don’t want to do it in public because if he should become upset—”

“Upset you haven’t told the whole truth? Oh, you betcha. This mess is going to blow up in your face.”

“Virginia,” James said. “Please.”

“It’s okay,” Brianna said. “I hate to admit it, but she’s right.”

Virginia's eyes beamed with glee. "Well, Yankee, you're not so dumb after all."

CHAPTER THIRTY-NINE

I sat alone in the emptiness, watching the storm passing by.
Dreams of a river were haunting me. I was tossed like a leaf on the tide.
~ Vertigo Rising by Roger Drawdy

"Damn it all to hell!"

Declan's throat ached from screaming. He hated being this helpless, unable to protect Brianna, unable to even talk to her. Cussing was all he *could* do. It didn't solve anything, but it sure as hell felt better.

Mighty mentor Connell had blocked him from any contact with Brianna or those in her life, including Begley. Only Riordan could give and send messages—a damn rookie.

And where was this protective rookie? Nowhere to be found. Not even now, when Begley knelt beside Brianna's Jetta with C4 and a detonator in his hand.

Why had Brianna taken her car anyway? He'd seen her go toward River Street. Why not walk? Or why didn't this guy she was dating pick her up in his car?

Declan slammed his fist into a massive oak and screamed once more.

No response, not even a slight breeze. Maybe he should try another way. He would try anything at this point—whatever would save his sister's life.

"Connell, sir, I know you have the ability to hear me. Please, I'm begging you. Get a message to Brianna. Have Riordan—or someone—draw a Celtic cross on her car window. Draw it, spray-paint it, I don't care. Just make it a Celtic cross. She'll know that means me, and it means my promise to protect her."

Declan waited, but the silence that followed was almost deafening.

CHAPTER FORTY

Three things cannot be long hidden: the sun, the moon, and the truth.
~ Buddha

Brianna stabbed her salad with her fork and dipped it in a side dressing of vinaigrette. Steven had met her at River House, a renowned seafood and steak restaurant on the west end of River Street.

She wanted one nice date together before she told him the truth. The truth that might send him running, though he'd surprised her by not fleeing when she'd told him about conversing with the dead. Maybe he would understand once he knew he could talk with his family with her help.

Or maybe he would be really angry.

An hour and a half later, Steven walked her to the square where she'd parked her car. She reached for her keys and—

"What the hell?"

"What?" Steven asked.

"That," she said, pointing to the finger-drawn Celtic cross in her foggy driver window. She spun around, looking in all directions. No one was nearby. But how could this be?

"We need to get out of here," she said, forcing herself to remain calm. Right now, the nausea and her nerves were so intense, she wanted to throw up.

“What are you talking about?” Steven asked. “I don’t see anything.”

I’m not crazy. “It’s a signal from Declan.”

“Brianna, I think you’re under a lot of stress—”

“Just trust me and do what I say,” she said, not hiding her impatience with his doubt.

Steven narrowed his eyes, but at least he paid attention.

“Back up a few feet and then run like hell into the square. Get as close to the oaks as you can. They’re sturdy and can protect us. On three, okay?”

“Okay.”

“One two three!”

She grabbed his hand. Channeling every ounce of energy available, she raced away as fast as she could.

Before they could reach the nearest oak tree, her car exploded into a fiery mass, the powerful shock wave knocking them both onto the cold, hard ground.

###

“Brianna?”

The voice was familiar, but not Steven’s. Who was it?

She tried to open her eyes but her eyelids felt like they were weighted down with cinder blocks. A pounding ache loomed in her forehead. Had someone kicked her in the teeth? She lay flat on her back. The last time she felt anything close to this was in the fourth grade, when Jenny O'Hare pushed her ten feet off the jungle gym.

A foggy male voice spoke. "You need to kill that fucking bastard for me, Riordan. You know I'm not allowed to go near anything in her life."

Wait a second. She knew who Riordan was, but who else was here? The voice wasn't Steven's. So who was it? The cops? Doubtful. Begley owned so many.

Riordan's calm Irish accent returned, though he didn't seem to be speaking to her. "She got away in time. Be glad she finally accepted her gift and listened to things most don't understand."

"Hell is too frigid for that greedy son of a bitch. I'll snap his damn neck without a second thought," the voice said.

Fog lingered and thoughts disconnected, like trying to remember a dream, but she knew the second voice. In her head, her heart, she couldn't quite place where she knew it from.

"Brianna?" the voice asked.

"Hmm?" She blinked fast to help open her eyes. When she did, all she saw were blurry shapes.

"How do you feel?" the voice said. "Please tell me you're okay. Please."

"I'm…foggy. Can someone sit me up?" she asked.

“Not yet,” Riordan said. “We need to keep you still. Do you remember anything?”

Remember? Thoughts. Blurry figures. Loud sounds. “Not really.”

“Tell her,” the voice said.

“You know there are rules to this,” Riordan said.

“Where the hell were you when we could’ve stopped him? I promised to protect her.”

Wait a second. That voice couldn’t possibly be—Declan? Impossible, right?

“You’re upset and I understand, but you know how this works. She has to defeat Begley on her own.”

“What the—?” she asked.

“Brianna,” Riordan said, his Irish accent warm and familiar. “Your car exploded. You managed to get away from the car, but the explosion—”

“Steven. Where is Steven?”

“He’s fine,” Riordan said. “He’s banged up but we’ve checked him. He’ll be awake any second now.”

“Get home. Lock your doors,” Riordan said.

“But what about Declan?” Her head continued to pound.

“Shh,” a voice said.

“What?” She pressed her arm to her forehead and opened her eyes. “Steven?”

“Hey, it’s me. You’re okay. Dennis is coming to bring you home.”

“Right…” Her eyes closed again.

“I don’t know how you knew back there, but—”

“I told you. I talk to ghosts. Declan left a sign on my car. I’ll never doubt my gift again. Steven, there’s something I need to tell you—”

“Shh. Wait until we get you home.”

###

After dealing with the fire and police departments, Dennis drove Brianna and Steven back to her house. Dennis managed to get photos of their scrapes and bruises and her car, and he’d sent everything to Piper, who’d promised she’d forward the info to the GBI.

“You sure you don’t need me to stay?” Dennis asked.

“Nah, we’re good. I’ll call you later. Right now I just want to stay with her for a while, make sure she’s okay.”

Time alone with Steven—well, time alone with Steven and his entire family.

At least her head had stopped doing the conga. For now. Steven had settled her onto the living room couch.

“Steven,” she said. “I need to tell you something.”

“Shh.” He went to the kitchen and returned with a cold cloth. The man was too sweet. She hoped he would understand what she was about to tell him.

"We have to talk," she said.

"Okay. I'm here. I'm listening." He reached out and held her hand.

Damn, this was difficult. Push the words out. She had to tell him. James, Virginia, and Amy stood along the back wall, keeping Plato occupied near his crate.

"Do you remember when I told you I could see and talk to ghosts?" Brianna asked.

"Yes."

"Tell him," James said. "He might be upset, but he'll come to see it's a good thing."

She wanted to believe James, but the man didn't know his own son in so many ways. How could he be so sure on something like this?

Best to blurt out the truth fast, like yanking off a Band-Aid. It may hurt like the dickens for a minute, but the pain doesn't linger.

She shut her eyes tight. "The ghosts of your family still live here, and they've been talking to me since I moved in. It's like I've had three houseguests all this time."

There. She'd told him.

Silence, except the slow tick, tick from the clock. Not a word out of Steven, but he released her hand. Crap. This wasn't good.

She kept her eyes closed for a second more. Opening them would mean seeing his reaction—and she wasn't sure she was ready.

Just do it.

She opened her eyes—and saw the glazed, wide-eyed terror in his.

"What the hell are you talking about? I thought maybe you were just a little confused when you told me about this gift of yours, but now you're claiming to be best buds with my parents and my sister? That's more than confused. That's screwed up."

He backed away from her, putting at least a two-foot distance between them on the couch. The withdrawal along with his words—*screwed up*—sent a throbbing pain into her heart.

"Please just listen—"

"To what? To how you've decided to mess with my head? We almost got killed tonight, and you're telling me about my family? You don't know anything about my family."

"I know more than you can imagine," she whispered. "Your mother is named Virginia. She sings off tune when she wants something, or to get her way."

Steven shot her a cold stare. "How do you know that?"

"I told you," she said. "I talk to ghosts. They talk back. I used to think it was a curse, but look at how it saved us tonight. That Celtic cross was a symbol. Declan said it would always keep me protected. It was too specific to not be from him."

"Your point?"

“My point is, because I finally starting accepting that I can see and hear ghosts, we didn’t die in a fiery explosion tonight.”

“What does that have to do with my family? You’re saying they’re here now?” He stood up and pointed around the room with large gestures. “Well, gee. What are they doing?”

Brianna glanced over to the Graysons, who all seemed as surprised by Steven’s outburst as she’d been. For once, they were tight lipped.

“They’re standing by the back wall, near Plato.”

Steven shook his head. “I can’t believe this. I thought I could handle this, but—”

“Please, I know it’s scary. Believe me, I’ve been there. But your dad James smokes pipes that smell like cranberry and roses, your sister Amy loves and misses you—”

With a chilling glare, Steven leaned over, inches from Brianna’s face. “You, of all people, know what it’s like to lose a sibling. I would never play with your mind like this.”

“I’m not. I swear.”

He shook his head, exuding disbelief. “You know, my mother taught me how to be kind to a woman when I was only three years old, but she never, ever taught me how to deal with something like this.”

“Look, we’ve both had a long day. Why don’t we just call it a night and talk more tomorrow?”

"No, I'm sorry," he said, a frown replacing his usual smile. "I don't think I can handle this. I don't know anyone who could."

With a nod, he grabbed his jacket and left.

CHAPTER FORTY-ONE

After a good dinner one can forgive anybody,
even one's own relations.
~ Oscar Wilde

Steven's head pounded as he walked away from Brianna's place. Damn it, why was he even calling the house hers? His family had lived there and should still live there. Now Brianna claimed their *ghosts* were living there?

An aching thought nagged at him. Could she have been more injured in the explosion than he'd thought? A concussion maybe? He'd assumed she'd been playing mind games, but maybe she hadn't. Oh god. If she wasn't playing games with him, he'd just been the world's biggest jerk.

Too many thoughts churned through his mind. He needed to take an aspirin and focus. The next few days were crucial to getting Begley behind bars. This wasn't the time to go all pensive. It was time to be on full alert.

He walked a few blocks before stopping to gather his thoughts. He sat on one of the squares, watching a clump of tourists take a walking ghost tour.

Ghosts. He didn't believe in psychics or fortune-tellers who wore bad scarves and ugly earrings. The paranormal was just too…paranormal.

Was Brianna messing with his mind or just his heart?

###

Brianna used her cold compress to wipe down her face after Steven left. "Gee, that went well."

"He'll come around," James said. "With the occasional overreaction comes a great passion for life, for his music. I was too blind to see it, many years ago, but I see it now."

She arched an eyebrow. Did James think the last few minutes were a good thing?

"I see that passion for life when he looks at you, Brianna," James said.

James's tender words reached into the most broken, jagged piece of her heart. She wiped away the tears spilling from her eyes.

"You're very sweet," she said, "but I think Steven has gone for good."

"That's crazy," Amy said. "He gets angry sometimes. He'll be back, honest."

Brianna liked to think so, but Amy was young, naive. "You don't understand. Men run the fifty-yard dash and keep going when they get to know the real me. Only difference is, Steven hung around a lot longer than most."

"He's a good man," Virginia said. "Despite what he said, I *did* teach him how to deal with all sorts of situations. A Southern gentleman adapts."

Brianna smiled and the corner of her lips tasted a salty tear. "You raised a wonderful man. I hope he can eventually accept this part of me, because this…thing, this gift, is my worst secret. I promise I have nothing else to hide."

Amy sat at her feet, giving Plato a belly rub. "Steven and I were close, but I always wanted a big sister, too. He'll come back. Sometimes he just needs to be alone, but he'll return. Wait and see."

Brianna wasn't so sure, but the thing she became clear on was how far she'd come in such a short time. Looking from James's distinguished face to Virginia's stubborn expression to Amy's young beauty, Brianna saw something new. They weren't just ghosts trapped in her house. They were like a new family, one she could depend on. These ghosts accepted who she was and needed her to help them.

If only Steven felt that way too.

CHAPTER FORTY-TWO

Vision is the art of seeing things invisible.
~ Jonathan Swift

Brianna thrashed about under the sheets, but sleep wouldn't come. Too many thoughts, too many images of Steven's handsome face, all raced through her mind.

Had the Graysons been right in their assessment? Maybe Steven had overreacted. After all, finding out she heard and spoke to ghosts would be freaky enough—but that she'd been talking to his dead family? The guy had a right to be a little wigged out.

But freaking out a little doesn't mean abandoning all hope for a relationship, especially with both their lives in danger. Steven had been about more than a handsome face, a sexy whisper. He'd been something she'd always yearned for but could never find—a soulful connection.

Plato whimpered and pawed at her foot. Normally, she didn't let him sleep on the bed. He tossed and turned like crazy, but given the recent events, she felt safer with him near her.

"I can't sleep. Do you need to go out?"

He barked and hopped off the bed. Guess so.

She pulled on a thick terry-cloth robe and put on his leash. Winter was almost here, and she didn't want to freeze outside in her pj's. The closer she walked to the back door, the more Plato spun around and bounced.

"C'mon," she said. "Let's go."

The night was calm but not as cold as she'd expected. Hydrangea blooms made the air smell sweet, and melancholy fiddle notes floated in the occasional breeze. Plato sniffed and walked, always wanting to find the precise spot to pee.

Clutching his leash, she looked up at the vast, starry sky. Something else twinkled, to her left. Fireflies at this hour? She tugged on Plato's leash and walked toward the lights, then stopped short.

"Riordan?"

What was he doing here? The lights weren't fireflies at all but were the moonlight's reflection on his guitar's tuning knobs.

Plato barked a greeting and rolled in the grass, lavishing nature's smells.

"I wanted to check on you," he said. "You dodged quite a bullet tonight."

She didn't have the energy to make polite chitchat. She wanted to be honest. "I'm feeling pretty lousy, to tell you the truth."

Riordan began to play his guitar, upbeat and comforting notes. "The truth is always better."

"Not really."

He stopped playing and watched her intently, as if trying to figure out what made her tick. "Why would you say that?"

She loosened her grip on the leash, giving Plato some room to walk. "I told Steven the truth and he bolted. I told the truth about Begley, and tonight my car exploded. Tell me, how exactly is the truth always better?"

"Because the truth is real. Lies aren't."

"I get your point," she said. "But what happens when the truth scares off the one man I can connect with?"

"Better than lying about who you are. Why fool yourself by being in a relationship and thinking he accepts you, when he doesn't even know the *real* you?"

She wondered if Riordan had been this astute when he was alive. "So, what should I do?" He continued to pick an Irish tune and avoided her pleading expression. "Maybe tonight's explosion, while dangerous, is supposed to be a catalyst for you. Maybe the point of all this is to not give up." He winked at her. "You may be surprised at what you find."

"Keep the faith, like Declan always said. Right?"

Riordan's eyes glowed. "Exactly."

She took a resolved breath. "Well, I have to keep something, because I think Begley's going to try to kill me again."

CHAPTER FORTY-THREE

Memory is the diary that we all carry about with us.
~ Oscar Wilde

Steven fiddled with the Band-Aid he'd finally put on the world's worst paper cut. As he replayed his conversation with Brianna in his mind—she not only claimed to converse with the dead, but she'd talked with his *family*—the Band-Aid took on a mesmerizing quality. He rolled up the edge. He smoothed it back down. Lifted up the cotton pad section to let air flow, and pressed it back down. Over and over.

"Brother, what's eating you?" Dennis said. He sat in the recliner and Steven could feel Dennis's eyes on him as he paced around the living room.

Steven gave a half shrug. How could he explain the truth, even to a journalist who seeks out the truth?

"Brianna may not be the woman I thought she was," Steven said. "She started playing games with my head."

"Thought you said she wasn't the type. That's what you liked about her."

"I didn't think she was," Steven said. "But she told me a huge stack of things which couldn't possibly be true." He ran his hands through his hair, wishing he could brush away all the bad memories. "I think it's time to just cut my losses where she's concerned. See Begley gets justice and then I'm done."

Dennis walked to the fridge, pulled out some bottled water, and handed one to him. "Getting out of town, as per usual?" Steven stopped pacing.

The comment, while certainly true, stung more than expected. "Meaning?"

"Do you want some hard truth, man?" Dennis sat on the couch and waited for a response.

"Uh, I think you're about to give me some whether I want it or not."

"I won't if you don't want to hear it," Dennis said. "But you need to hear it. It's best to hear it from a friend."

Steven guzzled some water and replaced the cap. "Go ahead."

"You run away too much."

"Wow. Nothing like honesty to slap a friend across the face."

"I'm a journalist. I don't dance around the truth," Dennis said, flashing a smile. "And you've run away ever since we were kids. First, you left Savannah. Then you travelled so much up and down the California coast that no one could keep up with you, not even me."

Steven's mouth went dry at his friend's blatant words. He reached for more water. "You don't understand—"

"Yes, I do. Anytime things got too complicated, you took off to start something new, be it a woman or a gig. You never stuck around to see things through when things got tough. I think you're making the same mistake with Brianna."

Steven didn't say anything for a minute. Dennis's words were harsh but true. But would Dennis stick around if some woman did this to him?

"Brianna is different—"

"Yes, you told me. So work through it. Give her a chance before you take off again. I hate to see you spend your whole life running. I know it comes natural, man, but damn it, I've missed seeing you all these years."

His buddy had a point. "I wouldn't say I miss everything about the South, but I have missed jamming with you."

"Good enough," Dennis said. "Now, one more thing I want to say."

There was more? There was already enough truth in the room to repel politicians for a decade.

He braced himself. "Go ahead."

"You need to make amends. I know it's too late to talk to your family, but write them a letter to say all the things you need to get off your chest. Do something. You survived. They didn't. And survivor's guilt sucks."

"Tell me about it," Steven said. "I carry on through all these incidents, yet my loved ones don't get the chance. What the hell is that about?"

"I don't know, man. But if I had to take a stab at it, I'd say you need to make amends with your past and move forward. Stop letting those memories choke you out of something good. You told me Brianna understood you more than anyone."

She does. He nodded.

"Then work through all this shit so you can give things with her a chance."

"I don't know where to start," Steven said. "It's too late to call her now."

Dennis arched an eyebrow. "It's not too late on the West Coast."

"West Coast? For what?"

"Call your old band leader. Tell him you're sorry his sister was killed."

"Tyler? He'd hang up on me within a second," Steven said.

"You can't control his reaction, only your actions. You've lost Amy. He lost his little sister, too. Offer your condolences. You'll feel better."

Steven cracked a half smile. "Since when did you become the Zen master of redemption?"

Dennis didn't smile, didn't laugh. "I was in a twelve-step program. Gambling had a pretty tight grip on me."

"I…I didn't know."

“Not many do,” Dennis said. “But the twelve steps make a lot of sense. So call your old band leader. It doesn’t matter how Tyler responds. What matters is, you made the effort. Then talk to Brianna tomorrow. You’ll be fine. I know you will.”

Steven gripped the water bottle and swirled the liquid around. “Been a long time since someone’s been this honest, man. I can’t say I liked everything you said, but thanks.”

Dennis handed him the phone. “What are friends for?”

CHAPTER FORTY-FOUR

Guilt has very quick ears to an accusation.
~ Henry Fielding

The next morning, Brianna poured herself a second cup of coffee. Today held double danger and she needed double caffeine.

After taking the first sip, someone knocked on her door. Great. Had Begley shown up to kill her before she even finished her coffee? Relax. He wouldn't be so stupid as to come to her house to kill her—would he? Then again, he'd killed the Graysons in their own home.

Best to be prepared, as the Scout motto said. She grabbed the butcher knife and looked through the door's peephole.

Steven?

Hope fluttered in her chest, sending her heartbeat into a rhythm all its own. Could it be? The Graysons were right. He was back to say he'd overreacted and he'd accept her for all her eccentricities.

No. Don't get the hopes up. He may be stopping by with an update from Dennis. Stay cool, stay reserved.

She opened the door and used her warmest voice. "Good morning. Want some coffee?"

"Sure."

He didn't seem surprised at her friendly demeanor, but he'd been raised in the South. People here gave reverence to the chitchat tradition, even though they'd argued the night before.

Amy stopped playing with Plato and walked into the kitchen. "Ask him if he wants his coffee with part half-and-half, part milk, and a smidge of cinnamon."

Brianna raised an eyebrow.

"Just do it."

Brianna pulled out the ingredients from the fridge, grabbed the cinnamon from the spice rack, and set everything on the counter.

"Would you like these for your coffee?" she asked.

His big green eyes widened and he gawked at the three condiments. "I haven't had coffee like that since I was seventeen."

Amy's expression beamed with pride. "Tell him it's a Steven special."

Okay. Let's see if this works.

"I hear it's a Steven special," Brianna said, watching for his response. Would he believe her now? Such a unique mixture for homemade coffee, rather than the holiday Starbucks special, couldn't be something she could've guessed.

His eyes narrowed to suspicious slits. "How could you possibly know that? I made it up. The only other person who knew what it was called was—"

"Amy," Brianna said.

His lips pursed to a thin line. "Amy," he repeated.

"I tried to tell you—"

"No." He grabbed the milk and pushed the other ingredients away. "I can't accept that my sister's ghost lives here and talks to you. There has to be a logical explanation."

She curled her lips into a smile.

"Something funny?" he asked as he pulled out a barstool and sat at the counter.

"Just your mention of needing a logical explanation," she said. "I used to tell myself the same thing until I met your parents. Eventually, it became healthier to accept who I am rather than running from something real." She sat on the second barstool down from him. Maybe a little distance was a good idea right now.

"My parents?" he asked. "Changed you?"

Brianna sprinkled Splenda into her coffee. "They've done much more. While annoying at first—your mother can't sing worth a damn—eventually, they grew on me."

He stared, not saying a word. Then he picked up the coffee mug and drank.

Maybe she was pushing the issue. Change the subject.

"So, any updates from Dennis?" she asked.

His shoulders seemed to relax at the mention of persons other than ghosts. "Yes. Piper's GBI contact is in town. They're interviewing Edwin this morning. I wanted to come by and make sure you were safe."

"Thanks, I appreciate it."

The sweet, concerned soul she fell in love with still lurked behind the cautious exterior. There was hope.

"Dennis thinks Begley learned the GBI was in town. That's why he panicked and set the bomb on your car."

"How would Begley know the GBI arrived?"

Steven shrugged. "Begley likely has a whole spy network on his payroll. I'm guessing whichever bellboy helped the GBI with luggage is the one who called Begley to give him the heads-up."

She took the last, delicious swallow of coffee. "There's no end to all his connections, all his lookouts, is there? He's got his greedy hands in everything."

"Only for a short time longer," Steven said. "Listen, I know I freaked out last night and said some things. I'm sorry."

The butterflies in her stomach danced once again. She and Steven were okay.

In the den, Virginia and Amy lifted their arms in turn, doing the wave. Brianna smiled. They'd been right all along.

"I'm sorry for not being fully honest with you," she said. "So, what do we do now?"

Steven set his coffee cup in the sink. "For today, stick together. Begley will be after both of us. He probably knows Edwin will roll over on him, and our testimony will only hurt his case further."

"I'd planned to take Plato to River Street. They're having a festival of some kind. Supposed to be tons of food and people, and I figured safe because it's so public."

Steven glanced around the room. "Probably safer than being a sitting duck here."

"Agreed."

James sat in a nearby chair, listening to their conversation. She'd tried to block them out while talking to Steven. Sometimes it worked and other times it didn't. Privacy with three ghosts in the house was difficult to come by.

"Tell him once Begley is arrested, we'll be free," James said. "I want time to talk to my son. I'm not sure how much time we'll have to spend together."

Oh boy. How was she supposed to convey this message without Steven freaking out again?

"Listen, Steven," she began. *Use the logical voice. Be comforting.* "After Begley's caught, your family says they'll be free to leave. They've been trapped in the house since the murder—"

"Brianna, don't go there," Steven said.

"But I—"

"I know I freaked out last night, but I can't believe what you told me. I refuse to."

Refuse to? His adamant denial only spurred more questions. What was he afraid of? So she talked to his family all this time. Yes, she'd omitted that detail in her confession. But did that warrant the extreme denial beaming off him like a gigantic spotlight?

"Tell me why you *refuse* to believe me. I can accept if you don't believe in ghosts. All relationships have their agree-to-disagree aspects."

"Good to know," he said, smirking. "Because I don't believe you."

"I disagree," she said. "I think part of you wants to, because you're so hell-bent on *not* believing me. Why?"

"Because it's crazy," Steven blurted out. Realizing he'd misspoken, he lowered his voice. "My parents and my sister were burned to death. They're gone. Dead."

"I'm so sorry for what happened to your family," Brianna said.

His chin started to tremble and he turned away from her.

"You have a chance to make peace with them," she said. "As strange as you may think I am, not many people get the opportunity to make peace with their dead loved ones. I want to help."

I want to make a difference.

He turned around, and she saw a rebel tear forming in his eye. "What makes you think I deserve to get any peace?"

She arched a knowing eyebrow. "You blame yourself for a fire Begley caused?"

He shoved his hands into his pockets. "No, but I shouldn't have left town without looking back. I didn't even know my own sister was dead. What the hell does that say about me?"

Out of the corner of her eye, Brianna noticed Amy starting to cry.

"I'd say it means you're human. A stubborn and rebellious one, perhaps, but human. I don't think Amy blames you."

"I don't," Amy said. "I miss him."

Brianna took a deep breath. "Amy says she doesn't blame you. She misses you."

For a split second, the edges of his mouth curled upward.

"At least you had the courage to follow your dreams," Brianna said, hoping she could bring his smile back. "You didn't settle for your dad's dreams on a silver platter." *Keep talking. You know what he's going through.*

"Perhaps I should've."

"Like Declan did? He joined the air force to please our dad. Now he's dead. You can't blame yourself for your loved ones dying."

Steven met her eyes for a quick moment before breaking away to stare at the floor. "I left the South, my family gets killed. I moved to California, Kate gets killed."

"You told me Kate was killed by a drunk driver. How is that your fault?"

He bit his lip. "She was, but I was driving her car. I survived. She didn't."

No wonder he wanted to block out any chance to make amends. He had a horrible case of survivor's guilt. Brianna had it after Declan died, but she'd forgotten how much harm it could do to someone who felt he didn't deserve to survive.

"Survivor's guilt. I'm sorry. I didn't know," Brianna said, reaching for his hand.

He looked up, his eyes focused on hers. In those soulful green eyes were oceans of guilt and regret.

"I don't want the third time to become the charm," he said.

"What do you mean?"

He cradled her face in his hands. “I fell in love with you,” he said. “Now Begley’s trying to kill both of us. Eventually, Brianna, I have to look in the mirror when assigning blame.”

“No, you don’t,” she said. “And Begley isn’t going to get the last word with either of us. That’s a promise. And believe me, since moving down South, I’ve learned to keep my promises.”

CHAPTER FORTY-FIVE

Of our conflicts with others we make rhetoric;
of our conflicts with ourselves we make poetry.
~ William Butler Yeats

Steven searched Brianna's face for any sign of doubt. Her warm smile, the newfound resilience in her glance, her willingness to trust him despite his track record—all things he loved about her. How could someone like her also understand him so well, know what demons he'd buried inside for so long?

Survivor's guilt. She'd nailed it in two honest words, just as Dennis had last night.

The questions still churned inside his mind. Why *had* he survived the crash that killed Kate? Why was he kept on this Earth while such a lovely soul got ripped from it?

He hadn't caused the accident, but he'd played a thousand scenarios in his mind, sifting through each one, wondering if he could have done anything differently. He didn't know, which became the curse he'd lived with.

Now Brianna claimed he could talk to his family through her? Make amends? He'd been skeptical but tempted. And yet, Brianna somehow knew things only he and Amy had shared. The coffee with cinnamon. Steven's special. He'd played around with condiments that day—his mother didn't even want him drinking coffee, but she wasn't home—and Amy suggested adding cinnamon because she'd learned the word in her spelling class.

It was their recipe. A private bond between siblings. Brianna couldn't have known, and yet she somehow did.

"Have a little faith," Brianna said, smiling ear to ear.

Apparently he'd been wearing a scowl, because she reached out her hand and smoothed out the lines. Damn, she was beautiful. He needed to do what he'd failed to do with his family and Kate—keep her safe. And alive.

###

Before leaving for River Street, Brianna moved several important papers from the house safe into her small-suitcase-sized purse. In case Begley decided to blow up her house. She didn't want to think about the possibility, but realistically speaking, it could happen.

"Hold on. Dennis is calling me," Steven said. He picked up his phone and began to talk.

James approached her. "My son is warming up to the idea of us. I think he believes you."

"Maybe," she said. "But I want him to be comfortable. I can't force him to accept my help, James."

"I understand." James walked over and put his arms around Virginia and Amy. "Be careful out there. We're rooting for you."

Warmth rose in her cheeks. "Thank you," she whispered.

Steven tapped his cell phone. "That was Dennis with an update. You ready? I'll tell you on the way."

She gathered her purse and snapped the leash on Plato. "Yes. Let's go."

CHAPTER FORTY-SIX

Hang the bard, and cut the punster,
Fling all rhyming to the deuce,
Take a business tour through Munster,
Shoot a landlord—be of use.
~ Advice to a Young Poet by Richard D'Alton Williams

"Let's take Habersham Street down to River," Steven said. "It's a more populated route."

"Sure," Brianna said, a nervous knot forming in her throat. She never thought she'd be forced to take one street over another in order to stay alive. "What did Dennis say?"

Steven reached for her free hand. "You were right about Edwin. He fell apart like wet newspaper when he realized he was caught. They're charging him with being an accessory, but he'll get a reduced sentence for nailing Begley, the big fish they want to fry."

"Southern metaphors are charming," she said.

Steven turned to her, taken aback. "You making fun of me, ma'am?"

"Yes indeedy." She laughed, and it released some tension in her muscles. "Seriously, though, what else did Dennis say?"

They kept a brisk pace along Habersham, though she paused for a moment when they passed the Cathedral of St. John the Baptist, a French Gothic building and part of Savannah's distinctive skyline.

Plato began to sniff around, but she led him along to the next block. Churchgoing types tended to frown on dog poop messing up their latest fashionable shoes.

"The GBI plans to interview Begley at his office at noon."

She glanced at her watch. Eleven. "So we need to stay incognito for the next hour?"

Steven turned to her, a gleam in his eyes. "I do love your trusting nature. I know it doesn't come easy for you."

"Thanks, but your point?"

"You don't honestly think Begley will wait around to be investigated, do you? He's probably collecting all his money and prepping to fly to Rio as we speak."

"True. I wouldn't put anything past him."

"Dennis will text me. We're all supposed to meet Piper and the GBI on the riverfront later."

Brianna nodded. They passed Colonial Park Cemetery, where random ghosts of those who'd died from yellow fever gawked at her from their graves. The men lifted their hats in respect; the women smiled and hugged young children. All of them seemed to cheer her on, like the Graysons had.

Savannah, its living and its dead, was slowly becoming home. If only she could see Declan too.

Steven's cell phone beeped three times.

"A text?" Brianna asked.

He pulled it out and read the message. "Piper in town for story. Begley MIA. Be careful."

"We will be, and when this is all said and done, I do want you to let me help reconnect you to your family. I'm stuck with this *gift*. I want to use it for the people I care about."

He nodded but kept a keen eye on their surroundings. Had he understood what she'd asked him to do? Or, like the parent immersed in a favorite TV show, had he offered a blasé nod to whatever request the child could invent?

The riverfront festival bustled with Southern food vendors, face painting for kids, locally brewed ales, and wine tastings for dads and moms. On the paddleboat going downriver, a fraternity of college guys drank beer and lifted their glasses in a toast to historic Savannah.

Seeing the crowds, especially the kids, at the festive outdoor event only confirmed Brianna's decision had been the right one. These young children, hopeful with the promise of opportunity, didn't deserve to grow up in a place controlled by Begley. Not when she could prevent it.

All the main businesses were open. People meandered in and out of shops and bars, enjoying the day. It was the perfect setting for her and Steven to blend in and stay safe.

Plato did okay with the crowds, but he'd always been the patient sort. For all a sheltie's quirks, barking at falling leaves and ants on the ground, they were also one of the most intelligent breeds. He sniffed the ground and walked, all the while scanning the crowds for danger.

Out of the crowds, a red-faced little boy, his tiny body filled with gleeful energy, charged toward Plato at full speed. "Mom, look. It's Lassie!"

Brianna darted her eyes in every direction. Kids always approached Plato in the park, and she was used to them mistaking him for a small Lassie. But today, when she was trying to remain hidden, the outburst seemed too…convenient.

Steven held her hand, apparently thinking the same thing. Yet when the mother appeared and the little boy came closer, Plato ducked his head and bobbed it upward into the child's outstretched hand without a care in the world.

"He likes me, Mom!" the boy said.

Brianna relaxed her shoulders and smiled at the boy's mother. "Shelties are great with kids. Don't worry. He won't bite."

"We saw one in the store last week. He wants a dog so much." The mom smiled. "C'mon, Scotty. Say good-bye to the doggy and let's go to the bookstore."

The kid rubbed Plato behind his ears. "Bye Lassie."

"Plato might never let you go," Brianna teased. "He loves being petted behind the ears."

From the tight-knit crowd, a pubescent girl appeared and pushed the little boy away.

"No need to push," Brianna said. "Plato is a ham for attention. Just wait your turn."

The girl's dark glare made Brianna's neck hairs stiffen. What kind of person pushes away a little kid when he's petting a dog? This girl was teen angst with a sprinkling of bitchiness.

Plato wiggled to get away.

"I don't wait for what I want," the teenager said. She punched Brianna in the elbow, ripped Plato's leash away, and ran off with him toward the waterfront.

"What the hell?" Brianna rubbed her arm and tossed Steven her purse.

"I see her. C'mon," Steven said.

Brianna sped ahead, weaving her way in and out of the crowds as she chased after them. Plato barked loudly and tugged on the leash, but the girl kept dragging him further down the sidewalk.

Steven was behind her, but the masses were thick and he was five or eight feet back, last she looked. She had to get Plato. Weaving around a family of six, she saw the teen girl trying to tug Plato toward the western end of the street.

“What the hell do you think you’re doing?” Brianna yelled.

The girl only shrugged, showing no hint of emotion in that lank face.

Brianna looked over her shoulder. About fifteen feet behind her, Steven clawed his way between people.

“This way,” she called to him, but when she turned around, Plato and the girl had disappeared.

CHAPTER FORTY-SEVEN

True friends stab you in the front.
~ Oscar Wilde

Something small but rock hard pressed against Brianna's rib cage. She looked down, expecting to see someone's heavy purse. Instead, she saw a 22 semiautomatic—attached to Begley's hand.

"Scream, and I shoot you right here."

Holy shit. Her mouth turned cotton dry. Begley had found her. This was it. He would kill her if she gave him the chance.

She gulped for air. It didn't comfort her parched throat. Nothing would. Wait, where was Steven? She turned her head, trying to locate him.

Begley grabbed her arm with one hand and shoved the gun harder into her ribs with the other. "You think your knight in shining armor is going to save you, girlie?"

She glared at him. "He has more honor than you ever will." *You bastard.*

Begley draped his coat over his gun hand. Smart move for him, bad move for her. Now any passersby would think Brianna and Begley were one of those couples who walked close together no matter where they went. The thought sent nausea churning through her. No one would see them for what this was—a kidnapping and murder attempt.

Begley prodded her forward—away from the main crowds and toward the western edge of River Street. "I knew you were naive, but I gave you more credit than waiting on a man to rescue you. You really are a stupid Yankee."

She didn't respond. Anything she said could get her killed. Best plan was to stall Begley for now. She didn't see Steven anywhere. *Please be witnessing this and call Piper. Get her to bring the GBI to capture Begley before the maniacal jerk pulls the trigger.*

"Just in case you're wondering," Begley said in his fake-sounding Southern drawl, "I intend on dealing with Steven in my own way. We have some scores to settle."

Crap. *Stay hidden, Steven, but follow us.*

How could she not have seen this coming?

"So, this was your master plan? Solicit a kid to kidnap my dog? Where is Plato?"

Begley's sinister laugh sent shivers down her spine. "The little boy wasn't even planned, but my niece wants to be an actress. She improvised quite well, wouldn't you agree?"

Oh yeah, she deserved a damn Academy Award.

Brianna took small steps, unsure where Begley planned to take her. The docks, maybe? They'd walked a few short blocks in that direction.

"I want my dog."

"Relax. He's fine."

"Why should I believe you?"

His icy stare flashed a hint of madness. "Because I wouldn't kill an animal. At least, not until you were there to watch."

"What kind of man kills someone's dog?" *You psycho. I can't wait to see your ass get arrested.*

"Shut the hell up," he said. "You've flapped your gums enough."

So much for fake Southern manners. She glanced over her shoulder. Had anyone seen Begley push her away from the festival crowds? Was Steven scrambling to find Piper and the GBI? Begley couldn't have known Piper and the GBI were supposed to meet them on the riverfront—could he?

Steven, figure out a way to get Begley in the crosshairs. Before he kills me.

CHAPTER FORTY-EIGHT

May you be afflicted with the itch
and have no nails to scratch with!
~ Irish Curse

Steven tore through clusters of giggling girls, couples holding hands, and parents moseying with baby strollers. Damn his polite upbringing. He needed to reach Brianna but not topple everyone over in the process.

Hell, he hadn't even been close enough to wrestle her out of Begley's grasp. The jerk planned his distraction perfectly. Plato was the only thing that could separate her from Steven at a time like this. Begley must've had a gun pointed at her. No way would she go with him as calmly as she did if she hadn't been forced.

He ran toward the western end of River Street and called Dennis on the cell. "Hey, where's Piper? We need to move, and fast."

"She's in back of the Hyatt, the River Street side, ready to meet up."

"Great, I'm almost there now." Steven picked up his pace and turned inward toward the Hyatt entrance. "Begley has Brianna."

"What? How the hell did that happen?"

"Long story," Steven said. "Does Piper have a GBI agent with her?"

"I think so. The other agent is at the office prepping for Begley's interview."

"That ain't gonna happen, brother," Steven said. "I'm willing to bet Begley's new plan is to kill Brianna so she won't testify against him. And possibly me, but I won't let either one happen. This jerk is going down for murder, for killing my family and plenty of others."

"I'll tell the agents to head your way. Where do you think he's taking her?" Dennis asked.

"They were headed toward the docks, but I don't know where. Wait. Shit. All those warehouses surrounding the docks—some of them have sat empty for years. Find out if Begley owns any of those properties. Tell the agents to go there. I'll find Piper and we'll meet up with them. My phone has GPS. Brianna's does too, but I'd bet Begley tossed it."

"I'll call you back when I have some news about the properties," Dennis said. "And hey, brother?"

"Yeah?"

"Be careful."

###

Steven found Piper standing next to a tall guy dressed in black. "This is Jack, my cameraman," she said.

They exchanged quick hellos. No time for basic pleasantries. They needed to find Brianna, and fast. Steven brought Piper up to speed on his call to Dennis.

"Where's your camera?" Steven asked.

"Here," Jack said, pulling out a black tube no bigger than a soda can. "Latest technology. Small but effective when we need to stay on the move."

"Good thinking," Steven said. "Where's the other GBI agent? Dennis said he was with you."

"Mike saw Begley lead Brianna away. He's about a block ahead of us. I'll text him with your info on the warehouses."

"Great, let's go. Once we get Brianna back, I want to take this bastard down," Steven said.

They started walking along the riverfront toward the docks. "By the way, Edwin's in custody," Piper said. "They're processing him now. Brianna was right about him taking the deal. He gave up Begley like a scared kid surrendering his lunch money to the school bully."

"Good. That's what Begley is, a bully. But Savannah isn't his playground anymore."

CHAPTER FORTY-NINE

I fear not the man who has practiced 10,000 kicks once,
but I fear the man who has practiced one kick 10,000 times.
~ Bruce Lee

The barrel of the gun dug further into Brianna's side. Her feet ached from the rapid pace Begley was forcing. The crowds had thinned out, and Steven was nowhere to be seen. Had one of Begley's accomplices picked up Steven? Where was poor Plato?

Begley inched the gun to the left. "No one beats me and gets away with it. I suggest you quit squirming and take a last look around. You're about to get my payback in full."

She kept silent, racking her brain for ways to escape. Stomp on his foot, elbow him in the gut, and run like hell? No way could she hope to outrun a 22 bullet. Even if the foot-and-gut attack worked, she'd need a bigger distraction to escape gunshot.

She needed Steven to bring the GBI.

"Turn left," Begley said, pushing her off River Street. They entered an industrial-looking area filled with white and cream buildings, all with chipped paint, random graffiti, and no windows.

She gulped. No windows? If Begley planned to bring her into one of these buildings, no one would be able to hear her scream or see her body crumple to the floor. *Steven, where are you?*

To the few remaining stragglers walking toward the festival, Begley put on a polite smile and used his Southern charm, saying, “Excuse us” and “So sorry.” His damn accent didn’t change the fact that he was the most evil man she’d ever encountered. Maybe he’d pulled these murdering and cremation schemes in other states. She wouldn’t put it past him.

“Where are we going?” she asked.

“This is the South. We’re just taking a little stroll.”

Yeah, right. More like a death march.

She swallowed hard. How could she distract him, get a head start, and find a way to escape? There was no one left on the streets of the warehouse district. Even if there were, she couldn’t risk signaling for help. Begley would kill them too. She couldn’t put others in danger.

“This is it,” he said, pointing to a red brick building with rusted trim. “Let’s go.”

“I need to tie my shoes.” She dug her nails into her palms to avoid wincing. Tie her shoes? Was that the best excuse she could come up with? Right now, in her panicked state, apparently so.

“Women really are more trouble than they’re worth,” Begley said. “Just hobble. You’ll be fine.”

“I can’t.” She pretended to stumble, hoping he’d stop. Anything to avoid going inside the warehouse, where she would surely die.

“Of all the—”

"Just let me tie it. Please?" she said. "Then you can bring me into the building. But I'm no use to you if I can't even walk."

Keep focused on what will benefit him. Pride and vanity were his weaknesses. Use them.

"Fine," he said with obvious exasperation.

Just as she'd hoped, his annoyance diverted his concentration for a second.

Great, this was her chance. A second was all she needed. With all the strength she could summon, she stomped on his foot and jabbed his rib cage with her elbow before running like hell.

Run in a zigzag formation. It was easier to shoot someone running in a straight line. Uncle Jack taught her that trick.

Begley chased after her, his heavy footsteps echoing off the asphalt. "Stop! Now!"

She continued to zigzag. Get someplace public and things would be fine.

A bullet zipped past her ear, barely missing her. Adrenaline pumped through her heart and into every limb of her body. She ducked and ran in the opposite direction. Begley chased after her. Every ounce of her energy rocketed her forward.

He sped up and was right on her heels. He pushed her to the ground. She lay flat on her stomach, her palms scraped from the pavement. He'd been in better shape than she imagined.

Begley shoved his foot into the center of her back. "You stupid bitch. Do you really think I intend to lose this fight?"

"I'm…I'm—"

"Shut your trap."

Shit. This was it. He was going to pull the trigger. She took a deep breath and braced herself to hear the crack from the gun.

Instead, he gripped her arm and jerked her up. He pressed the gun into the nape of her neck. Tiny hairs stood erect; primal instincts sent a shiver down her spine. No more fooling around.

"As I was saying before your stupid stunt," Begley said, "let's go into the warehouse. Any tricks and you die."

CHAPTER FIFTY

At his best, man is the noblest of all animals;
separated from law and justice he is the worst.
~ Aristotle

Steven had forgotten how all the streets in this section of Savannah looked alike. How could he have lost sight of Brianna? He'd lost too many women in his life. He wasn't going to let Brianna die. Not on his watch.

Piper's cell phone rang. "What have you got?"

Steven watched her countenance as she spoke. Seemed like good news, but he wasn't ready to let out a breath of relief—not yet.

She tapped her phone and ended the call. "That was the GBI. You were right. Begley owns a warehouse in the district. The GBI agent saw him leading Brianna in that direction. Other agents are on the way."

"Great, let's go," Steven said. "You have an address?"

"Yes." Piper pursed her lips. "Steven—"

"What?" The dark shadows behind her glance made his stomach turn. Something else was wrong.

"There are some discrepancies between what Edwin's telling us and what we suspect Begley's been up to. It would really help if we hang back. Get Begley to brag about his business on tape."

Steven could hardly believe his ears. "You want to use Brianna as bait? No. No way."

"Unfortunately, it's not up to me."

"Then who the hell is it up to?"

Did an agency get to decide the best way to gather evidence? Even if it put the woman he'd grown to love in danger?

"Listen to me," Piper said. "The agents that are moving in are some of the best on the force. They won't let Begley kill her."

Steven narrowed his eyes. "You can't promise me that."

She shrugged. "No, I can't, but I can tell you with ninety-nine percent of my being, these guys are at the top of their game. One agent is there now, and two others are meeting us there. If we can hold off going all tactical on Begley, and she can get him to open up, brag about his crimes, I'm saying we'll have a more solid case. That's what you wanted…justice for your family."

His shoulders tensed. She was right. He wanted that arrogant son of a bitch behind bars. But with the risk to Brianna's life? He loved her. If anything happened—even by accident—he didn't even want to think of the possibility.

"We're wasting time," Steven said. "Let's just get to the warehouse. Time to take down Begley once and for all."

CHAPTER FIFTY-ONE

Energy and persistence conquer all things.
~ Benjamin Franklin

Brianna glanced around the warehouse. Giant paper-mache dragons with menacing teeth lined all the walls. In the center stood a solitary chair. Her spot to die? She swallowed so hard, the sound reverberated in her ears.

"Welcome to my abode," Begley said.

Abode? More like hell.

Stall. Stall as much as you can. "What's with the dragons?"

"Parade floats for St. Patrick's Day, the biggest party in Savannah. I *do* have a sense of community, Brianna."

Right. A sense of doing whatever the hell he wanted—however illegal—to control the community he claimed to support.

With a firmer push of the gun into her neck, he led her to the chair. "Sit down."

Shit. Her legs trembled as she sat. He managed to tie her legs and hands with rope while holding the gun. There was no escape. This was it. She took a resolved breath. At least she had begun to make good on her promise to Declan. She'd helped the Graysons and she'd connected with Steven.

If need be, she was ready to face death. But that didn't stop every fiber in her being from hoping Steven would bring the GBI.

Begley didn't pull the trigger. Instead, with her safely tied up, he reached for some containers on metal shelves.

Holy hell. Kerosene?

"You're going to burn your own place? Kill me like you did the Graysons?"

She wriggled against the ropes to no avail.

His mouth curved into a wicked grin, one that sent fear into the depths of her bones. "I like consistency."

She looked up, around, and tried to formulate some form of escape. Wait. Who was behind the back door? Begley didn't seem to notice. He was too busy pouring flammable liquid into every corner of the warehouse.

The man, dressed in black and hiding in the shadows, pressed his index finger to his lips. He held up his badge and digital recorder.

She let out an audible sigh of relief. Steven had come through. She loved that man.

"What was that?" Begley asked, suspicion in his glance.

Shit. She'd been too loud. No one sighs with relief when they're about to die. Think of something to say.

"I just realized that if you kill me, I'll get to see my brother again."

Begley smirked. "You're sure one to remain positive, aren't you? I'll give you credit for that, you annoying Yankee bitch."

He poured more Kerosene. When she glanced at the agent, he motioned with both his hands to keep Begley talking, do what she had been doing—stall.

Okay. She could do this.

"Begley," she said, a newfound sweetness in her voice, "since you're going to kill me anyway, tell me something. Satisfy a Yankee girl's curiosity, so to speak."

He smiled, apparently amused at her question. "And that would be?"

"Why do you care about land so much? The Graysons, Bobby Ray, Riordan O'Shea—"

"The Graysons were a stubborn bunch of idiots," Begley said.

"So you killed them?"

"They lived on prime real estate," Begley said. "Hell, you live there now. You're aware of its potential. I didn't want to kill them. I'd hoped James would see reason, sell me the house."

She glanced at the GBI agent. "But James didn't want to sell," she prompted.

"No. Edwin and I made a deal. I killed them and he cremated the bodies. That damn scaredy-cat would do anything I say."

Oh, just you wait. He's going to do a lot of singing on the witness stand at your trial.

Begley's shoes clacked against the floor as he approached. "Any other questions before I kill you?"

Her stomach knotted up. Think. Keep Begley talking…appeal to his pride, his vanity.

She offered the sweetest smile she could muster. "Your charismatic personality helped buy off the cops, I presume?"

His eyes gleamed, and he seemed pleased she'd recognized his talent. "Easy as pie. I put a few extra thousands in their meager checks. Cops aren't paid enough, making them the perfect targets for bribery."

"Not all cops," Brianna said.

"You'd be surprised." Begley gave a half grin. "The only way to control someone, whether by bribery, blackmail, or murder, is to squelch their spirit."

"And how does one do that?"

He arched an eyebrow, seeming to question her motives. "Why do you care?"

Think. Appeal to his vanity. Keep him talking.

"I'm intrigued," she said. "Steven's friend Dennis tried to investigate you for years, but he never found evidence. It takes a bit of genius to get away with everything you have, Begley."

The flattering remark worked.

"Have you seen the elephants at the circus?" he asked.

"Yes." Where was he going with this?

"They're just like people. When the elephant is young, it struggles to get away. Something in its mind knows that being chained up is wrong, so it resists."

"And?"

"The chains used on younger elephants are thick steel. The elephants fight and kick but can't escape. Circus ringmasters do more than chain up the elephants. They imprint the psyche, controlling both body and mind."

I never liked the circus. "And you use this approach with people?"

His brows furrowed and he chuckled as if she was a village idiot who couldn't possibly understand his grand scheme.

"By the time an elephant weighs ten thousand pounds, those circus ringmasters can control those massive animals with a piece of string. If you control the spirit, the body follows."

She swallowed hard. Begley wasn't just a criminal. He was evil.

And he stood four feet away from her, smiling maniacally and cocking his gun. She had to keep him talking.

"What about Bobby Ray, the Elvis impersonator? You have something against Elvis music?"

Begley's eyes flashed with anger. "First of all, I love the King. Second, I'm not the villain you think I am."

"You're not?"

She steadied her breathing. If she kept him distracted, kept him talking, she could stay alive. Either she would talk him to death or the GBI was going to arrest him. At the current pace, she didn't know which would happen first.

Maybe the GBI needed all this info on tape despite Edwin's confession? At least she knew there was an agent who could shoot Begley if the jerk lit a match.

"That Elvis impersonator learned about a well-to-do couple I killed two years ago," Begley said. "Said he was going to go to ask the feds to investigate their death."

"Anyone who got in your way, you murdered," she whispered.

"I'm striving for a better Savannah, a new kind of community."

She didn't want to ask what he meant. The man was a sociopath.

"What about Steven? You did a terrible thing, killing his family and never telling him," she said.

Begley rolled his eyes. "That kid bolted out of the South like a bat out of hell. I didn't think he'd ever come back, so I didn't try very hard to find him."

"He had a right to learn his family was dead. But you didn't care about that, did you?"

Begley raised his eyebrows, but he lowered the gun as he defended his position as one of the great leading men of Savannah. Ah, pride. The sin that always brought people to their knees. Catholic school had taught her something.

"I don't understand what you see in Steven," Begley said. "He's just a no-good annoyance."

"No, he's not. He's a good man, a man I've come to love."

Begley burst out laughing. "Thanks for the chuckle, but it's time to say good-night, sweet princess."

Go for his pride. "Everyone in Savannah thinks you're a monster. If you kill me, you just make it worse."

Begley's ears turned flaming red. He'd become focused on his anger, and his gun still hung at his side, not pointed at her.

Two other GBI agents appeared from behind a paper-mache dragon. With practiced precision, they crept into position behind Begley.

Don't let on. Keep eye contact with Begley. If she darted her glance away—even for a second—he'd suspect something. No. Focus all eye contact on the maniacal creep in front of her: his blond perfectly gelled hair, icy-cold blue eyes, football-player neck.

Her intense stare into Begley's face turned her stomach, but the trick worked. Begley continued to defend his good name. She'd been right. Pride would be his eventual undoing.

"I'm not a monster," Begley hissed. "I'm a visionary. Someday, the good people in Savannah are going to see that."

"Not today, asshole. Freeze." One of the agents gripped Begley's arm, sending both men and Begley's gun to the ground. "GBI. You're under arrest for the murders of James, Virginia, and Amy Grayson, Riordan O'Shea, and Bobby Ray Canters. And the attempted kidnapping, assault with a deadly weapon, of Brianna McNeil."

Piper came running. "We got everything on tape. How does it feel to be the most powerful man in Savannah now, Mr. Begley?"

Begley glared up at her and thrashed on the floor as they read him his rights. "I'm a pillar of the community! You can't do this to me."

She laughed. "Yes, we can. And you'll be on the news tonight. Famous, just like you always wanted."

Brianna's shoulders slumped, all tension fading away. Begley was in handcuffs. She was safe.

"Thank you," she said, her mouth dry.

The GBI agent untied Brianna. Piper picked up her cell and said, "Yeah, we're good. Tell Steven he can come in now."

Steven? Brianna's heart fluttered. "He's here?"

Piper nodded. “They made him stay outside with another agent. He should be here right about—”

“Now.” Steven ran to Brianna’s side, cupped her face in his hands, and kissed her. “I’m so glad you’re safe. I don’t know what I would’ve done—”

“I know. Thanks for getting the GBI. I love you.”

He stroked his fingers along her face, such a tender touch after Begley’s harshness. “I love you more, Brianna McNeil.”

She buried herself in his muscled arms. Never before had leaning against a man’s chest felt so amazing. She was home, truly home.

CHAPTER FIFTY-TWO

Life cannot subsist in society but by reciprocal concessions.
~ Samuel Johnson

Declan fidgeted in Columbia Square, not quite sure how this meeting would go. He didn't often ask for favors, but this one was well deserved. But would Connell see it that way? Declan hadn't exactly been in his mentor's good graces in recent weeks.

"Good afternoon, Declan," Connell said, appearing from one of the large oaks. "I don't think I've seen you this much in months. To what do I owe the pleasure today?"

"Hello, sir." He hoped he didn't sound like the brown-nose he thought he did. "I wanted to ask if you'll consider—"

"Consider…what exactly?"

Declan lowered his eyes in hopes Connell would see the gesture of respect. "I have a favor to ask."

"You're one of the bravest souls in my charge, I'll give you that. Not many would ask a favor only days after breaking the rules."

"It's important, sir," Declan said.

"Tell me, does this favor concern Brianna?"

"Yes, and also Steven Grayson."

Connell strolled to the fountain and the droplets spilled through his transparent form. “Favors—especially in regards to family—require a sacrifice. You know this.”

Declan followed him and kept a reverent stance. “I’m aware. This is the right thing to do, Connell. I’m willing to pay whatever price you see fit.”

Connell gave a half smile. “I’m listening.”

CHAPTER FIFTY-THREE

Be happy for this moment. This moment is your life.
~ Omar Khayyam

As they left the warehouse, Brianna didn't let go of Steven's hand. She'd had a gun shoved in her rib cage, a heavy foot pressed into her spine, and been tied up at gunpoint. In Steven's passionate eyes she saw life, hope, dreams. All the things she wanted. She didn't want to let her newfound resolve for life or him slip out of her grasp—ever again. Life would be different going forward. Better.

She and Steven were safe. Begley and Edwin were under arrest. The GBI closed Restful Oaks during their investigation, but they'd said she could open it again once she had her director's license.

"Let us give you a ride home," Piper said. "It's the least we can do."

Suddenly she remembered. "Where's Plato? Did anyone find him? Get Begley's niece?"

Now that things were looking up, she didn't want the day to end with her dog getting killed.

"I was so busy chasing after you," Steven said. "Does he have tags on his collar? Or a microchip?"

"Yes, but we should still look for him." Her stomach cramped. *Plato, where are you?* He couldn't be dead. He just couldn't.

A soft breeze blew, carrying music through the trees and into her ears. She pressed her fingers to her ears, opening and closing them. The music continued, but it wasn't violins. It was…Elvis? Singing "a hunka hunka burnin' love"?

She glanced upward where the words seemed to come from. Sitting on a large oak limb was Bobby Ray Canters's ghost.

"Bobby Ray?"

Steven grasped her hand tighter. "Are you okay?"

"Give me a second," Brianna said. "Bobby Ray? Is that you?"

"Yes, ma'am. I just wanted to tell you that Plato's in the City Market. He's fine. That's where you'll find him."

An Elvis-impersonator ghost was telling her where her dog was. After the month she'd had, this didn't seem strange. She breathed a sigh of relief. "Thanks."

"No, ma'am. Thank you, thank you very much."

Brianna chuckled, and her laughter blended into the breeze as Bobby Ray faded from sight.

"Who were you talking to?" Steven asked.

She turned to face him. "Plato's in the City Market. He's fine."

With narrowed eyes, Steven said, "Listen, we can search for Plato in every corner of Savannah. But I think we have to remain pragmatic—"

"You are more like James than you think." She smiled at him.

Steven's eyes went wide with horror. "What?"

"Trust me. Plato's in City Market."

"Hop in," Piper said. "We'll take you there."

During the five-minute drive, Steven didn't say much. Guess she'd taken him aback with the comment about James, but he'd looked so adorable—just as James did. Both men, both pragmatic, yet both wanting their own dreams in life. She didn't find it surprising that they'd clashed on numerous occasions.

"City Market is on the right," Piper said. She pulled over the sedan. "I'll be in touch soon for an in-depth interview, plus the coverage during Begley's trial. Meanwhile, his arrest will make the six o'clock news."

"I wouldn't miss it," Brianna said. "Thank you again for all your help."

"Yes, thanks," Steven added, and he clasped Brianna's hand in his. "So, where do we look first? City Market covers four blocks."

Brianna scanned the crowds. There were cart vendors selling flowers, water, and snacks. Shops and alfresco eateries lined the pedestrian-only streets. Near one of the hamburger eateries, she saw a gaggle of ten-year-old girls. They wore red corkscrew-style wigs, green sequined outfits with shamrocks on the chests, and clogging shoes.

"There."

Steven's eyebrows shot upward. "The cloggers? Strange. It's not St. Patrick's Day yet."

"They must've performed at the festival," Brianna said. "Savannah is doused in Irish culture, remember?"

He smiled, seeming to relax a little more. "I remember."

"It's Lassie," one of the girls said.

Steven arched an eyebrow.

"People always mistake Plato for a small Lassie," Brianna said. "C'mon. I have a feeling Plato is being his usual attention-hungry self."

When they approached, Brianna laughed so hard that she hiccupped. There, in the center of these curly-haired girls with rouge on their cheeks, laid Plato, flat on his back and begging for tummy rubs from anyone and everyone.

She squeezed Steven's hand. "I told you Plato was here."

Steven winked. "Guess I should believe you more often."

"Yes, yes you should." She kissed him on the cheek. "Come on, let's get him before he gets too spoiled."

Steven pulled her into him for a long kiss. "I don't know if that's possible. I intend to spoil you and Plato for a long, long time."

Her pulse raced and she couldn't stop herself from grinning ear to ear. "I'll hold you to that. C'mon."

"Plato?" Brianna called, using her high-pitched voice.

Plato scrambled to stand up, his nails clicking against the cobblestones. When he saw her, his legs ran in place before ever moving. The eagerness in his wiggling body made her heart smile. There was nothing like a dog's expression when he's happy to see his human. He bolted out of the circle and sprinted to her legs.

"Is the Lassie dog yours?" one girl asked.

"Yes, I lost him this morning." She snapped on the leash she'd kept in her purse. "Thank you so much for taking care of him for me."

Another girl with red freckles stepped forward. "He was hungry, so we all pitched in and got him some food. He really likes hamburgers."

Steven chuckled. "We'll keep that in mind."

After several minutes of petting Plato to his full satisfaction, she glanced into Steven's eyes. "Come to the house with me. There's something I want to do."

CHAPTER FIFTY-FOUR

If you don't believe in ghosts, you've never been to a family reunion.
~ Ashleigh Brilliant

Steven couldn't believe they'd found Plato—safe—in City Market. Just like Brianna had said, and the news reached her by a ghost. Suddenly, his hometown and its supernatural legends didn't seem so hokey anymore.

And what had she meant when she said he'd sounded like his father? It hadn't been her words that threw him for a loop. It had been the way she seemed to have known with such confidence.

They strolled through the historic district, making their way past the squares, away from the crowds, and back home.

"C'mon. This won't be too painful," Brianna said with a glimmer in her eye.

Maybe for you it won't. I have no idea what's lurking behind that door.

"Sure."

She unlocked the door and let Plato inside. Steven followed, shut the door behind him, walked into the den—and froze. What on Earth? Nothing could've prepared him for this.

"Ah, Yankee, I see you're back. I'm cooking grits. James and Amy, get me some napkins."

Brianna looked toward the kitchen and smiled at the three—ghosts!—before sitting on the couch. As if everything was normal.

Steven forgot to breathe. Seconds later, he gasped for air.

"Are you okay?" Brianna stood and whacked him on the back.

"No." He pointed to the kitchen and tried to choke out the words. "My family?"

The pot of grits his mom had been cooking crashed to the ground, shattering glass and grits across the floor. "Steven?"

Brianna darted her gaze between the den and the kitchen. "Steven, you can…*see* them?"

"Yes. Isn't that why you brought me here?" He sank onto the couch, dazed.

The bewilderment flashing from her eyes told him no. "I'd just planned to translate whatever each of you wanted to say to each other," she said. "I had no idea you'd be able to see them too. This is…not my doing."

Steven's knees trembled and he leaned against the counter to steady himself. Maybe this was a hallucination. Maybe those earlier drug-hazed days on the road had come back to haunt him. This couldn't be real.

"Trust me," Brianna said as if she could read his mind. "They're real, but you probably won't be able to touch them since they're semitransparent."

Steven looked into the warm, caring faces of his mother, his father, and Amy. "I'm going to find out."

He rushed toward them and gathered them in a group hug, just like they were still alive. No missed grasps, no disappointment, only open arms of love and forgiveness. He had no idea how this could be, but now was not the time to question such special occurrences.

"I've missed all of you. I'm so sorry I left and never came home."

"We're thankful you're safe," his mom said.

"You did it, son," his dad said. "You brought Begley to justice."

Amy's tiny voice was muffled by tears. "I missed you so much."

Steven didn't want to let go. He'd yearned for this moment for so long—the chance to make amends, the chance to make things right, the chance to say good-bye.

His father broke free from the group hug first. "Son, our time is limited, and there's something I want to tell you—"

"I didn't mean all the things I said when I left—"

"All's forgiven, son." His father's warm cheeks and blue eyes hadn't faded, not even in death. "I wanted to say how sorry I was for not having more faith in you. For not trusting you to know your dream and believing in your talent to make that dream come true."

A lump formed in the back of Steven's throat. "Thank you, Dad."

He patted Steven on the shoulder. “I’m proud of you, son. Remember that.”

Steven’s chin trembled. The precious words he’d longed to hear all those years ago. He reached out to hug his father once more, but this time, only chilled air embraced his arms. James Grayson had faded from sight.

Steven swallowed hard. Dad had been right about the short time. No more time to waste.

He looked into his mother’s eyes. “I love you, Mom.”

Her eyes lit up. “I love you too, son. My boy.” She walked a few steps away, almost as if knowing she would fade out at any moment. “And despite her Northern roots, Brianna’s a decent catch.”

Out of the corner of his eye, he noticed Brianna smiling wide.

“Thank you, Mom,” he said.

“But one thing. Teach that Yankee to make a decent pot of grits, will ya?”

As Steven laughed, Virginia Grayson faded and disappeared, leaving only a cold gust of air behind.

Now came the hardest one to say good-bye to—Amy.

The auburn curls draped off her shoulders and her big blue eyes trusted him. She’d grown up in his absence. He’d missed too much.

“Forgive me,” he said, “for not protecting you.”

Amy smiled a wide grin that made his tense shoulders relax. "I never blamed you, Steven. I only missed you."

"I should've come back, should've called more."

"You had the guts to follow your dream. I loved your music, even the hard rock stuff," she said.

He smiled wide. "I've shifted over to ballads."

Amy twisted her curled hair with her fingers. "I'll like any music you make. You taught me it was okay to follow my heart, Steven. You're not someone I blame. You're my hero."

Tears spilled down Steven's cheeks before he could even attempt to stop them. "Scarecrow, I will miss you most of all," he said.

"From the *Wizard of Oz*," Amy said with a twinkle in her eye. "The first movie I ever saw, the one you took me to at the Savannah Theater."

"One of the best times we had," he said. "I've missed you more than you know, Amy."

"Me, too."

He knew what came next. She would fade out. He tried to brace himself for the inevitable. Any second now, she'd go.

Five seconds passed. She remained in front of him, her face as perplexed as he felt.

Brianna tiptoed over. "I think y'all should hug."

Would it work? Worth a try. He put out his arms, expecting to grasp nothing but cold air. Instead, he was able to hug her for too brief a moment before she began to fade.

“Keep playing your music,” she said, growing fainter by the second until only her happy laughter remained, followed by silence.

CHAPTER FIFTY-FIVE

Patience is also a form of action.
~ Auguste Rodin

Brianna's heart warmed seeing Steven make peace with his family. She'd been able to facilitate the meeting, though the hugging part had not been her. She'd made a difference, kept her promise.

And yet, she couldn't deny the growing ache in her stomach. She hated to be selfish, but what about *her* wish? She'd seen nearly every ghost in Savannah, risked everything for them, and Declan had not appeared. Not once. She hadn't even been certain she'd heard his voice after the car explosion.

"You okay?" Steven asked.

"I'm fine. Turn on the six o'clock news. Piper should be on." He wrapped an arm around her and they stood in front of the television.

He flipped to the channel.

Piper sat behind the news desk. "And tonight, we have a special story to bring you. One of corruption, but also of courage. Longtime real-estate guru Sam Begley was arrested earlier today for allegedly murdering six people and kidnapping another. He remains in prison tonight, without bail."

"Good," Brianna interjected. "If he'd made bail, there is no justice."

Piper continued. “Sam Begley’s cohort, Edwin Lawson, manager of Restful Oaks Funeral Home, has been accused of cremating the murdered remains. He has agreed to testify against Sam Begley in exchange for a lesser charge, but he also faces years in prison after being part of an eerie cover-up scheme for the last eight years.”

“Amazing they got away with it for so long,” Steven said.

Piper continued. “But in a heroic gesture to learn the truth about his murdered family, son Steven Grayson returned to Savannah, and with the help of Restful Oaks cosmetologist Brianna McNeil, garnered enough evidence to put Begley and Edwin under arrest.”

Piper paused for effect and flashed a smile at the camera. “That’s heroism, and this reporter is touched by his commitment to family. Hug your families tonight, Savannah. They’re the most precious thing.”

Brianna clicked the remote to turn the TV off.

“You okay?” Steven asked.

“Her words struck a nerve. Will I ever get to see my brother? You know, family being the most precious thing and all?”

Plato scratched his paws against the back door and whimpered to go out.

“Sure, boy.” She snapped on the leash. “Steven, you want to come outside?”

He shook his head. "I'm good…just need to absorb everything that's happened in the last few minutes. Yell if you need me."

She and Plato walked into the backyard. The weather in Savannah had changed. There was a crisp chill in the air, familiar to winter, but the sun shone so bright, she could've sworn it was late summer. One of those beautiful days where nothing was what it seemed.

Plato burrowed his nose into a pile of leaves near the wilting hydrangea. She held the leash, her mind going numb from the day's events, and waited for him to finish exploring whatever fascinating creature he'd found in the dirt.

While she waited, the crimson sun began its descent behind a patch of cypress trees.

"Bree?"

Her breath caught in her throat. Only one person called her Bree. She spun around, adrenaline rushing through her.

Declan stood five feet away, with the same charming smile and mischievous expression she knew as a kid. "Hello there, little sis. Mo Éireannack Cailín."

The Gaelic words for My Irish One. She'd missed him speaking in Gaelic to her.

The *D* in his name rested at the tip of her tongue, ready to leap into speech. She opened her mouth but nothing came out. Enthusiasm and shock deluged through her simultaneously, making words difficult to think of, much less string together into a sentence. Even a name.

What if this was a figment of her imagination, something she *wanted* to see and hear, rather than something real?

He cocked his head to one side, the way he always did when interrogating her about the boys she liked.

"What, I come all this way, and you can't give your big brother a hug?"

She raced toward him and flung her arms around his neck. Then she held on for dear life. "Declan? I can't believe you're here. I've wanted to see you all this time—"

"I know, Bree."

He held her tight. There was no cold air, no missed contact—only a real hug, like he was alive again. "Family contact is complicated. I've been trying to reach you for a long time."

"And now you're here. I can talk to the dead. This is going to be fantastic. We're both in Savannah now."

Declan's grip around her loosened, bringing in a hint of cold air.

She stepped back. Dread coiled in the pit of her stomach. "You have to leave too, don't you? Like the Graysons did?"

His large blue eyes, desperate to formulate an explanation, answered her question before he ever said a word.

"Why do you have to go? I've only just found you."

"That was the price," he whispered.

"Price?"

He gave her a warm smile. "For Steven to make contact with his family, have his peace. For you and I to have one hour together today. For the chance to hug our loved ones again."

Her mind reeled. "I knew the hugging part with Steven hadn't been me, so thanks for that. He's a good man."

"You're welcome. I like him. He's certainly better than those O'Malley boys you used to run with."

She slugged him in the arm. "C'mon, I was a normal kid."

He laughed and a gust of wind blew across the tops of the trees. "You were anything but."

A few seconds of silence hung between them. She didn't want him to leave, even in an hour's time.

"I have to," he said as if he'd read her thoughts. "Ian and I start a new assignment."

"What are these…assignments?"

"Hard to explain, but let's just say, the living and the dead are a lot closer than you may think. Some people, like you, are able to see and talk to both sides. People like you are a rare jewel, Bree. Rare jewel indeed."

"Sure hasn't seemed so at times," she said.

His jaw clenched. “Do you know the worst part about being dead, besides the obvious complications?”

“No, what?”

“Seeing our loved ones suffer and being unable to stop it.”

“I did miss you,” she said.

“I missed you too, but that isn’t the suffering I was referring to.” The intensity in his gaze seemed to look directly into her soul, to secret places long hidden by dark shadows.

“I…I don’t understand.”

He reached for her hand and held it in his. “I saw what they did to you.”

Tattered images, splices of her past, reeled through her mind like a broken home movie. Needles. Forced restraints. Screams. Windows with steel bars. No escape.

She swallowed the hard lump in the back of her throat. “Like what?”

With the stern glare only a big brother could give, he asked, “Do you really want to bullshit me right now, when our time is so limited?”

“No,” she said. Tears spilled from her eyes. “I hadn’t thought about that place in so long. Occasionally, it bubbles up in my mind, but I push it back down.” She sniffled. “Where it belongs.”

Declan hugged her tight once more. "I know you were just trying to keep a promise to me. I am so, so sorry you went through that and I couldn't stop it."

The heartwarming cry on Declan's shoulders had long been overdue. After a few minutes, she collected herself and looked at her watch. Thirty minutes left.

"I know you'll miss me, Bree," he said, "but I think you'll be relieved to know what my assignment will be."

"I will?" She didn't want him on any assignment except in Savannah, where she could have regular contact with him.

"To help others like you, those who can hear the dead. Make sure they don't get locked away in some insane asylum. If we can help them embrace their gift, not reject it, their lives will be better."

Brianna chuckled. "Good luck with the embracing-voices-as-a-gift part. Took me a while."

"You weren't as difficult as you think," he said, slugging her playfully.

She bit her lip. "Thanks for believing in me. This whole experience has been…surreal, to say the least."

His eyes twinkled. "I'll always look out for you, even when I'm not in Savannah. You may not see me as much, but I'm always here. I love you, little sis."

"I love you, too. I wish you could stay longer, but thank you for everything you've done for both me and Steven, seeing our loved ones."

"Speaking of which," Declan said, and he pointed toward the back door. "Looks like your man's coming this way."

"Brianna?" Steven asked and stepped a few feet into the backyard. "You okay?"

"Better than ever," she said. "Come over here. There's someone I want you to meet."

Steven approached them, and Plato sauntered to his side.

"Steven, believe it or not—but after today, I guess you will—this is my brother, Declan. Declan, this is Steven."

Steven's eyes widened. "Wow, it's been a day for the supernatural. I'm Steven Grayson. I'm honored to finally meet you."

"You too," Declan said, and he shook Steven's hand. Brianna noticed their hands locked for a long second, as if trying to determine who was tougher. Men.

"I appreciate your looking out for her," Declan said. "You've proven yourself pretty damn worthy in my book."

The color rose in Steven's cheeks. "One older brother to another, that means a lot. Thanks, man."

Declan nodded. "Take care of her for me."

"I will." Steven put his arm around her, and his touch made her heart flutter. "I promise."

Declan cocked an eyebrow. "Be careful, Steven. No one breaks a promise to the dead without retribution."

"I know," Steven said, pulling her closer to his side. "Don't worry. I don't intend to break this promise."

Brianna smiled wide at Steven's words. Everything had worked out. Savannah had been the new start, new life she'd wanted—with a few detours and ghosts along the way.

"You've got a good man here, Bree," Declan said. "Have a little faith in things, and you'll be just fine."

"I will," she said. "Promise."

Plato snuffled at her feet. "Plato promises too," she said.

Declan laughed, sending a gentle wind across the treetops. "Well, doggy promises aren't my area of expertise, but I'll pass the note along."

She threw her arms around him for one last hug. "Thanks for everything."

Cool air blew between them and lingered.

"You two take care of each other," Declan said.

"We will," she and Steven said in unison.

Then, as the fireflies began to appear and dance around the hydrangea, Declan faded from sight.

CHAPTER FIFTY-SIX

Is not a kiss the very autograph of love?
~ Henry Finck

Four Months Later

Winter had loosened its frosty grasp, awakening the plentiful azaleas. As Brianna strolled toward the river, the delicate white blossoms lining Savannah's long streets made the whole city look dressed up for a special occasion.

Nature had perfect timing, for tonight *would* be special. Steven was playing his first gig since returning home, and she wanted to be there—front and center.

As she walked across Bay and descended on cobblestones toward the river, ghosts from different times and places meandered past. Children laughed and played hopscotch. Older gentlemen tipped their hats before returning to their card game. Even ghost carriages wheeled past between modern buses and motorcycles.

She was home, connected to Savannah and even the Southern customs she'd once avoided. Steven even taught her how to make cheese grits, though of course, Virginia remained the queen bee of the grit world.

Minutes later, she entered the River Street venue where Steven was scheduled to perform. Every seat was filled, with the exception of one table in front Steven had reserved for her, Dennis, and Piper. The two journalists had struck a chord after the intense investigation, and in the last four months, Brianna and Steven had often double-dated with them.

Brianna weaved between chairs and tables to sit down. What an amazing turnout. She breathed easy, thankful her persistent effort to spread the word about his opening performance had paid off.

Persistence had paid off in more ways than one. Begley had been sentenced to life without parole, barely avoiding the death penalty. Good riddance. Edwin was offered twenty years in exchange for turning on Begley. Restful Oaks had been reaccredited and she'd received her license to run the place last week.

The South had become the magical place Declan always said it was.

Brianna greeted Piper and Dennis before sitting across from them.

Steven adjusted the microphone. "Good evening, ladies and gentlemen. Welcome to the River Café. My name's Steven Grayson, and I'll be playing for you this evening. I'd like to thank my good buddy Dennis for his help in putting the melodies together. I hope you enjoy." Steven pointed to the table, and Dennis stood up and took a bow.

Once Dennis sat back down, the café turned quiet. Steven's delicate fingers moved across the strings with such precision and talent, she became transfixed. He'd played some tunes around the house before, but she'd never seen him perform live. But here on this small stage, with crowds of awed people, he did more than make music. The room came to life.

His skillful hands wielded the guitar like they had her body so many times—melodic, haunting, irresistible notes that left her wanting more. When his sweet voice came across the speakers, she had to catch her breath. Dressed in a black leather jacket, his captivating presence sent pleasure-filled jolts through her body.

She'd fallen in love with him…again.

As the notes died away, Steven cleared his throat. "Thank you. I hope you'll indulge me for a moment this evening. I have a special song I'd like to sing to a very special woman, who not only changed her own destiny but mine as well."

A collective "Aww…" filled the room.

Brianna's cheeks turned hot and she couldn't stop smiling. She hadn't expected anything like this. A front-row table was all she'd wanted. But a personal dedication? The man was amazing.

Steven's green eyes gazed at her with adoration. "Brianna, I wrote this one for you."

The happy tears in her eyes made him look like a watercolor painting for several seconds, until she was able to regain her composure. His song spoke of love, of having a little faith, of understanding another's pain—all the experiences they'd had together. And he'd crafted all their madness into the most beautiful melody she'd ever heard.

With the last strum from his fingers, the entire room burst into applause.

"I didn't expect that," Brianna said to Dennis.

Dennis and Piper only grinned at her like they were part of a large secret. Were they?

She glanced back to Steven, who'd stepped down off the stage and approached her. Why was he off the stage? Holy cow. Why was he getting down on one knee?

"Brianna," he said, looking up at her with the most beautiful face she'd ever seen.

"Yes?" she asked, her voice quivering.

"With you in my life, Savannah has become my homeland once again. Marry me?"

The place was so quiet, a pin dropping would sound like an explosion.

Tears fell from her eyes. "Yes."

He stood and took her in his arms. She clung to his embrace, knowing without a doubt, she was home.

THE END

Dear Reader,

Thanks so much for reading No Grits No Glory, the first book in the Southern Ghosts Series. I have ten books planned for this series and several books are available now.

To learn when additional books will be released and to receive coupons, join my readers list on my website at www.elainecalloway.com.

I appreciate all reviews and love to hear from readers. Please leave a review at your favorite retailer.

Additional Books by Elaine Calloway:

Southern Ghosts Series:

- Ticket to Die, Book Two
- Krewe of Souls, Book Three

Elemental Clan Series:

- Water's Blood, Book One
- Raging Fire, Book Two
- Earthbound, Book Three
- Windstorm, Book Four
- Penance, Book Five – Coming Soon

Made in the USA
Columbia, SC
26 August 2023